NEVERLAND'S LIBRARY

A Library Anthology

Edited by
Roger Bellini

NEVERLAND'S LIBRARY
All stories within copyright @2014 their respective authors.
This edition reprinted, 2020. All rights reserved.

Published by Outland Entertainment LLC
3119 Gillham Road
Kansas City, MO 64109

Founder/Creative Director: Jeremy D. Mohler
Editor-in-Chief: Alana Joli Abbott
Senior Editor: Gwendolyn Nix

ISBN: 978-1-947659-69-8 (Paperback), 978-1-947659-73-5 (E-Book).
Worldwide Rights
Created in the United States of America

Series editor: Alana Joli Abbott
Original editing by Roger Bellini and Tim Marquitz
Cover Artwork: Jeremy D. Mohler
Cover Graphic Design: Michelle Dreher & Angie Bayman
Interior Layout: Mikael Brodu

Printed and bound in the United States of America.

Visit **outlandentertainment.com** to see more, or follow us on our Facebook Page **facebook.com/outlandentertainment/**

CONTENTS

— INTRODUCTION —
Finding Fantasy, Again

THE FIRST TIME one of our cave-dwelling ancestors came back scratched up and bleeding from a rough day of hunting or gathering and someone asked, "What happened?" literature was born. But the first time someone painted something on a cave wall that nobody else recognized, and explained it by saying, "I saw it in a dream" –well, that was the birth of fantasy.

For a very long time in human history there wasn't much difference between what we experienced and what we imagined. When blind Homer was reciting his poems about the Trojan War, did he think his semi-historical warriors like Achilles and Hector were more "real" than the gods who stand behind every scene in The Iliad? That's a hard question to answer even today, when we call the creations of our mind "imagination," and wall them off in a separate category from Truth. But what we see when we look at another human being is still only the tip of a great iceberg. What is in that human's head is a lot bigger and a lot stranger than the physical reality. We used to know that better than we do now.

What we experience. What we imagine. For a long time the two were pretty much equal in importance. There were witches in our villages, monsters in the forest, and dragons at the edges of the maps.

The growth of Reason, a belief that the universe could be understood by sheer hard work, drove the first wedge between these two types of reality. You may have noticed that a great deal of fantasy writing takes place in pre-industrial settings. That's because it's not the trappings of industry that discourage fantasy (Steampunk does very well in that world) but the growth of understanding. Reason spawned science fiction, a literature of human doings and human interaction with a bigger universe, stories based on ideas that seemed as if they might be possible one day. Humans (some of them, anyway) began to believe that everything we saw and heard and touched might be part of a larger, logical system, that we might understand everything if we could only tease out the truth.

Fantasy, though, is a literature of things beyond explanation. It calls us back to childhood, either the childhood of our species, before we knew those map-dragons were imaginary, or our own individual childhoods, when shadows held scary stuff, when things lived under our beds and in our closets or in that one part of our journey home where we had to walk through the dark woods.

The title of this anthology, "Neverland's Library," comes from Peter Pan, a famous story about not growing up—about continuing to see the world as children see it. We live in this modern age with a conflicting but ever-growing set of logical explanations for almost everything, for rainbows and eggs and evil. If somebody does something horrible beyond our understanding, we don't just assume that person been possessed by a demon or touched by malign gods, we try to track the genes and influences that created the monster, to find out where everything went wrong.

But the childlike part of us will never be entirely satisfied with this modern world of reasons and explanations and facts. The child in all of us, the part of us that used to paint dreams on cave walls because dreams were just as real as the animals we hunted, still lives in that world, even in this era of instant information and high-definition science. Somewhere, deep down, we still want to believe in gods and monsters, because even if gods and monsters don't explain reality as well as science does, they explain how reality *feels*.

Good fantasy writing takes us straight back to that important part of us—straight back to the past, straight back to childhood. The darkness beyond the fire becomes meaningful again, and the shadows under the bed are once more dangerous. But—and this is very important—if the danger and darkness are real, then so is the power of bravery, of hope, of simply being good. We don't want an inexplicable universe that's entirely against us, we want an inexplicable universe that might help us, too.

Ultimately, fantasy is about reducing the world to human size again, while expanding *what might be* to the greatest extent we can imagine. We can do it, because the human imagination is still the single biggest thing there is: it can encompass this entire universe, and several others beside.

Come and join me here, in a human-sized world that is much bigger than the everyday one we know so well. Read these stories. Come visit other places, other times, and other realities that only exist for certain in imagination, and see why we all need more than just "facts."

Find fantasy. Be in awe again. Be afraid again. Be human.

Tad Williams
September 2013

— A SOUL IN THE HAND —
by Marsheila Rockwell
and Jeffrey J. Mariotte

I N THE DREAM, Kord *was* Panther. He moved through the trees like an unmoored shadow, lithe and black, paws lightly brushing the earth with each step. This was not the hardwood forest he had been born in, at the empire's edge, or the swamps he had come to know in later years. It was jungle, densely wooded, steamy, thick with life at every layer, from the worms and insects underfoot to the birds inhabiting the highest canopies, their plumage flashing, brilliant as it caught sunlight that only reached the floor as a muted and filtered green haze.

Panther followed a scent trail he couldn't name. It was rich, heady, familiar and strange at the same instant. Whatever it was, the scent was clearer in this place than the few signs of passage left behind by his prey: a crushed leaf here, there a vine yanked free of a tangle. Panther's eyesight was sharp; he missed nothing. But odor was the only trustworthy guide, and Panther filled his nostrils with it at every step, confident that he was closing in.

That confidence vanished when a sudden surfeit of smells confused his senses. He tried to sort them, but he was unused to the jungle and most were scents he had never encountered before. The only ones he knew for sure were blood and human flesh. The trail he had been following had vanished into the olfactory chaos, and he didn't know which way to turn. One path would lead toward…something, he was not sure what. Something he wanted, at any rate. Any other path might make him something else's meal.

Standing still was not an option. He would have to choose a course and count on wits and strength to keep him safe. He decided to continue as he had been, always keeping the sun before him. Soon enough, he found it again, the trail he'd been following, and an image of the creature that had left it almost came together in his mind, but then blew apart like seeds in the wind. It was as familiar as home… but Panther hadn't had a real home in so long. He inhaled the scent and continued on. The scents of blood and flesh were stronger this way, too, and he had not covered much ground when he saw why: a human arm, caught in the fork of two branches, with blood spattering the trunk and the leaves below and the soil beneath those.

Then a foot, ripped off at the ankle, a line of ants looking like stitches against its pale skin.

Most of a face, limp and curled like drapery, dangling from a thorny bush.

And Kord realized he was human, no longer Panther, and whatever had strewn these parts about—not the same thing that had left the tantalizingly familiar scent trail, surely?—wasn't far away, hunkered in the shadows, waiting.

He'd had a choice to make, and he had made the wrong one.

Story of his life…

A boot in the ribs woke him.

Eyes closed, he waited, listening.

When it came again, he caught it, an inch away. Its owner tried to yank free, but Kord hung on, looked up.

"Kordell. He wants to see you."

Kord released Bragga's foot. The man stomped down once, an oddly petulant gesture for someone of his size and station. Bragga, bearded and burly and missing more teeth than he had remaining, was the trusted Second to Captain Antrem, Commander of the Red Legion, Glory Squad, in service to His High Autarch, Celaeus of Glaeve.

Fancy titles these mercenary bastards gave themselves, Kord thought as he pushed himself to his feet from where he had been sleeping against a tree, on one of the few spits of solid ground for miles in any direction. Antrem was captain of nothing but hired swords, and was himself hired out to Celaeus, a noble with more gold than brains, who hoped to use his paid army to overthrow an emperor and to award himself the stolen crown.

"In his tent?" Kord asked.

"Aye."

Kord leaned close enough to smell the rot that always wafted from Bragga's toothless maw. "Next time, you'll lose the foot," he said. "Just say my name. I'll wake."

The tent was pitched at the farthest point from the murky water. The stink of the swamp was everywhere, fetid and thick. Cloying.

The smell carried him back. Years. Memories with every breath, some of them even good ones.

Kord nodded to the woman standing guard outside the large crimson tent, which would have looked more impressive had it not been stained with brown smears and patched in a hundred places. He didn't care that Antrem was spending his inheritance playing at being a wealthy officer, and he didn't care about the politics of the fight. It would make no difference in his life whether Celaeus succeeded, or if Puell held onto his title and his empire. All that mattered was that the coins he was paid each week still spent.

The guard stepped to one side and pulled open a flap, and Kord ducked inside. Antrem's pipe blocked the smell of the swamp with a sweet, woody scent. It less successfully obscured the odors of Carna, Antrem's woman (who stayed, Kord knew, for the same reason he did: a weekly pouch of coins to make the memories of Antrem's blunt hands and plump red lips fade), and Nestor, Antrem's First. Carna was always so perfumed she made Kord want to gag, and Nestor was a giant of a man who sweated enough in a day to refill the swamp outside.

Whenever Kord encountered either of them, together or—more infrequently—separately, he gave thanks to the gods of the Thirteen Mountains of Creation that Panther's senses only ever fully manifested in his dreams, for if he had to smell those two with the much more sensitive nose of his totem, he truly would gag.

The three of them sat together on silken pillows in the rosy gloom. Carna was nude, her long black hair braided and greased with rank tallow into an upright wedge. Antrem and Nestor were dressed in loose tunics and leather leggings. "You sent for me?" Kord asked.

"I did." Antrem—*Captain* Antrem, Kord had to remind himself—was a slender man, wiry and tough, with a reedy voice. His quick movements were reminiscent of a snake's flicking tongue, and Kord could not help but wonder if one of those cold reptiles were the man's totem. Or if the self-styled leader of men were even in touch enough with that part of himself to have one.

Antrem relied on casual cruelty, base cunning, and the loyalty of Nestor and Bragga rather than on his own fearsomeness, to keep his crew in line, but it worked all the same. "I'm told you know these swamps, Kordell."

"Like you know Carna's breasts," Kord said, knowing the words were flippant, and not caring. "I grew up in them. Not as an infant; that was in the coastal forests to the north of here. But as a boy, until my fifteenth summer." He tilted his head toward the southwest. "Not ten miles that way."

"So I've heard," Antrem said. "You were tutored at the scriptorium there?"

"Yes."

"By Murdis himself?"

"That's right."

"Murdis?" Carna asked, her wedge of greasy hair rising off the pillow, where it had left a dark stain. "He's the one who's dying, right? The one with the Hand of—"

Dying?

Nestor's huge hand landed on her thigh and squeezed. She flinched but stopped speaking. Nestor's hand stayed longer than necessary, and his fingers stroked her once as he took it away, leaving Kord to wonder if Antrem shared her, and if so, whether he knew it.

"He's quite the scholar, Murdis," Antrem said.

"So people say."

"And you can read? Cipher?"

"I can."

"And yet, here you are, earning your keep with your shoulders and back instead of your brain."

"I go where someone will pay me," Kord said. He was tired of standing while the others sat, but had not been invited to join them. "These days, more are hiring soldiers than scholars."

Nestor chuckled, a sound that rose from deep within his massive chest, and came out sounding more like a belch than a laugh.

"Such will always be the case," Antrem said. "Where there are human beings, there is strife. Where there is strife, killing will always be more valued than learning." He ran a thin finger up Carna's cheek. She didn't quite shudder at the touch, but she didn't look far from it. "Loving will, no doubt, always run a close second. Learning, I'm afraid, comes rather far down on that list."

Kord was getting impatient, and the masking effect of Antrem's pipe was beginning to wear off. He didn't know which was worse, Carna's perfume and the grease in her hair that the fragrance of over-ripe fruit was inadequate to fully cover, or Nestor's sour musk, but he knew he'd rather breathe swamp fumes than stay in the tent much longer. "The swamps?"

"Right, yes," Antrem said, as if he had entirely forgotten why he'd sent for Kord. Given the way he was gazing at the fresh bruise rising on Carna's thigh, he probably had. "I understand that there's a detachment of Puell's soldiers somewhere in the vicinity. There can't be many routes through this forsaken hellhole that could accommodate such a large group. Get with Bragga, figure out the likeliest place, and plan an ambush."

"If they have skiffs—"

"Assume they don't."

"There are easily six or seven passable routes through—"

"The *best* one, Kordell. I'm sorry, you prefer Kord, no?"

"Whatever your pleasure, Captain."

"That's better. Go." He put a hand on the same thigh that Nestor had earlier, and waved his other toward the flap. "I've more pressing matters to attend to."

The smile that worked its way across Carna's face wasn't altogether convincing, but neither was it entirely false. As Kord left the tent, he didn't hear Nestor being similarly banished. Maybe the sharing was approved, then.

Maybe it was the whole point.

Antrem's guard would never say. Only women protected the captain's person, and they all sacrificed their tongues before being granted that privilege. Kord had never learned what they got in return for pulling the worst duty, and at such a cost.

He hoped he never would.

As he walked along the narrow, sandy, bark-strewn stretches looking for Bragga, he remembered what Carna had said about Murdis having "the Hand." Could he really? He had long sought it, Kord knew. And what other sort of hand could interest a woman as mercenary as any of those who sold Antrem their swords and perhaps their lives?

What other sort of hand, for that matter, would Nestor want kept quiet?

And perhaps most germane, what other sort of hand would Murdis want to possess?

There was, Kord thought, one good way to find out.

After all, he was only a hired man. He owed Celaeus nothing, nor Antrem, and Bragga and Nestor even less.

But he owed much to Murdis, and it had been years since he'd seen his old mentor. He'd sworn he'd never return, but if Carna was right and the old man really was dying, then Kord wanted to be there— though whether to mourn Murdis's passing or to spit on his grave remained to be seen.

He glanced at the sky. Hours yet before sundown. He kept looking for Bragga, determined now to plot out the best ambush he could. It would, after all, keep the Glory Squad of the Red Legion busy. And if Puell's troops could kill some of Antrem's, and maybe the captain himself, so much the better.

Though he had told Antrem there were several passable routes through this part of the jungle that Puell's men could use, most of those were only known to natives of the area. If Puell hadn't been able to buy or coerce a guide—no mean feat in these parts, where remnants of the Wild Ones still dwelled—then his men really had only one choice.

The road to Murdis's scriptorium had been paved with stones from the nearby Godsbreath Mountains, so-called for the dense fogs that wreathed their peaks even in the dry season. The old man had paid for the work himself, a decades-long project that saw completion when Kord was still a Spring Child. At the time, he'd imagined the construction had taken all the years and backs and coin in the world, but he knew better now, and the thought of Murdis spending so much of his own money just to ensure the safe passage of manuscripts to and from his care no longer filled Kord with wonder, but with a vague, unsettling distaste.

And perhaps, if he were honest with himself, with a bit of envy as well. With wealth like that, Kord could retire from the soldiering business himself, pay off well-appointed thugs like Antrem to either leave him alone or do his bidding, and embrace his true love—the texts Murdis had introduced him to as a child, when he first found him wandering the streets of Uxelte and brought him in as a foundling.

But Murdis, for all his generosity, had never offered to share anything more than his knowledge and his home with Kord. As a child, that had been enough. As a young adult, it had no longer sufficed.

Kord shook the bitter thoughts out of his head as he rounded the corner of a tent and saw Bragga harassing another mercenary, a youngster by the name of Julion, recently joined up and sending what little coin he made home to an even younger wife, pregnant with their first child.

"Bragga," he barked, distracting the older mercenary from a blow that would have left Julion's lip split for no reason other than the bearded man's dim amusement. "Leave the new blood alone and come help me round up some men. The captain wants to serve up a little surprise for Puell and his troops."

Bragga's eyes narrowed as they darted from Julion to Kord, and back again.

"Unless you want me to tell Antrem you were too busy pleasuring yourself with this boy to do his bidding? Because that works for me, too."

The other man's eyes narrowed further, becoming mere slits, and he muttered something vile but not quite decipherable into his beard as Julion cast a grateful look Kord's way.

"Fine." Bragga looked at the younger mercenary, who'd already wisely used his reprieve to back out of arm's reach. "I'll settle up with you later."

Then he looked over at Kord.

"What do you have in mind?"

It was a simple plan, really, but then, Kord was hardly a tactician. Planning ambushes wasn't generally a task that fell to a lowly mercenary, regardless of whether or not he had devoured Kalomte's complete *Treatise on Warfare* as a book-loving youth.

Simple, but sound, and easy to implement besides. Antrem would be hard-pressed to argue with his recommendations, and wouldn't realize the danger it would put his own men in until it was far too late.

Or so Kord hoped.

Puell's officers were no fools; they'd know following the road would leave their men open to attack, and would be especially alert where it funneled them through various chokepoints along the way. But even they would not anticipate an ambush where the road crossed through an open expanse of swamp, along the only firm ground for a quarter-mile stretch. The emperor's troops, having passed through the more dangerous jungle in seeming safety, would relax their guard as they entered the tree-free portion of swamp. Not much, of course— they were battle-hardened professionals, after all—but enough. And if they did look for trouble, their eyes would go naturally to the high canopy that ringed the cleared section, or to the dense trunks that lined it.

Not having been raised in the swamp, they'd never expect an attack from below it.

Antrem approved the plan without question upon hearing it, and even Nestor and Bragga could find little fault with it, though neither of them was particularly enthused about having to lie in wait just beneath the surface of the mucky swamp water, with only thin reeds and moss crammed into their nostrils to keep them from drowning. But since Kord would be there in the mire with them, they could hardly complain.

What Kord didn't tell them was that they wouldn't be the only ones in the water. As long as they were still, they'd be unmolested by the swamp's somnolent inhabitants, but once they swarmed up out of the muck and the blood of Puell's men began to fill the water, the sleepy alligators would rouse and enter the fray, and they'd be indiscriminate about who they feasted upon. Human blood and flesh foot, all tasted the same to them, untainted by that human's alliances or aspirations.

And what the alligators didn't eat, the Wild Ones would pick off with their bows, for Puell's men were right to fear the canopy, even if they weren't correct about who hid therein.

Some of them would get away, of course, but that wasn't Kord's concern. Both Antrem and the empire would suffer losses, none of which could be pinned directly on him. And with any luck, when the survivors couldn't find him, they'd assume Kord had perished in the ill-fated ambush, his remains filling the belly of a satisfied gator, or perhaps adding to the strata of life and death that made up the muddy bottom of the swamp.

Either way, he'd be free of the mercenary life—free of Bragga's bullying, of Antrem's posturing and machinations, of the rank and petty existence that he shared with a hundred men just like him. Men who, like him, might have once had dreams beyond the sword and the battlefield, dreams that had long ago withered and died in the face of practicalities like having food and a bed, and maybe someone to warm it occasionally.

Dreams that might yet live again, if he could reconnect with Murdis, the man who'd taught him to hunger for such things in the first place.

The ambush was easily set, with thirty men on either side of the reinforced roadway, their positions at arm's length from one another masked from anyone who might bother to look by the patches of reeds that grew sporadically throughout the swampy water.

Kord was one of the last to slide his head below the muck, after shoving enough tree moss up his nose to make him feel like he'd been buried alive. Usually, the stuff was porous, but when mixed with the bluish clay-like soil that blanketed much of the jungle, it hardened into a waterproof plug that the men would have difficulty removing when the time came. Especially since Kord hadn't bothered to share with them the little trick of coating the inside of their nostrils with snail slime first.

He took one last look around, listening through the ever-present buzz of insects for the telltale bird calls that would signal the presence of the Wild Ones. Though he heard none, he could still feel the weight of their regard on the back of his neck. He hadn't been sure they'd come, of course, so he'd taken the precaution of having the other men paint their faces with streaks of the azure clay. Camouflage, he'd told them, and that was true enough, as far as it went, for the swamp water here was slick with a film of the bluish sludge. But the real truth was that the Wild Ones—primitive tribesmen who still adhered to the ancient customs of their long-abandoned homeland—considered the clay to be sacred, and if the mere presence of Antrem's men hadn't already attracted their attention, and their ire, the outlanders' liberal use of the sacrosanct clay would.

As Kord slipped beneath the surprisingly cool water, he noted several bumpy logs near the tree line—logs that would prove to have legs, and tails, and large maws full of very sharp teeth when the time came.

The thick water oozed around him like the unwelcome but insistent embrace of a spurned lover, sending chills through him. He shrugged them off and eased forward until his hand touched one of the large chunks of stone that had been sunk here to provide a solid foundation for this stretch of what he had come to think of as Murdis's Folly. Kord was at the end of his line, closest to where Puell's men would enter the open space. Since he could neither see nor hear beneath the swamp's brackish surface, he had to rely upon feel alone to tell him when the emperor's men were nearing. When he felt the vibrations in the stone that heralded their approach, he would reach out to touch the next man in line, as would his counterpart on the other side of the roadway, and the signal would get passed down from each soldier to the next until they were all ready. He would send a second signal once the main body of Puell's troops had passed his position, and Antrem's men would surge up out of the water to attack, first with long spears, and then with swords, should they become necessary. Those who'd already crossed the expanse would be unable to turn back to help their comrades, and the empty road behind would provide an easy escape route for Antrem's forces once they'd done their damage.

If the gators and the Wild Ones didn't get to them first, that was.

Kord felt the first shivers in the cold stone that bespoke the impending arrival of Puell's men. They became steadily stronger until his fingertips felt like they were being pricked by a thousand tiny pins and needles, and he fought the urge to snatch them away.

Then he felt the barest slackening in the vibrations, and knew the end of the column had passed. He reached out to the next man in line and then counted to thirty, one second ticking off for each man who passed the signal down.

And then he burst out of the brackish water with fifty-nine other men, the majority of their spears finding targets in the groins and thighs of Puell's men.

But unlike his fellow mercenaries, once Kord's first blow struck home, he didn't draw his sword for a second. As his target cried out and grasped at the spear now piercing his leg just behind the knees, Kord slipped back into the water and swam for a thick stand of rushes he'd marked when Antrem's men had first entered the cleared section and begun taking their positions. The long stems would hide him as he climbed from the water into the jungle overgrowth, masking his escape from anyone who might glance his way.

He took a route that would keep him well clear of the alligators he knew would already be heading toward the roiling, bloodied water and reached the rushes without incident. There, he pulled the plugs from his nostrils and took a great gulp of air. As he did so, he heard the shrill cry of a scarlet macaw and the answering whistle of arrows being loosed from a multitude of strings. He climbed up the bank on his hands and knees, fresh screams filling the air behind him. Only when he was well within the cover of the jungle itself did he risk a glance back, just in time to see a blue-faced man take an arrow through the eye. As the man fell into the water, nearly into the gaping maw of a waiting alligator, Kord realized it was Julion, the young mercenary he'd tried to protect from Bragga.

He felt a momentary pang of regret, then quickly pushed it aside. If he got what he wanted from Murdis, he could make it up to Julion's family. If not, at least he could tell them that the young man had died quickly and honorably, which was more than most mercenaries' wives ever got.

Unsure that the rationalization was enough to convince even him, Kord turned his back and disappeared into the jungle, the accusing sounds of death and horror slowly fading behind him.

The scriptorium appeared first as a kind of mirage: glimpses of stonework fairly shimmering behind a screen of trees. Brilliantly feathered birds took flight as Kord approached, their squawking and the flutter of wings the only counterpoint to the rustle of a warm breeze skittering through the leaves. This had always been a quiet place, Kord remembered. Murdis stressed contemplation, reflection, even reverence.

As a boy, that had seemed an unreasonable demand. Sometimes the tales Kord had read, of heroes and gods, had made him want to run, jump, fight, or simply cry out in youthful exuberance. Murdis chided him on those occasions, and more than once had taken away the book that had inspired such behavior, making him instead read something as dry as Moulten's *Mathematical Principles*. Since most of the people Kord knew of, even then, were illiterate and could not count past ten without taking off their shoes, he had wondered how an entire book could be written about the topic. As it turned out, Moulten had filled his pages with the most mind-numbingly boring ideas Kord had ever encountered, before or since.

Now, however, after the never-quiet of the swamp and the brutal racket of killing, he thought silence would be a welcome change. To sit undisturbed for hours and read from one of Murdis's texts—even if it was the Moulten instead of, for instance, his boyhood favorite, *The Lives of The Warriors*.

As he neared it, the landscape became more familiar. The trees were taller than they had been, and seemed to grow closer together. But the walkway wending between them had not changed, nor had the surprising way the scriptorium appeared after he passed the last bend. He knew it was close; he had seen it peeking through the trees. But there was still a startling moment when he saw a massive edifice of stone that looked like it would surely sink, sitting on a grassy hillock that rose from the soupy flats like a red welt on a maiden's cheek, something that shouldn't be there. The hillock almost seemed to defy the laws of nature, but as Murdis never tired of pointing out, there it was, so it had to be real.

The last time he had been here, Kord had been too young to appreciate the graceful intricacies of the scriptorium's construction. His eyes picked out some as he neared it: the way it was built on a platform of stone that held it just above the high water mark on the hillock's shore, the precise joining of stone to stone that kept out the rain, the arched doorway and windows that lent the walls strength to hold back the wind. He realized that Murdis had, in building this place, designed it not just as a place of learning but as a fortress. Reading, he'd said, strengthened the mind against whatever the world might hurl at it. Just as surely, this place stood as a bulwark, dedicated to preserving his intellectual ideals against the world's unlettered hordes.

It was as quiet as ever. Even the birds had gone still. Kord stopped outside the doorway—open, as always—and raised his voice, albeit reluctantly. "Ho the scriptorium!" he called. "If Murdis be present, let him greet one he may have forgotten!"

He stood, waiting. The silence seemed suddenly oppressive, unnatural, and he felt the fine hairs on the back of his neck rise up. Was he being observed? As much as he wanted to look over his shoulder, he did not care to betray any weakness, so he kept his eyes locked on the dark doorway. After several moments he heard something from inside, a sound that revealed itself to be the shuffling of sandaled feet, and then a guard appeared, blinking away sleep.

"Did I disturb your nap?" Kord asked.

The guard held his spear diagonally, from his left knee to just above his right shoulder. Although Kord didn't recognize him, he might have been old enough to have been serving when Kord had studied here. His neck was thick, his belly ample. Chances were his duties consisted of little more than eating and sleeping and checking the door from time to time. Murdis had never been overly concerned about security, and time had demonstrated the wisdom of that. Thieves went after treasure, and most didn't know the value of ideas. Some even thought of Murdis as a kind of sorcerer, and superstitious terror kept those from his door.

"Never you mind," the guard said. "State your business."

"I already did."

"Again, then!"

"Enough, Beril," a familiar voice said from inside. The guard kept his spear at the ready, but his attention was split between Kord and someone approaching him from behind. A moment later, Murdis himself appeared in the doorway, and it appeared that Carna might have had the right of it.

Murdis's coppery hair had gone mostly white, with threads of pale orange here and there. He was leaner than Kord recalled, his stubbled cheeks gaunt, his eyes hollow. A gown hung off bony shoulders; Kord thought that in a high wind, his limbs might clack together like a skeleton's. But in those deep-set eyes a glimmer of intelligence remained, and more—recognition. A mouth with very few teeth in it opened in an unexpected grin.

"So you remember me, old man?"

"Forget that impertinent air? The careless disregard for cleanliness? The slovenly posture? Never, Kordell!"

Murdis started forward, his stride ungainly, his left leg dragging. He broke into a coughing fit, covering his mouth as his cheeks flushed, a ghostly shadow of the hale man Kord had known in his youth. When he was finished, he hawked and spat off the trail, then threw open his arms. "Come here, boy!" he said, his voice even more gravelly than it once was. "Let's have a proper look at you."

Kord stepped into his feeble embrace, and tried not to break any of Murdis's ribs when he returned it. When it was over he stepped back.

"What of Kenaris?"

"Dead," Murdis said. "Years, now."

"Kenaris gone, and you not well," Kord said. "I'm sorry."

"Nine hells!" Murdis replied. "I'm well enough for a dying man."

"You don't look so near death to me," Kord lied.

"I thought that's why you'd come."

It had been, but Kord would be damned by the Lords of the Underworld before he'd admit to it.

"I was nearby, in the swamps, fighting battles that were not my own. I remembered you were close, and wanted to pay my respects."

Murdis coughed again, and wiped his mouth on the back of his hand. Some spittle remained at the corners, white and foamy but flecked with red. "You never could lie for shit."

"Truth!" Kord said. "I was reminded of you, so here I am."

"Reminded by what? A bad case of the runs?"

"You sell yourself short, old man."

"Last time I saw you, Kordell, you compared me to a weeping sore. Don't think I've forgotten."

"I was young, foolish, and rude." Kord left it at that. Murdis had taken something from him, something it hurt to give up. He had been furious and in pain, and he wasn't entirely sure that he had forgiven the old man yet. Or that he ever would. "I'd had enough of reading about adventures and wanted to live some. What did I know?"

"*Did?* You've learned something since?"

"Not everything worth learning comes from books."

"Prove it." Murdis started to laugh, but his laughter turned into a wet, racking cough that doubled him over. He beckoned with a gnarled hand. "Inside," he managed, between coughs. "Come, boy."

I'm no boy, Kord almost said. *Not anymore.* But as he followed the old man into the cool of the scriptorium, he knew that by comparison to Murdis, he always would be.

Inside, memory lay thicker.

The place might have been a frieze, cast from Kord's recollection. Stone walls were lined with thick plank shelves, shelves stacked two deep with books. Scrolls were stacked on other shelves like logs beside a fireplace. The same chairs were scattered throughout, worn and threadbare now but holding together, as Murdis seemed to be, through willpower and stubborn resistance to change. Tables were thick with candle wax in places, worn smooth in others by arms sliding across their edges as books were painstakingly copied. A few people filled the big chairs, reading books. One ancient sat hunched over a table, copying the text from one volume into another.

"By the Thirteen," Kord said. "Has nothing changed here in the years I've been gone? I think he was working on that volume even then."

Murdis had brought his cough under control. He looked at Kord with glistening eyes, and clapped his palms together thrice. "Oh, some things have," he said. "Some have changed quite a bit."

The echo of his claps had scarcely died when she entered the room. Kord wondered if his eyes were playing tricks. He had seen plenty of women here—Murdis had always liked women—but none had looked like this one. She was young, older than Kord had been when he left, but younger than he was now, by several years. And she was beautiful.

"Your daughter?" Kord asked, though he doubted that could be possible. Murdis had never claimed any children that Kord had heard about, and it had only been fifteen—no, seventeen—years since he had left the scriptorium behind. "A niece?"

"Elinore, my companion," Murdis said. "Meet Kordell. One of my less successful efforts, which I attribute more to his dull nature than to my inability to teach. But a reasonably pleasant lad, just the same."

"I'm sure." Elinore took a half step in Kord's direction, as was traditional, then stopped and extended her left hand. Kord closed the gap, went to one knee, grasped the proffered hand and brought it briefly to his lips.

"Elinore," he said as he released it. "Lovely."

And she was. She was dressed like Murdis, in the fashion he preferred at the scriptorium: a loose gown of some flimsy material, with nothing on beneath it. Murdis hated false modesty, but allowed that absolute nudity might distract from the place's mission; therefore, he settled on simple garb that left little to the imagination but at least covered the basics. The form this gown both revealed and hid was lush, as feminine as could be, but also strong. Her bare arms were muscular, her neck taut. Kord could tell from her hands and feet that she'd led an active life, a physical one. She was no pampered scholar, that he knew.

Her face, too, was both lovely and contradictory. Intelligence was evident in the slant of her brown eyes, in the set of her mouth and her firm jaw. Her features were as finely crafted as one of Murdis's most prized books, and her auburn hair was loose, framing her face, hanging past her shoulders. She was not dolled up like one of Antrem's favored whores, but wholly natural and prettier for it. Yet, in the slight upward tilt of her head and what was probably an unconscious compression of her full lips when she smiled at him, he read ambition, and perhaps a tinge of resentment, as if she knew why he had come, and disapproved.

"Call me Kord," he said. "I'm honored to meet you."

"Call me Elin," she replied. "He talks about you all the time, Kord."

"Liar," Murdis said.

"Ignore him, Kord."

"I always have."

"Smart man."

"Not to hear him tell it."

"I'm certain," Elin said, "that you'll have plenty to tell me about our mutual friend Murdis. I trust you'll share?"

Kord ignored Murdis's glare, tempered as it was by a grin he half-heartedly tried to conceal; the old man was clearly glad his former charge and his new friend were getting along. "Lady," Kord said. "Once I start, you won't be able to stop me."

Elin waited until Murdis's breathing was as even as it ever got these days before slipping carefully from their shared bed. He'd been a virile man when she first met him, though many would have considered him well past his prime, even then. But the lung sickness he now fought took all his energy, and though she still lay with him, it was for comfort only. His days as generous lover were over; how much longer he would remain as generous patron remained to be seen.

As she stood over him, gazing down at the unsteady rise and fall of his chest, she thought about how easy it would be to end it for him. A pillow, applying the strength of arms more used to swordwork than scribing, perhaps a brief, ineffectual scrabbling as he fought. But perhaps he wouldn't fight, at that. He had to know he'd be greeting the Sixth Lord sooner rather than later. If he'd just been willing to leave the scriptorium, with its heat and humidity that hung in the air like the scent of decay, and gone somewhere cool and dry, the illness might not have progressed to the point it was now—the point of no return, no healing, no end other than a slow, painful loss of strength, and vitality, and hope.

But Murdis was as stubborn as he was wealthy, and so they stayed, and she watched him waste away, and her opportunity to find the Hand of Uxlabal along with him.

And now Kordell had shown up, complicating matters. Though the old man spoke of him roughly, it was the harshness of hurt that colored his words, not that of hatred. Murdis had wanted Kord to stay on at the scriptorium—maybe even run it after he himself had gone—but his foundling had had other goals in life. Goals that did not include fighting a never-ending and unwinnable battle trying to save old books and manuscripts from the ravages of time and the jungle, and from the arguably more deadly disregard and forgetfulness of men.

That Kord had returned now, when Murdis was so ill and she was so close to finding what she'd spent years looking for was no coincidence, of that she was sure.

The man was a study in contradictions. He was older than her by several years, though you'd never know it by the way he moved—trim and fit, he carried himself with the confidence of a trained swordsman who didn't need to swagger to prove it. Dark hair and heavy stubble showing the occasional glint of silver gave some clue to his true age, as did the creases around his deep-set blue eyes, but were it not for the fact that she knew when he'd left the scriptorium and how old he'd been at the time, she would have pegged him as being much younger.

It was his eyes, she decided. There was nothing of defeat in them, despite what could not have been an easy life once he'd left these walls. Instead, they shone with spirit, and humor, and intelligence. And given what Elin had already learned about his upbringing here, she knew that intelligence was formidable, perhaps even more so than his well-muscled right arm and the blade it wielded.

There would be no middle ground with this man—he'd either be a valuable ally or a dangerous opponent when the time came. That Elin hoped he'd opt for the former was not simple mercenary efficiency on her part, though in truth, such considerations were never far from her thoughts—she couldn't afford for them to be. But Kord's lips on her hand had stirred something unexpected in her, something neither Murdis nor any of the multitude of men before ever had, and she was intrigued by it, and him.

But not so much that she'd let him stand in the way of acquiring the Hand. She'd come too far and worked too long and hard to allow that to happen, fascination or no.

If she could get him to help her, so much the better. If she couldn't, then she'd get rid of him, by whatever means necessary. What she worked toward was more important than any one person, after all. Or any two.

She let herself out of the room, closing the heavy wooden door as quietly as she could behind her—no easy task, given the way it had swelled from years of exposure to moist air and so no longer fit well in its frame. The hallway she walked down was lined with more of the ubiquitous shelves, stuffed to overflowing with yet more books and scrolls and even clay tablets reminiscent of the homeland, inscribed with ciphers whose meanings Elin, for all her own education, could only guess at. In between some of the shelves hung tapestries, heavy curtains of fabric better suited for a northern keep than a jungle fortress. The scenes they depicted were equally out of place—thick-furred bears the likes of which she'd only seen in Murdis's books, speckled wolves, snowy landscapes. Where the old man had acquired them was a mystery—why, a greater one still.

The long corridor opened up onto a sunlit salon, full of more shelves and books, and many well-cushioned seats besides. Elin stopped short when she saw that one of those seats—moved up against the wall to give a clear view of the room's exits and windows—was occupied.

Though Kord had to be aware of her presence, he did not look up from the book he read. His feigned indifference gave her a chance to scrutinize him more closely.

Unlike many so-called learned men, Kord did not move his lips as he read and his brow never furrowed in concentration or confusion. He scanned the text with an ease and confidence that reminded her, fittingly, of the man who had written it, for when he turned a page in the leather-bound book, the slight movement revealed a bit of its title. *The Shared Essence of a Single Soul*, by Murdis.

"He postulates that soul essences are more easily shared with those whose totem animals are compatible," Kord said, still not bothering to look up at her as he spoke. Deliberately refusing to accord her the respect he would an equal, she thought, though to what end, she wasn't certain. "His is the serpent eagle. What's yours?"

Elin blinked at the question as much as at the challenging tone behind it. A person's totem animal—or lack thereof—was an intensely personal matter, one that some people did not even share with trusted lovers, or spouses, let alone with complete strangers. That he would dare to ask her such a thing so baldly spoke much of his arrogance. Or, just possibly, of his concern for his former mentor.

"The black pantheress." She strove to keep her own inflection neutral, but could not quite keep a slight tone of conceit from her voice. It was a rare totem for a woman, said to be reserved for queens and priestesses. That such a spirit had chosen her was a source of great pride, though normally she did a better job of hiding it.

Kord did finally look up at that, his gaze sharp.

"Panthers eat eagles," he said after a moment, closing the book with a thump that echoed off the room's stone walls.

She pursed her lips at the implication, then countered with one of her own.

"Only when there isn't any easier prey available." She smiled, her chin lifting to draw his eyes to the curve of her neck, and beyond. "And there is almost always...*easier*...prey available."

Kord surprised her by laughing out loud.

"Truth, Lady. And I can see why Murdis chances being devoured by one such as you, in any case. The reward appears well worth the risk."

He stood and replaced the book on a nearby shelf, then crossed the room and held his arm out to her.

"Speaking of devouring things, I'm starving. Care to accompany me on the hunt for some of that easier prey?"

Elin's smile widened and both it and her laugh when she took his arm were genuine.

"Lead on, dear Kord. I shall be more than happy to follow."

The kitchen was the busiest room in the place. Pale, scrawny Galetha stirred a huge pot over a fire, tasting her spoon after every ingredient she tossed in. Cheerful Cael, as round as he was tall, shaped balls of dough into vague representations of jaguars, fish, and birds before sliding the trays holding them into an oven. The blended aromas struck Elin with an almost erotic force. She had gone along with Kord out of curiosity more than anything, but now she found that she was just as hungry as he claimed to be.

On the far side of the kitchen were long tables with bench seats. More visiting scholars occupied those than the reading chairs in the other rooms, as if it had been the culinary delights offered by Galetha and Cael, and not Murdis's library, that had brought them.

Perhaps it had been. In the empire's towns and cities, patrons at a tavern or inn had to pay for their meals. Never here; Murdis's beneficence provided beds and sustenance for any who came to study or to help with the never-ending work of transcription.

Releasing Kord's arm, she crossed to Galetha's side and looked into the big pot. "That smells divine," she said. "Is it soup, or stew?"

"Call it what you will," Galetha replied, showing her snaggle-toothed grin. "If I had two more hares, I'd definitely say stew. As it is, something in between. Stewp, perhaps."

"You've always been good at making do, Galetha."

"Comes from practice, dearie."

Elin's mouth watered, but her gaze sought out Kord. That, she had a feeling, could easily become habit. When it landed on him, though, she realized that he was tense, the muscles of his powerful back and shoulders bunched and rigid. He was looking toward the serving tables.

Steam from the pot clouded her view so she stepped away from it and regarded the guests. Two guards, a man and a woman she had known since her first day with Murdis, sat at the end of the nearest table. At the next were a group of scholars she had seen many times; as ever, they were arguing over some arcane philosophical concept about which she had no opinion or interest. Beyond them, a trio of quiet men tore into the bread Cael had already served up. One of them dunked a bird-shaped loaf, headfirst, into a bowl of Galetha's stewp, then decapitated the sopping thing with his teeth. In the farthest corner sat a pair of female scholars, together yet separate, each immersed in her own book.

The only strangers to Elin were the three men so busily eating. They were dressed like any of those the scriptorium served, and she saw nothing about them that should have put Kord on edge.

But he was. Though she didn't know him well, she could see that.

A few more moments passed, and then he turned away from the tables and started toward the door, seemingly oblivious to her presence. For some reason, that bothered her.

She hurried to his side. "Kord? Don't you want to eat?"

"I'm not hungry," he said, brushing past her.

"But a minute ago—"

"I'm not hungry." He spoke those words with a flat, declarative tone that left no room to argue. But she was, now—famished. And perhaps, she thought, watching Kord go, not just for food.

After she had eaten, Elin looked for Kord again. From the corridor near Murdis's study, she heard the old scholar suffering another one of his spells.

He'd cough until he was dizzy and his gown was flecked with blood and bits of tissue from his lungs. Then he'd grow faint, and if he were fortunate and there was somebody nearby to help him, he could make it to a chair or a bed before he fell down.

He was less and less fortunate as time went on, and some of the worst falls had resulted in cuts and bruises to his head, which left him dizzier still. So when she heard him start to cough—not the light coughing she knew would quickly pass, but the core-deep, brutal hacking she'd come to fear—Elin always hurried to his side, no matter what else she'd been doing.

Now she wanted desperately to question Kord, to learn what he had seen in the kitchen that had so disturbed him, but Murdis was barking and wheezing and from the sound of it, would be on the floor at any moment. She rushed into his private study and found him bent over double, hand over his mouth. When she entered, he looked at her with panicked eyes that seemed not to recognize her. He lowered his hand and she saw wet blood on it and more around his lips and staining his teeth.

"Sit!" she ordered. "I cannot understand why you don't sit whenever you feel this coming on."

"It...it's just—"

"You hate to show weakness, is what it is," Elin said. "Even to me, who has only ever cared for you, and will only, whether strong or weak, sick or well. As you would for me."

That hadn't always been true, and she was fairly certain Murdis knew it. But though she'd originally come here seeking his knowledge—and later, his power—she had first found his respect, and kindness, and even tenderness. She had not lost sight of her goal—was closer to it now than ever—but even so, she could do no less than repay his affection in kind.

She took his arm and led him to the chaise against the only wall of the study that wasn't packed with books.

"You are too good to me," Murdis said, the thinness of his voice betraying his frailty.

"I know," she said. "Now lie back." Elin enforced her command with a gentle shove against his shoulder. He allowed her—not that she left him any choice—to press him down. With the hem of his own gown, already stained, she wiped his face, glistening with sweat and damp with blood. She ignored the skeletal body exposed by her act, so different now than the one she had once enjoyed so thoroughly.

His coughing subsided. She sat beside him, stroking his brow and whispering phrases that had long since lost any meaning: "You'll be fine," "There, there," "Don't worry, darling," until he had fallen asleep again.

When he had, she covered him with a thin blanket and left him there to rest. He would be fine until he awoke.

She hoped.

In the meantime, Kord was around somewhere, and he had questions to answer.

Elin padded, barefoot and silent, through the arched doorways and high-ceilinged rooms of the scriptorium. Some scholars looked up from their books as she passed; others, more deeply immersed, remained unaware of her presence. Finally, she heard voices from a rarely used hallway that led to a supply room, and recognized the low rumble that was Kord's among them. By the time she was near enough to make out words, though, another man was speaking. She froze, around the corner and out of sight.

"...interested to know you're here and not rotting inside some alligator."

"Bodies rot in the ground," Kord answered. "Or in open air. In the belly of a beast, they don't stay long enough to rot."

"You know what I mean!" the first speaker snapped back.

"You did not know I was here," Kord said. "So you haven't come for me. That means—"

"What we came for is none of your concern," another man's voice said. "Traitorous dog."

Kord ignored the jab. "You're here for the Hand, then."

Elin heard the distinctive metallic rasp of a blade being partly drawn from its scabbard. "Try to keep us from it, and we'll—"

"Keep you from it?" Kord asked with a laugh. "My ambush plan was a disaster. Seeing that, I knew it would take a miracle to get back into Antrem's good graces. A miracle...or the Hand. Since I know old Murdis, I decided that would be easier to arrange."

"You'll take it for yourself."

"And try to escape the swamps alone? With Antrem's force and Puell's army both after me? I did not escape the battle just to embrace suicide."

"Where is it, then?"

Kord hesitated, and Elin's breath caught. Did he know? He *couldn't*. Elin had been at Murdis's side for years, ever since whispers of him collecting his own soul-shards had begun circulating among a certain crowd. Understanding the power that would be his when he was finished, and maybe even before—that would be contained within the Hand, the vessel in which Murdis's soul would be stored— she had made her way to his side, and, after his wife Kenaris had died, to his bed.

Elin had watched him amass the shards over time, watching how it pained him to extract them from Kenaris, knowing all along that she would not survive the effort. But to possess one's entire soul, every last fragment of it, was among the rarest feats of man. Kenaris had understood, and willingly offered the many shards she possessed, though the agony of removal grew with each extraction. Anything to see him succeed in his goal.

And succeed he had. But he had hidden the Hand too well. And now she wasn't the only one after it.

"I'll find out," Kord said.

"*We'll* find out. Twenty minutes with us and the old buzzard will be begging us to take it from him."

"No, that won't work."

"What, torture? Always has before."

"You don't know Murdis. Even sick, he's the toughest man you'll ever meet. And he's close enough to death that he'd choose that over giving in."

"I say give me a chance, and—"

"No," Kord said firmly. "I know him. I can find it."

"When?"

"Give me...give me five days. I'll get the Hand and bring it to Antrem's camp."

"Three days. And you'll meet us in the swamp, just at the end of the paved walkway. We'll all go to Antrem together. Or the three of us will go, bearing the Hand and your head."

"Three days, then," Kord said. "Now go, before you bring the old man's suspicions down on me. One only has to talk with you for an instant to know you're no scholars."

"We'll go," the first voice said. "But not far. You have three days."

Elin went back the way she had come until she reached the first doorway. She stepped through it and waited in the shadows until the false scholars had passed. Kord came by a minute later, and Elin stepped into the hall behind him.

"You bastard," she said, her voice low and angry. "How could you?"

Kord turned slowly, and she didn't miss the flexing of his hand, as though his first instinct was to reach for a weapon. But his face, when she could see it, was relaxed, and his blue eyes were calm. Guileless.

"You heard them, then."

"I heard *you*."

Something not so calm flashed across his eyes then, though it was so fleeting she couldn't identify it. Fear? Anger? Regret?

"Then you heard me doing my best to keep those louts from storming in and flaying the flesh off of the frail bones of your lover. *My* old mentor."

"I *heard* you plotting to steal the Hand from him," she replied with equal heat. But she found herself hesitating. He *had* convinced them not to hurt Murdis.

She gave herself a mental shake. Why did she want to believe him so badly?

Kord frowned.

"More like buying time to find a way to save it—and Murdis—from Antrem. You think a man like that has any use for a place like this? The first thing he'll do when he gets the Hand is reduce the scriptorium to rubble. And he won't care who's inside it when he does."

Elin had heard of Antrem, of course. In a way, he was part of the reason she was here, him and all the others who sought to overthrow Puell and put Celaeus—or themselves—in his place. The thought of one of them getting his greedy clutches on the Hand after all her work to find it—and what they might do with it—was unconscionable. She couldn't let that happen.

Even if it meant trusting a man she'd just met. One who already made her feel things no other man ever had, Murdis included.

She reached out to pull him into the room behind her, not wanting to continue the rest of this discussion in the hallway, where any passerby might hear. As her hand touched the bare skin of his arm, a sudden musky scent overwhelmed her, both strange and tantalizingly familiar.

She gasped at the power of it, and might have stumbled if Kord had not reached up with his other arm to catch her and pull her close. From his face, she could tell he couldn't smell it himself, and she understood then that it was her totem animal reacting to something she could not perceive with her own human senses.

The scent strengthened as Kord's arms encircled her and she moved unthinkingly closer to him. She couldn't look away from his eyes, which had lost any pretense of calm. Her breath quickened and she could feel her heart racing beneath the thin cloth of her robes. As she breathed in his nearness, she realized belatedly that the musky odor emanated from him.

And that she recognized it, though she had never encountered it before. Like a wanderer lost in the desert, blind and deaf, yet still inexorably drawn to the promise of water somewhere beyond sight or hearing.

It was the scent of Panther—very nearly the same one she exuded when she dreamt of her own Pantheress totem, but deeper, somehow. Sweeter.

Irresistible.

She jerked away from him, and he dropped his arms, the answering intensity she'd glimpsed in his eyes quickly hooded over. She pushed away the pang of regret she felt when she saw it; she had a job to do, and she couldn't afford the kind of distraction Kord's embrace promised.

But she trusted her totem, and knew now that she had no choice but to trust him, as well.

"Come," she said, glad her voice did not waver as she motioned him through the doorway. "If we're to find the Hand before they return, we have much to discuss."

Kord followed her into the small, unlit alcove, struggling to swallow the bitter and entirely unexpected disappointment he'd felt when she pulled away from him. He'd gone from being ready to talk his way out of her wrath to wanting to talk himself into her bed in the space of a few breaths, and the suddenness of it unnerved him.

As did the quickness with which she had appeared to change her mind about him. He wasn't sure he could trust the about-face, but what choice did he have? She clearly knew more about the Hand than he did, and his best chance of finding it was working with her. And if there was a part of him that thrilled to that thought for reasons completely unrelated to Antrem or Murdis...well, he was only human, wasn't he?

Inside, she turned to face him again, her voice low and even and her eyes hidden in a slant of shadow. "What do you know of the Hand?"

"Not much. I know that it's powerful, a vessel for soul-shards. I know that Murdis has long sought it, and Antrem wants it. And that's all I *need* to know to want to make sure he doesn't get it."

Elin cocked her head to the side, as if considering her next words. The movement placed her face even further in shadow and Kord found himself wishing he could see her eyes.

Silence stretched out for several long moments before Elin finally responded, and when she did, Kord almost wished it had remained unbroken.

"Not just for soul-shards—though it confers more power with every one collected, and so would be valuable for that reason alone. No, the Hand is much more than that. It's a vessel for an *intact* soul. Specifically, for Murdis's intact soul."

Kord closed his eyes at the words, trying to wrap his mind around the terrifying implications.

Most people shared shards of their souls with others, usually their families and friends, but sometimes with people unknown to them—people who, many scholars theorized, were meant to be in their lives from the start, but whose destinies had taken them away from those who shards they'd been born to share. Sometimes they even shared shards with certain animals, which more learned minds than his claimed was the origin of the totems that guided them.

Rare indeed was the man or woman born with a fully intact soul—rare, and powerful, and usually completely insane. It was said that no one person could hold that much power for long without losing both his humanity and his mind. That Murdis, the man who had taken Kord in and treated him as a son, might finally be close to amassing such power, was almost more than he could grasp.

And for another to seize that power—the power of an intact soul belonging to one strong enough to claim his own—well, that was unheard of, in Kord's experience. Presumably it would confer the soul's power to he who had taken it.

He had known the Hand was powerful. He had not understood just *how* powerful.

Or how powerful it would have been, had it, in fact, been complete. But only he and Murdis knew the truth of that.

He opened his eyes to look at Elin, only to find that she'd shifted, and her face was no longer wreathed in shadow. Her dark eyes regarded him intently.

"What does he intend to do with it? Heal himself?"

She gave a small, delicate shrug.

"If that's all he'd intended, he would have done it already. No, I'm sure he has something much grander in mind, but whatever it is, I haven't been able to learn." Her lips compressed a fraction and Kord forcibly pushed away the thought of kissing them back to fullness. "Nor have I been able to discover where he keeps it. But you knew him before me—better than me, probably. Maybe you can help me find it."

"And what do *you* intend to do with it?"

Elin's lips curved into a wry smile, and her eyes sparkled in a way that only made Kord want to kiss her more, and he found himself biting the inside of his cheek to stay focused.

"The same as you. Keep Antrem from getting it."

"And after?"

She gave a husky, amused laugh.

"I guess we could wrestle for it."

Before Kord could get lost in *that* vision, she stuck out her hand.

"Partners?"

He didn't hesitate.

He reached out and clasped her hand in his, and though it should have been just a momentary touch, neither of them let go.

"Partners," he said at last, wondering just exactly what he was committing himself to.

Kord had been honest when he'd told Antrem's men that physical intimidation wouldn't work on Murdis. Now that he knew the old man's power was more profound than he could have guessed, he was even more convinced of that.

Trouble was, that would have been his first instinct, too. He had made his way with his sword and his strength for so long, he sometimes forgot that he was more than either; he was also smart, and had been well-educated.

Right here in this very building. By the man he now needed to outthink.

He and Elin sat in side-by-side chairs in the main library. A few greasy candles sputtered around them, bathing them in warm but uneven light less likely to be seen from the corridor than the room's oil lanterns. They'd waited until the last of the scriptorium's scholars had gone to bed, and while there was no guarantee that someone might not suffer a bout of sleeplessness, or be struck by a late-night inspiration and return, for the moment they were alone.

"Where would he hide something so precious?" Elin asked, leaning toward him.

"I...I have no idea," Kord admitted. "Remember, it's been years since I've seen him."

"True. But some things don't change. As long as I've known him, Murdis has been a constant sort. When he talks about you—"

"You said that before. I'm still not sure I believe you."

"Start believing. He told me that besides Kenaris, one of his former students knew him better than anyone. It took me a while, but eventually I figured out that he meant you. And now here you are, in the flesh. It's almost as if you were..."

In that instant, he caught her aroma and a dream came flooding back into his mind, one he'd forgotten. He had been Panther, chasing a scent he could not name. But now he could—that smell belonged to Pantheress. To Elin. "As if what?" he asked, his voice catching in his throat.

Elin turned her head away, drew back from him. "Nothing. Never mind."

Kord wanted to press her, but he recognized that doing so might just drive her away. There was something about her, something he could not define any more than he could ignore, that made him not want to risk that.

He was about to say something else, anything, to shift the subject in a more constructive direction, when three sharp claps sounded, echoing through the silent structure.

"He wants me," Elin said.

"For what?"

"How do I know? He's sick—far sicker than he lets on. He has his servants, but he prefers for me to attend him."

"Go to him, then."

She pushed herself up out of the chair. Was it reluctance he saw in her eyes, in the deliberate, dilatory pace of her motions, or was he only trying to convince himself of that? Either way, she had barely taken three steps when Kord heard the dry rasp of Murdis's bare feet coming toward them with his characteristic shuffling. "Elinore?" the old man said, his voice barely more than a whisper.

"Coming, my dear."

Murdis chuckled, then coughed. "Stay," he said. "And save your endearments. I'm afraid I am past the point—" He coughed again, this time longer and harder. When he finished, he stepped into the library "—past the point where they matter." The old man's gaze took in the room, empty but for Elin, halfway to the door, and Kord sitting in one of a pair of chairs pulled close together, and the candles that cast their glow on those chairs. "Good, you're here too."

"What is it, darling?" Elin asked, taking another step toward him.

Murdis froze her in place with a glare. "I said to save it. We need to talk."

"I can go," Kord offered.

"No! *We* need to talk. You and I, Kordell."

Elin's head swiveled between the two men. Kord rose from his chair, at a speed at least as desultory as hers had been. "Can she—?"

"Go to your chambers, Elinore," Murdis ordered. "She's quite comfortable there," he said to Kord. "Right next to mine. She has everything she needs."

"Yes, *milord*," Elin said. If Murdis caught the edge in her voice, or her choice of words, he didn't let on.

When she was gone, Murdis turned his attention to Kord. "I need it," he said.

"Need what?"

"You know. Don't toy with me, boy. I haven't time."

"You didn't used to be so impatient."

"I didn't used to be almost dead."

When Kord didn't respond, Murdis said it again. "I need it."

"Haven't you taken enough?"

"You know I haven't, Kord. I *will* die, if I don't get it. With it, I could save myself. And more."

"And the cost doesn't matter to you. It killed Kenaris, didn't it?"

Murdis glanced away. It was the closest thing to shame Kord had ever seen him exhibit. "She volunteered. Neither of us knew what the price would be. And she had so many shards, more than we could have known. With you, I'm only asking for one."

"The last one. For all you know, that'll kill me."

"I know it'll be easier given than taken. Easier on you."

"You know? Truly? Or you believe?"

"Kord, you learned much, when you were here. But you didn't learn everything. Don't pretend that you did."

"I never do. But the one lesson I learned best is not to trust you. If you want the damned shard, you'll have to take it. If you can."

A wheezing cough escaped Murdis's lips, leaving behind a wet streak. He wiped it with the back of his hand, where the scabbed, mottled skin looked as thin as old paper. "Oh, I can—" he started. Another cough interrupted him, this one coming from deeper within. Others followed, a series of them, each stronger than the last, exploding from his core. He doubled over, and when he looked up there was panic in his eyes and blood hanging in red streamers from his nose and mouth.

"Elin!" Kord cried. "Elin, come quick!"

Murdis coughed again and his legs gave out. He dropped in a single motion, too fast for Kord to catch him. His legs spasmed and his hands fluttered and the coughs continued, each one arching his back and causing his head to slam against the stone floor.

"Elin, damn it!" Kord shouted. He got a hand under the old man's head, but he feared it was too late. The coughs were becoming weaker, but so was Murdis's breathing. Blood and snot glistened on his cheeks and chin.

"I'm here," Elin said before she was even in the room. "What is—oh!"

"He's had some kind of attack."

"He does, sometimes," Elin said. "But this one—what happened? Did you get him worked up?"

"Not by design. But yes, we argued."

"By the Thirteen, Kord! He's not a well man."

"I can see that. What can we do?"

"Lift him—gently, you ass! Take him to his bed and we'll try to make him comfortable. I've a poultice there that sometimes helps, but…"

Kord scooped the old man up in his arms and rose. It was like lifting a child, or a large bird; no weight to speak of. Murdis's coughing fit was over, but his eyes stared, unblinking, into the distance. His muscles were stiff and his breathing was shallow and strained. "But what?"

"I've never seen him this bad, is all."

Kord carried Murdis to his rooms. When he put the old man down on the bed, Murdis's eyes had lost some of their panicked look. But they were filmy, glazed over, and Kord didn't think that was an improvement. Elin busied herself at a nearby cabinet, and after a few moments she came bearing the poultice she had mentioned, a gray mound of something, veined with black. She pressed it against the old man's forehead. "This will make you feel better."

Murdis gave a soft moan and relaxed visibly, tension running off him like water from a man stepping out of a stream.

"That's remarkable," Kord said.

"It will ease his pain, that's all. It won't make him better."

Kord recognized the unspoken undercurrent there. One thing could make him better—the power of an intact soul. And despite whatever Murdis had told Elin, he didn't have that. Not fully intact. Not yet.

Lost in thought, he was startled when Murdis's bony fingers clutched his wrist. "I…I am dying, Kord," he said. His voice was weak, and Kord had to bend close to make out his words. "I see that now. There is no help for me, even with…"

The reality of the situation struck Kord with the force of a mallet. Before, he had responded like the boy he had been when he left this place; still angry, unforgiving. But Murdis had given him so much. How could he refuse the one thing that could save him?

"You can take it," he said. "Take the last shard. Use it to save yourself."

"No," Murdis said. "It is…yours, now. All of it."

"The Hand?" Kord asked. He felt Elin's presence, close beside him. This was what she had come for, and once Murdis revealed the location, it would be a race to claim it. And now that she knew the soul wasn't complete—could not be, until Kord gave up the last of Murdis's soul-shards, the one he carried inside himself—if she got the Hand, she would want to take that shard as well.

He might have been willing to give it to Murdis. He'd said he would, at any rate, although on some level he must have known the old man was too weak now to take it by force. But could he give it to Elin? Let her have the Hand and all the power it promised? She was a beauty, and smart, and she had worked hard to get in Murdis's good graces. In a surprisingly short while, he had come to feel drawn to her in a way he never had before, to any woman.

But she was a thief, just the same. A patient one, a lovely one. But a thief. If she got the Hand first, he doubted that she would be interested in sharing.

"The Hand..." Murdis said.

"Where is it, then?"

"Well hidden."

"Where?"

The old man's eyes rolled up in his head, and his mouth went slack. Dead? No, he breathed yet, and then his jaw worked again. But his voice was a mere whisper, like a light autumn breeze passing through a dried-out husk.

"Clues. Follow..." Before he could finish, his mouth sagged open again. A thin stream of bloody spittle ran from the corner. He was still breathing, and when Kord put two fingers against his neck he could feel a faint heartbeat. But Murdis was through with words, he thought.

"Follow what? The clues?" Elin asked.

"That's what he said."

"What clues?"

"How would I know? You've been here with him. I've been away."

"If I knew, Kord, I would tell you."

He doubted that. But what if he was wrong about her? Perhaps she had come as a thief, but had turned into a true lover, or an acolyte. He had come as a child and left as a scholar, after all. People changed.

Not often, or easily. But they did.

"Kord, I heard what he said. It's yours. The Hand belongs to you, now. If we can find it."

"You won't try to take it?"

"If I help you find it, I'll expect a reward. Of some kind. We can work that out when the time comes."

She held her gaze with his, and her full lips were parted ever so slightly. She breathed heavily, her breasts rising and falling, and he wondered if the reward she wanted was power, or gold, or something more common, more base, and yet precious all the same. She could have that, regardless, he thought. And there was every chance she knew exactly the effect she was having on him, and it was meant only to distract him long enough for her to get away with the Hand.

He looked at Murdis, who appeared to be sleeping. A sleep, Kord suspected, from which he wouldn't waken. "Do you have any ideas?" he asked. "What do we do now?"

"What is most important to him?" Elin asked in return. "That's the place to start."

"When I knew him, these. Books, scrolls. The wisdom of the ages, he called it. His life's work."

"Yes!" Elin said. "Yes, that. His books, his scrolls. Where he would hide his most valued possession—it would be in those somewhere, wouldn't it?"

"I don't know. He's collected so many. Over years. Decades. A few, he wrote himself, but if he's written any since he acquired the Hand, I wouldn't know."

Elin sighed. "He's always working on something. Some he doesn't finish, and those he burns, taking care to scatter the ashes to the four winds. I remind him how precious paper is, how dear, but he won't listen."

"We're wasting time here, Elin. Will he be safe, alone?"

"Whatever is yet to happen to him will happen whether we're here or not," she said. "Back to the library, then?"

"Back to the library." He spared a last look for Murdis, and started toward the hallway.

"And when we get there," she added, "you'll tell me what that was all about? The last shard?"

Kord's turn to sigh. "I'll tell you."

Standing in the middle of the library, Kord stared at the overflowing shelves of books, wondering where to start. There had to be thousands upon thousands of volumes in the scriptorium, and most of them were collected here, in this room. How in the name of the Thirteen was he supposed to find Murdis's clues in this vast hoard?

"If he told you about the clues, then it must be because he thought you could figure them out," Elin said when he voiced his doubts. "So maybe they're hidden in books that were meaningful to the both of you in your past, when you were here?"

Kord nodded; that made sense, and he should have thought of it himself, instead of being overwhelmed by the sheer number of books and scrolls—and, if he were honest with himself, by the memories of that shared past.

"There were several." He walked over to one shelf and bent down to reach a section of leather-bound books whose covers had been well-worn by smaller hands. He pulled two off the shelf—*The Lives of the Warriors* and Moulten's *Mathematical Principles*, the first decidedly more worn than the second.

He handed the Moulten to Elin.

"He was always after me to read this one, though he knew I found it dry as an old whore's—" he stopped himself before Elin could do more than raise an eyebrow. "He knew I hated it. So it would be just like him to stick a clue in it somewhere."

"And that one?" Elin asked, graciously ignoring his slip. Perhaps because she'd heard worse from Murdis, who'd taught Kord that particular pejorative in the first place.

"My favorite. Which means I'll likely find nothing in it. But these are the two most likely choices out of all of them. As good a place to start as any."

She took in a breath as if to respond, but Kord turned back toward the table where they'd been sitting together earlier. He'd promised he would tell her about the last shard, but he wasn't ready to dredge those memories any further out of the muck of his past than Murdis and his illness had already done. He knew she wanted answers, and she deserved them, but she was just going to have to be patient. Something he didn't think she'd have a problem with, considering.

He sat in his same seat, and after a moment, Elin sat beside him. A companionable silence fell over the library as the two read, the flutter of carefully turned parchment pages the only noise to disturb the stillness.

The warmth, quietude, and familiar words almost served to lull Kord into a dream of his childhood, when he'd sat in this very room, with this very book, imagining himself in the midst of the battles so vividly portrayed in the meticulous script. His favorite story had been that of the warrior twins, Hunah and Balank, who had used their wits as well as their arms to vanquish the Lords of the Underworld.

He skimmed over the once-beloved tale, knowing the shape of the words so thoroughly that he no longer needed to read them, having committed them to memory long ago. So it took him a moment to realize that something had been altered in the last line of the story.

It had once read, "...and so the brothers passed into legend, lauded as heroes and venerated as saints where they had sought only to do what is right, as we all should." But a word had been changed, carefully erased and recopied in a script different from the original. Now it read, "...sought only to seek what is right..." Which made no sense, and was redundant besides. Why would anyone alter the words...?

Of course.

"That wily old bird," Kord said aloud, shaking his head in bemused admiration.

Elin looked up from her own text.

"What did you find?"

He showed her, and explained the change.

"But how is that a clue? It's nonsense."

Kord smiled at her, knowing his expression verged on the predatory, but not caring. He'd caught their prey's scent. The hunt was in his blood as Kord now, just as surely as it was as Panther.

"Not nonsense—a title. *To Seek What is Right*, by Wardon. It was one of Murdis's favorite punishments when I'd done something he thought was wrong. Which was frequently."

Elin's slow smile matched his, in both approbation and excitement.

"It's brilliant. Changes only you would catch, in volumes only you would know. I'd never have been able to find these clues on my own."

Which reminded Kord that there would be a price for her aid—aid he may not even have needed in the first place, but a price he was fairly certain he'd be happy to pay, regardless.

"Come on. The Wardon is in a different section."

They found the book quickly, a thick volume bound in layers of brittle hide. As Kord brought it back to the table and began skimming through it, he couldn't suppress a groan.

"This thing is a thousand pages long! I have no idea where to even begin to look."

He looked over at Elin in frustration. She pursed her full lips in thought and tilted her head so that the candlelight caught her dark hair and made it shine like spun silk. Kord bit the inside of his cheek so he could focus on her words.

"Are there particular passages he made you return to over and over? Favorite topics?"

Kord shook his head.

"Sometimes he'd just open the book up at random, point at a line without looking, and tell me to start reading." But as he said it, he realized that wasn't entirely true. It had been that way at first, certainly, but as Kord grew older and better able to at least hide his transgressions from Murdis when he couldn't refrain from them entirely, the old man's method had changed. More and more of Kord's reading came from the back of the book, where the heavier philosophical discussions lay.

When he said as much to Elin, her eyes lit up.

"Of course! That has to be it!"

At his puzzled look, she explained. "He altered the last line of the first book, right? So check the last line of this one."

"But I don't know this one like I know *Warriors*. Even if he did change the last line, I'd have no way of knowing what that change was."

Elin waved off his protest impatiently.

"You grew up in a scriptorium; surely you'll be able to detect physical signs of alteration? And the pattern seems to be book titles you know, so that should make it relatively easy to pinpoint, even if you can't ascertain where the changes were made."

Kord couldn't fault her logic. Turning his attention back to the book, he flipped to the last page, and read the closing line.

"In the end, the most difficult task that faces any man is not in understanding the difference between right and wrong; it is in acting wisely upon that understanding."

He frowned.

"If there's a book title in there, it's not one I'm familiar with." And though he examined the script carefully, he could see no signs of tampering.

Elin leaned over to look at the words herself, the smell of her catching Kord off-guard as she did, suddenly strong in their close quarters, musky and yet somehow sweet. The scent of Pantheress, achingly familiar in a way he couldn't define or deny. A way that made him ache in return.

"I was so certain that was the key..." she murmured as her eyes scanned the page in vain for some hint as to Murdis's clue. "Maybe it's a different sort of message? Not a book, but something you need to do?"

Kord laughed, and with that, Elin's scent was no longer in his nostrils, tantalizing him with a longing he couldn't begin to understand.

"I've never been particularly good at acting wisely."

But even as the words left his mouth, he was struck abruptly by a memory of another time he'd said them. To Murdis, in this room, while arguing over this very book. This very line.

It had been a few days before Kord had left the scriptorium—for good, he had thought at the time.

A few days after Murdis had extracted all but the last soul-shard from him.

"I've given you the tools, Kordell," Murdis had said, his voice so much stronger then, his back so much straighter. "You know the difference between right and wrong. Use that knowledge wisely."

Kord had laughed then, too, but with considerably less humor.

"By which you mean, do what *you* want me to do."

Murdis, his hair still full and red, had shrugged.

"That would be the wisest course."

"Well, as you are so fond of reminding me, I've never been particularly good at acting wisely."

"No," Murdis had said, and it seemed to Kord now that what he'd taken for arrogance then had really been resignation. Perhaps even sadness. "But you have always been good at following your heart. It will lead you on a more circuitous path, perhaps, but I have to believe you will wind up in the same place, regardless."

"Believe whatever you want, but I'm leaving and you're not getting the last shard, and there's nothing you are ever going to be able to do or say that will change that."

He'd been wrong, of course, and Murdis had been right, for here he was, in the very place the old man had always wanted him to be, trying to find a way to offer up the exact thing he'd fled from here to keep.

"Tell me."

Elin's soft words pulled him out of his reverie and he looked at her questioningly.

"You've been somewhere else for the last few minutes, obviously remembering something. Tell me. It could help us figure out what the clue is."

So he did, knowing that he'd have no choice now but to also tell her about the last shard.

But to his surprise, she didn't ask about that. Instead, she asked him to repeat Murdis's exact words, slowly. It wasn't hard to remember them; they'd been the last the old man had said to him before he'd left the scriptorium. The last words he'd ever thought he'd hear Murdis say.

"…lead you on a more circuitous path, perhaps…"

Elin stopped him with an impulsive kiss, her lips there and gone again before he could react. But not before their touch was burned into his owns lips like a brand.

"That's it! *A More Circuitous Path.* That's the book he's been working on for…forever, it seems. The one he says is never quite done, though I never see him working on it anymore and he hasn't yet burned it to ashes, despite its unfinished state. That's *got* to be the clue."

Kord nodded in agreement, her excitement contagious.

"Where does he keep it?"

"Locked up in his study. It was one of the first things I looked at when I started searching, but whatever clue is in it was obviously meant for you to find."

She pushed back her chair and stood, reaching out one hand toward him and picking up a slender candlestick with the other.

"Come. I'll show you."

In the study, Elin pulled the chair from Murdis's desk over to one of the bookshelves and stood on it, reaching for a wooden box that was holding a pile of scrolls in place. She pulled the box out, careful to keep the rolled tubes of paper from falling as she did, mindful of Murdis's love for them and all they represented, even if she didn't always share that love herself.

She stepped down, a bit unsteady now with the box in her hands, but Kord was there with a hand on her arm, his touch all the hotter now that she'd let her excitement get the better of her and foolishly kissed him. She knew he wanted her to do it again—possibly as much as she wanted to—but there was no time for that, and no point in it, really. She'd already as much as promised him that he could keep the Hand—she couldn't take it from him, now. Wouldn't. But without it, she would have to find another way to achieve her larger goals, and there was no way to do that here. With him.

Once both feet were firmly on the floor again, she twisted a bit, casually, just enough so that his hand fell from her arm, leaving a cold spot where it had been. She didn't want him to think she was rebuffing him—not when it had been her kiss, and her stumble before that, that had ignited this longing, this ache of the Pantheress for her Panther. A desire that would never be satiated, alas. It wasn't his fault that her plans went beyond just acquiring the Hand, or that there was no place for him in them.

It wasn't hers, either.

Back at the desk, she wiped a thick layer of dust from the top of the box. Murdis hadn't touched it in months, maybe longer. Whatever clue he'd hidden inside had been placed there long before Kord had even been in the vicinity—perhaps before he'd even begun working for Antrem. How the old man could have known that Kord would return here was a mystery to her. She had thought she understood him, and knew him better than anyone now living, but now she saw the stark arrogance in that assumption. Murdis had known what she was and what she wanted all along, and if she had a part to play in this final act of their story, it was because he had written it for her.

Thumbing a hidden mechanism, she unlocked the wooden box and raised the lid. Inside, an unbound manuscript lay, looking no different from the last time she'd seen it, years ago. She carefully lifted it from the box and set it on the desk, then stepped aside for Kord.

As she'd been opening the box, Kord had retrieved the chair from near the bookshelf, pulled it closer to the table, and sat on it. He didn't immediately touch the manuscript, though. Instead, he placed both palms flat on the surface of the desk, one on either side of the neatly stacked pile of papers. For a moment, Elin thought he might be praying, but as he drew in a deep breath and let it out again slowly, she realized he'd been fortifying himself for whatever he might find in the pages of his old mentor's last book. The one Murdis had clearly written just for him.

As with the other books, he turned to the last page, reverently lifting the rest of the pile and setting it upside down on the desk beside the box. Elin, looking over his shoulder, skimmed the text. Though she'd only seen it a few times before—not enough to have memorized it—she still knew it better than Kord would, seeing it as he was for the first time.

She couldn't be completely certain, but if she'd had to lay a wager on it, she would have bet that the page had not been changed since the last time she saw it. The final lines, at least, were still the same as they had been; there was no way she could have forgotten them, prescient as they had proven to be.

"In the end, whatever path we take, we end up where we began—naked, helpless, knowing nothing. If we are lucky, we will have been loved at some point along that path, perhaps more than once, and perhaps even well. And if we are luckier still, we'll have found forgiveness for at least some of the missteps we took while traveling it. And the truly fortunate soul may have one blessing further—to leave this world as he entered it, in the arms of a woman who gave his life meaning. I do not think I will be that fortunate; my greatest hope for you, my son, is that you will."

Kord stared at the page for a long time—long enough to have read it several times over, and perhaps have committed it to memory. Elin wondered what he was thinking, but didn't dare ask.

"There's nothing about the Hand," he said at last, and Elin thought she heard a tightness in his voice, one that might have been reining in tears. She couldn't see his face, though, so couldn't be sure. "Nothing about soul-shards at all."

"Did you really think it would be that easy?" she asked, placing a hand on his shoulder, even though she knew she shouldn't, that it wasn't fair to him. Still, the desire to comfort him outweighed her caution. Or maybe it was just the desire to touch him again; her uncertainty in regards to her own motives was disturbing, yet strangely exhilarating.

He didn't answer, but neither did he shrug her touch away, and she realized it wasn't the fact that there was no mention of the Hand or of soul-shards in the book's last paragraph that was bothering him.

"Did you really think there'd be an apology?"

Kord's muscles tensed beneath her hand, and she knew she'd guessed right.

"Tell me about the last shard, Kord."

If she had thought him on edge a moment ago, it was nothing compared to the stress that now radiated off him in waves. Almost of its own volition, her other hand rose to join the first on his shoulders and she began trying to knead the strain away. It was a tactic she'd used successfully in the past to get information—and other things—from men. And she wanted information from Kord, too, but she found that even more than that, she wanted to caress the worry from his bunched muscles and replace it with tension of a different—and far more dangerous—sort.

But the gentle pressure of her fingers seemed to do the trick, for after a moment, he let out another long sigh, and some of the tightness fled from his shoulders along with it.

"I'm sure you've pieced most of it together by now. When I was fifteen, Murdis decided he wanted to try and collect all of his soul-shards—or at least all of the ones that I held. I didn't know anything about the Hand back then, and I don't know that Murdis had even acquired it yet. I think he mostly just wanted to see if it could be done."

Once the words finally started coming, Kord couldn't seem to get them out fast enough, almost like a boy racing to confess his sins to his parents before his sibling could beat him to it, in hopes of earning himself the lighter sentence.

"He brought me here, into his study, sat me down in a chair, and gave me a glass of wine. He said it would relax me and make the transfer easier. I should've known he would drug it—he didn't want me relaxed, he wanted me compliant. When I'd had about half a glass, he took it away—probably so I wouldn't break it and try to use the jagged edge to slit his throat. Then he placed one hand over my mouth and the other on top of my head, and started to chant."

She felt the shudder that coursed through him, but let it pass without comment. This tale would be hard enough to tell without interruptions from her, however well-intentioned.

"Growing up here, I'd been exposed to dozens of languages, and those I couldn't speak, I could at least recognize. But not this one—whatever tongue he was using, it wasn't one meant for human mouths.

"It wasn't so bad at the start. Like when you've eaten too much food and need to vomit—the first bits come up easily, and it's actually a relief to get them out of you. Except he wasn't pulling the shards out of my stomach, he was pulling them out of my brain. Out of my heart.

"But the painlessness lasted only for the first few shards. Soon enough it was like having the dry heaves, with nothing coming out but bile and stomach lining, no matter how hard my muscles strained. Nothing but the shards, of course, and what seemed like gallons of blood. It poured from my nose and mouth, even my ears, and I was howling in pain, trying to beg him to stop but unable to even speak. And still he kept on, and there was a gleam in his eyes I'd never seen before. A touch of madness that brightened just a bit with every shard he pulled from me."

Elin couldn't see Kord's face from where she stood behind him, but his body language was easy enough to read. Though he held his back stiff even through her ministrations, she could see that his hands had balled into fists, thumbs clenched tightly inside. He was angry, yes—who wouldn't be?—but the unconscious placing of the thumbs inside the fist instead of outside was a classic sign that he still felt vulnerable all these years later. Betrayed.

"He could easily have taken the last shard then—I was too weak from the pain and the blood loss to stop him. I don't know why he didn't, unless it was because he realized it would probably kill me, or at least leave me crippled. A qualm he apparently overcame easily enough when it was Kenaris's turn.

"Whatever the reason, he stopped without finishing the job. He was about to take that final shard, had his hand ready to pull it out of my mouth, his own mouth open to say the chant one last time, and then he just…stopped. His eyes cleared for a moment, his mouth snapped shut, and he let go of me. He stood and stared at me, and if I didn't know better, I would say he almost looked horrified at what he'd done. But that of course would require a conscience, and if he'd had one of those, he would have stopped far sooner. Or never started in the first place.

"And then he turned and rushed from the room, leaving me there bleeding and incapacitated. I think I tried to get up—I fell out of the chair, at any rate, and must have hit my head, because the next thing I remember is waking up in my own bed, clean, in a fresh set of clothes, as if nothing had happened. I might have thought it all a dream, in fact, if I hadn't had a raging headache and felt an emptiness inside me like nothing I'd ever known. I drifted in and out of consciousness for the next several days, and sometimes Murdis was at my bedside when I woke, but it was like he was a stranger."

Kord's hands opened now, and his shoulders slumped, and his next words were quiet, and almost forlorn.

"Whatever closeness we had had before, whatever affection, it was just…gone. And not because he'd taken the shards from me by force, though that would have been reason enough, but because the shards themselves were gone, all but that last one. It was like they were what had forged the bond between us—or maybe the bond had been between *them* all along. Either way, once they were gone, so was it. And so was I; I left as soon as I could walk again, and never looked back."

Elin's hands had grown tired as she worked to massage the stress from his back and neck, but she kept it up as silence filled the study and then stretched on interminably. Gradually, Kord began to relax into her, her touch and his confession combining to drain the last of the pent-up anger from him. When he tilted his head back to rest it against her, she stilled her fingers and slid her hands down his shoulders and across his chest, leaning forward to embrace him from behind as she did.

"I'm sorry," she murmured into his ear, and meant it. It was one thing for an adult woman to willingly go through such an ordeal for the man she loved; it was another thing entirely for that man to force a boy to do the same. She'd known women who'd been violently assaulted by men who professed to love them, and what Murdis had done to Kord carried the same vile stench. For the second time today, she thought about killing the old man, but there was nothing of mercy in the idea now.

"Wasn't your doing," Kord replied, uncomfortable, shrugging against her. She drew back a little.

"I can be sorry that something happened without having had a hand in it myself. It's called compassion. Empathy."

Kord snorted.

"Think I lost that with the shards, too."

Elin knew that was a lie. He'd returned to pay his final respects, hadn't he? And she'd seen how he reacted when Murdis collapsed, how willing he'd been to return the last of those shards, if it meant saving the old man.

"You still have one."

Kord made a disgusted noise.

"For all the good it does me. I should have let him take it the first time."

"Don't say that," Elin snapped, dropping her arms and stepping around the chair to face him. "Don't ever say that."

Kord looked up at her, his blue eyes wide and startled at her vehemence. She was a little startled at it herself.

"Well, it's certainly not helping us figure out this clue."

Elin frowned down at the manuscript, glad for the distraction. Her eyes scanned the last paragraph again.

"It has to be here. We're just not seeing it. Yet."

Kord leaned forward, his eyes on the paper. After a moment, he gave a bitter laugh.

"What is it?" Had he found something?

Kord waved his hand at the manuscript, but it seemed to Elin he included the whole room, the whole scriptorium, in that simple gesture.

"Murdis. This ridiculous path of clues he has us following. 'A more circuitous path,' indeed. He could hardly have left us a *less* circuitous one."

A More Circuitous Path...Murdis had lifted that title verbatim from his conversation with Kord. And then repeated the word 'path' in the final paragraph of the book, where all the past clues had led them to believe they would find the next one: *In the end, whatever path we take, we end up where we began.*

Surely that couldn't be a coincidence?

"Does it matter?" she asked slowly, puzzling it out aloud. At Kord's raised eyebrow, she continued. "Murdis wrote it himself—'whatever path.' Does it matter if it's more or less circuitous, as long as it ends up in the right place?"

"But what *is* the right place?"

Kord's question brought the answer into sudden, sharp focus for her, and she smiled brightly as the realization of what Murdis must have meant hit her. She pointed at the words on the page.

"Where we began."

Kord looked at her askance.

"Our mother's wombs?"

She chuckled.

"No, silly. All of the clues have led to books, and this one does, too." She could tell from his expression that he wasn't quite there yet, so she added, "Where does a book begin?"

"The first page? Where the story actually starts?"

Elin shook her head. "For the reader, yes. For the writer—for Murdis—it begins before that." She picked up the stack of papers Kord had left face down on the desk and flipped it over, so that the title sheet was on top. Then she carefully peeled it off and set it aside to reveal what was underneath.

"With the dedication."

Kord looked down at the page, wondering if she could be right. He had to admit, it was just the sort of twisted solution that would have amused Murdis back in Kord's youth; the old man had always been trying to get him to think outside the usual patterns and approach problems from less obvious directions.

But when he read the short inscription, he couldn't hold back a rush of disappointment. It was nothing but five lines of unpronounceable gibberish.

"That's new," Elin said, sounding surprised. "There was a dedication before, but it was written in Kichic, just like the rest of the manuscript—I'm sure of it. I can't even read this. What language is it?"

"It isn't a language. It's nonsense. Just like this whole foolish endeavor."

"No." Elin shook her head, a look of determination on her face. "I don't believe that. Every single clue has tied back to your past with Murdis somehow, almost as if he's been taking you on a tour of your lives together. This must relate to you, too. We just have to figure out how."

Kord sighed. She'd been right about everything else so far. He had to trust that she was right this time, as well.

What other alternative was there?

Kord examined the words more closely, trying to sound them out in his head, but they made no sense. It was like they were syllables not meant to be fashioned by human tongues...

His grin came fast and hard and held more than a touch of grudging respect.

Murdis always had been a cunning bastard, but this time he'd outdone himself.

"You've figured it out?"

"It's the chant he used to extract the shards from me. Well," he amended quickly at her look of disbelief, "not exactly the same, I don't think. But it's the same language. I'm sure of it."

"So it's a spell of some sort," she said, her dark eyes thoughtful. Kord nodded. "But what does it *do*?"

He shrugged.

"Only one way to find out." And before she could caution him against it, he lifted the dedication page and began reciting.

"Ahj-chah-quay sic-eej koy-oh-pah kee-ahb..." Even as he sounded out each syllable, Kord somehow knew they'd been phonetically rendered, and the letters he saw on the page bore no resemblance to how the words—if words they were—were actually spelled.

And as each alien sound passed his lips, one building on the other, he somehow knew, too, what the words meant:

"The Master summons the Hand of his Soul
From the Darkness behind the Earth.
Let it shine forth in Power;

A Scepter for him who has Wisdom to wield it,
A Noose for him who has not."

As he uttered the final word, Kord's right hand rose of its own accord, palm upward, fingers outstretched. There was a bright flash from out of nowhere that momentarily blinded him even as an intense heat seared across his upraised palm. Kord blinked furiously, trying to restore his vision as the fire in his hand dissipated, replaced by something cool and hard and pulsing with life.

The sight that greeted him when he could finally see again filled him with wonder.

A five-pronged crystal rested in his hand, each iridescent finger refracting the light from the study's lone candle into a thousand vibrant rainbows. But even that dazzling display paled next to the fleeting radiance that shone from with the Hand itself, as though a guidestar had been plucked from the night sky, shrunk down, and encased in the most flawless of diamonds.

"The Hand of Uxlabal," Elin breathed in awe beside him, reaching her own hand out as if to touch it, but pulling back at the last moment. "It's the most beautiful thing I've ever seen."

Seeing the dying light from the Hand playing off her eyes and hair, Kord was about to disagree, when suddenly a brash horn sounded from somewhere outside the scriptorium—three short blasts, followed by silence, and then repeated again.

Elin's wide eyes met his over the now-quiescent Hand and Kord swore.

The scriptorium was under attack, and there was only one person who could be leading the assault.

Antrem.

Kord pinched out the candle and took Elin's hand in the same instant. "My chamber," he said. "Quickly."

Her only response was a brief squeeze of his hand. Until this moment, he hadn't been sure he could still navigate the building in absolute darkness, but now he knew he had not lost that ability. He took seven steps, reached out, and felt the cool stone of the doorway arch with the knuckles of the hand holding Murdis's prize. In the hall, he turned right, away from the main entrance.

Sounds of battle filtered in and Kord increased his pace, moving with the same assuredness that he would have in full light. With Elin padding along beside him, he made one more turn, left this time, brushing the corner with his free hand to confirm what he already knew. Nine more paces brought them to his door. He worked the handle and pushed Elin in ahead of him. A lantern glowed from a table near his sleeping mat.

"Why are we here?" she asked.

"To hide the thing. And my sword is here."

"Just one?"

"One usually suffices."

"Hide it well, then." Elin spun on her heel and left the room. Kord wondered if he had said something wrong. He had no time to fret about it, though; the Hand needed to be concealed, and the sounds of combat grew ever closer.

He studied the chamber. The room contained his sleeping mat, a low table with a pillow beside it and the lantern on top, and a basin and pitcher of water for bathing. His clothing was folded in a neat pile, next to his sword and dagger. High on the wall opposite the doorway was a barred window. He could set the Hand back on the ledge, between the bars—but he would have to put it there by feel, reaching well above his head, and the slightest miscalculation could mean dropping it outside the building.

Finally, he dropped it into the pitcher of water, instead. Light from the lantern barely penetrated the bottom half, and the crystal object nearly disappeared inside.

It would have to do. Kord strapped on his belt and drew his sword from its scabbard. The grip had been fashioned to resemble intertwined serpents, and although long use had smoothed their scales somewhat, they remained prominent enough to make his grasp all the surer. The serpents' heads formed the pommel, their mouths open and touching as if biting each other. A leather thong was looped around the guard and grip, and Kord wrapped it twice around his right wrist, to ensure that the sword would never be out of reach. Then he extinguished the lantern and stepped into the hall, pulling the door closed behind him.

As he headed toward the scriptorium's entrance, he wondered where Elin had gone to hide, and when he might see her again.

Kord had just passed the door to Murdis's suite—here, lanterns blazed in their wall sconces—when the guard named Beril stumbled around the corner toward him. Beril ran a hand along the wall to steady himself, and left a bloody trail there. He saw Kord ahead of him, looked up with frightened eyes, and opened his mouth to speak.

Blood, not words, was all he could spit out, and when he pitched forward onto his round belly, Kord saw two arrows in his back, both snapped off but buried deep.

If Antrem's soldiers were already inside, it would be a hard fight in narrow spaces. Holding the entrance was the only guarantee of victory. The thick stone walls and small, high, barred windows were virtually impenetrable, at least without a lengthy siege. And siege engines were something Antrem didn't possess, and couldn't have brought through the swamps even if he did.

Kord sidestepped around the fallen guard and was about to round the last corner before the entrance when he heard Elin's voice. "That's all? A sword and a belt?"

He stopped. She had emerged from a door behind him, next to Murdis's. Though he shouldn't have been, Kord was momentarily surprised to see that she had donned a heavy leather tunic with iron rings worked through it, and leather bands encircled her forearms and upper arms, thighs, and ankles. A round shield with a pantheress's head painted on it was strapped to her left arm, and that fist held a short spear. In her right was a sword, fully as long as Kord's, though with a narrower blade. It shone in the lantern-light, but nicks along its length proved that it was not new, only well cared for.

"I was in a hurry," Kord said, leaving out the fact that he had no armor of any kind. He'd left it back at Antrem's camp, explaining to Antrem's men that he wanted to be able to move freely underwater when the ambush was sprung. Others had followed his lead, no doubt to the delight of the alligators.

"As was I," Elin said. "But not to reach the nine hells."

The interruption likely saved Kord's life. Instead of running headlong around the corner, he approached cautiously and peered toward the entranceway. Four of Murdis's guards fought there still, but two were down—and Beril, so that made three. A woman named Aranth, who'd been introduced to Kord as one of the resident scholars, fought alongside them. As Kord watched from the corner, a long dart struck her in the throat. Her knife fell from her hand and she took two steps back before crumpling to the floor.

The guards went next, as spears and arrows and an axe struck them down. Kord held an arm out, trying to block Elin from moving around the corner. She pushed against it enough to see the guards fall. "Back!" he whispered. "We have to protect Murdis. The building's breached."

"He's dead anyway," she countered. "Or will be, soon enough. The Hand's the thing. He'd want us to save it, save ourselves. So let's take it and go."

"There's no other way out, but into Antrem's waiting arms."

She eyed Kord, surprise written on her visage. "Are you sure you lived here as a boy? I'd have thought any boy would have found the other exit."

"There's another exit?"

With her hands full, Elin couldn't take his, though she clearly wanted to. Instead, she nudged him with the spear. "The Hand," she said.

He went with her, back down the hall toward his chamber. "It's hidden."

"Murdis's guards are done. There's no one left inside but us, a few ancient servants, and scholars who're doubtless cowering under their beds and praying to gods they're too sophisticated to believe in. Unless you think you and I can stop all of Antrem's soldiers—"

"There might not be many left, after the alligators fed."

"I wasn't serious! We get the Hand and get out, or we die here and Antrem takes it, after all."

When Kord's hand touched the door handle again, he heard the rush of soldiers through the entryway. They shouted in triumph, and challenge, as if the battle were already done and they the victors.

If Elin was right—and he'd no reason to think otherwise—they were, or nearly so.

He pushed inside, crossed to the pitcher, and plunged his hand in.

It was gone.

Kord pawed at the water, panic rising in him, but then he felt it, small and solid, and breathed a sigh of relief.

"You have it?"

He closed his fist over it. "Aye."

"Have you a pouch to carry it safely? If not, I do."

You'd like that, he thought. *For me to hand it over for "safekeeping."* But he had a coin-purse, dangling from his belt. Empty, since he'd deserted Antrem's squad before being paid. "I have one," he said. He pushed a finger inside to widen the opening and dropped in the Hand, wiggling it to make it fit, then drawing the purse closed again. "There. Where's this other exit?"

"In the main library," Elin said. "One of the bookcases swivels out. It conceals the opening to a passageway that runs the width of the building. On the outside, the door looks just like four stones, at the corner. You'd have to know it's there to see it, and even then it's not obvious."

"So if Antrem hasn't surrounded the building, we might yet escape."

"If we hurry."

He gave the purse a last tug, to satisfy himself that the Hand was secure. "Lead the way."

Loud voices and the heavy footfalls of armed soldiers echoed through the corridors. The scriptorium was a warren, with several paths leading to almost any destination. Elin and Kord tried the most direct route, but spotted Antrem's men hurrying through an intersection ahead. They took cover in the recess of a darkened doorway until the soldiers were gone, and tried a more circuitous path. Kord almost laughed out loud when he made the mental connection to Murdis's book, but he bit it back.

It grew impossible to tell where Antrem's soldiers were and were not, given the echoes and the shouting, the crashing of furniture being upended and the shrill screams of scholars torn from their rooms. From the sound of it, interrogations were swift and brutal and ended, often as not, with a body hitting the floor.

As Kord and Elin made for the library, a pair of soldiers, apparently having finished searching a guest's room, emerged from a doorway just ahead of them. Blood glistened on their tunics and ran from the blade of the first man's sword.

Seeing Kord and Elin running toward them, that man planted his feet wide, blocking much of the corridor, and braced for battle. The other followed him out the door and took up a position a couple of steps behind. Elin, a pace ahead of Kord, threw herself to the floor at the last moment, sliding feet-first into the man in front. She crashed into his left ankle as he tried to swing his weapon down toward her, but the impact threw off his aim and the blow slid harmlessly off her shield. He fell as his ankle was knocked out from beneath him, and Elin drove her blade up into his sternum. She skidded past him as he tumbled over her.

Kord barely dodged the falling man by bouncing off the wall. He maintained his speed, and when the second soldier thrust a spear at him, trying to shout an alarm at the same instant, Kord sidestepped it and caught the man's wrist. He planted his feet then, yanking the soldier forward and onto the point of his blade. The sword cut through the soldier's padded vest and sank deep. By the time Kord withdrew it, splashing blood onto the hallway's smooth stone floor, the soldier's mouth was open and his eyes rolled back in his head. Kord cuffed him for good measure, and the man fell in the pool of blood he'd already spilled.

A glance at Elin confirmed that she was unhurt. She gave a brisk nod and they continued to the library. Before they entered, they could hear the sound of books being dashed to the floor, handfuls at a time.

The noise broke Kord's heart and enraged him at the same time.

Inside, one man held a torch high while two others tore books from the shelves, checked them quickly for hidden compartments, and tossed them into a growing pile. One of the men was Bragga.

Bragga paused with a book in his hands and gave Kord a cruel, gap-toothed grin. "I was hoping I would be the one to kill you," he said. He let the covers of the book dangle, holding it only by some of the pages, and gave a ferocious jerk. Pages ripped from the spine as the rest of the volume fell onto the pile, and Bragga let the pages drift down atop it.

"I could say the same," Kord replied. "About you."

The man with the torch held an axe in his other hand. Bragga and his companion both whisked swords from their scabbards. A reading table, some straight-backed wooden chairs, and the mound of books separated the combatants. "You can have both the others if you want, Elin," Kord said. "But Bragga's mine."

"You're too kind."

"You've earned it." He let his shoulder glance against hers, simply for the pleasure of the touch, then started toward the far side of the table. Bragga moved that way as well, though it meant crossing in front of his fellow soldier. Elin went left. When Bragga's gaze shifted toward her for an instant, as his bulk blocked the other swordsman, Kord swept up one of the chairs with his left hand and hurled it at Antrem's Second. Bragga raised an arm to deflect it, sending it crashing into the other man.

Kord and Elin both attacked at that moment, Panther and Pantheress moving as one.

Kord sprang onto the table and off it again, soaring over the discarded books. Bragga tried to bring his sword up, but he had not anticipated the sudden change of direction, and as he swiveled to meet the charge, his foot landed on some of the pages he'd just dropped. The papers slid beneath him. When he threw his left arm out for balance, it struck the other swordsman. Kord, airborne, slammed into Bragga, driving him against the other man, and both of them into the bookshelves.

As he was falling atop Bragga, he glimpsed Elin slipping around the table the other way. The soldier with the torch had raised his axe to ward her off, but clumsily, with one hand. He seemed unsure of what to do with his torch. Elin took advantage of his confusion and feinted toward his right side. He swung the axe that way, to parry her blade, but she corrected and thrust at the center of his chest. He brought both arms in, with torch and axe, but too late to block her attack. The point bit deep. She drew it out again and followed it with a second thrust, lower in the man's gut, to make doubly sure.

Unable to spare Elin any more attention, Kord hung onto the collar of Bragga's vest and smashing the heavy pommel of his sword into the Second's face over and over. They had landed on the pile of books, which skidded and shifted beneath them. Kord got in one last shot with his pommel, splitting the skin beneath Bragga's right eye. Blood ran from the wound, and Kord knew if Bragga lived even a few minutes more, his eye would swell shut.

The big man got in a few blows of his own, and scrambled to his feet while Kord was still off-balance on the books. He drew his sword back, but before he could drive it forward, Kord threw a handful of the tomes at Bragga's face. Bragga flinched away, and Kord swung his blade into the man's wrist as he rose to his feet, lending extra momentum to the slash. Bragga screamed and dropped his sword, clutching at the hand that suddenly dangled perilously from a few strands of muscle and flesh. Blood spurted onto Kord and the scattered volumes and torn pages.

Out of the corner of his eye, Kord saw that Elin had engaged the other soldier. Their blades clashed as they traded thrusts and parries. At Bragga's agonized scream, the soldier glanced toward his superior—a moment's distraction, but all Elin needed. While Kord ended Bragga's misery with a slash across the throat, she cut the soldier's thigh with a quick jab. His sword dropped to defend his groin, and she thrust high, the tip of her slender blade penetrating his eye and punching through the back of his head. He was dead before she could yank it free.

Elin met Kord's look, panting from exertion, a fierce grin on her face. She was bathed in blood, and Kord reckoned he must look the same. But he shared her exultation over a hard fight won. "So where's that passageway?" he asked.

"You won't need it, Kordell," another voice said. "You'll not be leaving here, not in this life."

Kord and Elin whirled toward the door. Nestor stood there, with a dozen soldiers. Swords, spears, and arrows all pointed at them.

"You do, however, have a choice," Nestor said. "You can give me the Hand now, and die easily. Or you can resist, die slowly and with immense pain, and I'll take it anyway."

"What makes you think we have it?" Kord asked.

"You wouldn't be in such a hurry to go if you hadn't acquired it."

"As much noise as you made coming in, we thought the entire Red Legion had arrived. Staying would have been suicide."

Nestor shrugged. "Suicide either way. Fast or slow, those are your only options now."

Kord caught Elin's eye. "Can you take six?"

"If they're all as easy as those last," she said.

"I see Antrem's not with you, Nestor," Kord said. "He sent you to die, and kept Carna for himself? I thought him more generous than that."

A couple of the soldiers snickered. Nestor's face grew red. "Antrem and the rest of the squad surround the scriptorium, so even if you could get out, it wouldn't mean you had escaped. And delaying the end won't make it any less painful," he cautioned. "Quite the opposite, in fact."

"We can take many of them with us," Elin whispered. "I'd rather go down fighting than under torture."

"Wait," Kord said.

"For what?"

Kord's mouth opened, but before he could answer, he heard shuffling steps from the library's other door, steps he had somehow known to expect. He dropped a hand to the pouch on his belt, fingered it open. "Take it," he said. "It's yours."

"Kord, what…?" Elin began, no doubt thinking he was talking to her.

Then Murdis came into the light. He looked skeletal, as if he had died months ago. His jaw hung slack, and a line of spittle dangled to his chest, and it was clear he couldn't speak. But his eyes were bright and aware, and he moved with more speed and determination than Kord had seen since he'd been back.

"What's this?" Nestor asked.

"Your host," Kord said. "Murdis, take it."

"No!" Elin said, apparently realizing he didn't mean the Hand. Or *just* the Hand. "You can't. That's what killed Kenaris, giving up the last one."

"We'll die anyway if I don't," Kord said. "Besides, Kenaris had more than me to begin with. Having so many taken at once is probably what really killed her. I've had just the one for so long now, taking it won't hurt me any more than taking the others did." He believed that was probably true, but it was a guess all the same.

"Take it," he said again, looking at Murdis. "I offer it freely."

"Kord, *why*? After all he's done to you, he—"

"—still deserves a chance to avenge everything he's lost," Kord said, his eyes locked on Murdis. "To redeem himself."

He didn't add that if he did die giving up the last shard, he couldn't think of a better place to do it than at her side.

Kord moved toward Murdis, the ancient words coming back to him as he grew nearer. "Ahj-chah-quay sic-eej koy-oh-pah kee-ahb…"

Murdis's mouth closed and he began to mutter along. After a few seconds, Elin, seemingly caught up in the moment, joined in. Nestor and his soldiers watched, confused or dumbfounded, as the three continued the chant. Before the end, Murdis had placed one hand atop Kord's head.

Kord's gut heaved. Blood pooled in his mouth, filling it with the taste of copper and running out the corners as he chanted. He thought, too late, that it had been a mistake, perhaps his last and worst decision in a lifetime full of bad ones. But it had begun and there was no turning back now. Blood spilled faster as Murdis's voice gained strength. Kord lurched forward, releasing a jet of crimson onto the floor and the books and the bodies there. As he did, Murdis shoved bony fingers into his open mouth, deep in his throat. Kord gagged, spewing even more blood.

At the same time, though, he reached into the pouch and grasped the Hand. When Murdis's fingers were jammed so far into his throat that he thought he would surely choke to death, he forced the crystal into the old man's other hand. Murdis withdrew his hand and the last shard, and raised the other, the vessel, high into the air. Kord, wretching and spitting, caught a glimpse of his mentor and saw that he looked impossibly stronger, even younger, as if all the years had been a dream and Kord, still fifteen, had never left the scriptorium.

"Kill him," Nestor said, his voice quaking. "Kill all of them."

"No!" Murdis boomed. Dust fell from the ceiling, and a book, precariously balanced on a shelf where Bragga had left it, plummeted to the floor.

Kord, bent over double, hands on his knees, and Elin hurried to his side. They watched as Murdis seemed to grow, his actual self only a core now while a second, outer self expanded to fill the room, and then some.

"Kill him," Nestor squeaked again. A couple of soldiers let arrows fly, but they traveled only inches before running into the spreading essence of Murdis and dropping to the ground.

The outer Murdis appeared insubstantial, but that, Kord knew, was illusion. Where his form touched pillars, those pillars were beginning to buckle. Where it touched walls, the walls bowed and cracked. The ceiling overhead began to split, more plaster and dust raining down every second.

Kord spat blood, then grabbed Elin's hand. "That passageway," he said. "Quickly!"

"But...the Hand!"

"Doesn't matter," Kord said. "We have to go!"

Nestor's soldiers were abandoning him, breaking from the library and running for the building's entrance. Kord heard screams as the walls gave way, blocking their egress, probably crushing some. "Now, Elin!"

She blinked, as if she'd been sleeping. "Yes. This way." She went to the bookcase next to the one Bragga had been emptying, felt underneath a shelf for a hidden latch. When she tripped it, the bookcase swung out. She eased behind it. Kord followed, slowing just long enough to take one more look at Murdis—the real one, the core still faintly visible within the ever-expanding outer. He looked back, caught Kord's gaze, and mouthed two words. Kord wasn't sure, but he thought the words were "I'm sorry."

Then Elin caught Kord's wrist and pulled him into the passage. Stone walls formed one side, wood and plaster the other. Here, too, the building shook and split, bits of broken rock tumbling in toward them, plaster crumbling.

They ran, ignoring the destruction. A wooden beam splintered and fell in, cutting Kord's cheek as he tried to run past. A stone bigger than Kord's two fists bounced off the back of Elin's neck.

But soon she was pawing at the large cornerstones, and when she found the release, they swung away as easily as the bookcase had. She stepped through the gap, Kord right behind her. "Run!" she cried.

She took her own advice. Kord did too, keeping pace with her but unable to pass. They had come out on the scriptorium's back side, and their course took them higher up the rise that kept the building dry despite the swamp waters surrounding it on three sides. Some of

Antrem's Glory Squad stood by, but their attention was riveted on the building and they seemed not to even notice the escapees.

When Kord risked a glance over his shoulder, he saw why. Murdis, or his seemingly insubstantial form—Kord could see right through it, and see Antrem himself on the other side, standing near the swamp's edge with Carna and a small contingent of female bodyguards—had grown ever larger. The scriptorium was barely ankle-high on Murdis now, and his feet thrust out through the walls. His head touched the clouds, grayed as they were by dawn's light at the eastern horizon. The earth trembled and spasmed, and just before Kord turned back to watch where he was running, he saw the waters of the swamp swelling, impossibly. They engulfed Antrem and Carna and the men around the scriptorium, swallowed the scriptorium itself, which was even then collapsing in on itself, walls shattering and roof caving in. And still the waters kept rising. Kord and Elin raced up the hill, the swamp water reaching them and lapping at their ankles before they finally outdistanced it.

They stopped, finally out of breath, after the water had begun to recede. Kord collapsed on the hillside, his mouth tasting of metal and bile, and Elin fell beside him. She had her feet spread out, knees up, and she leaned forward and caught her face in her hands.

"What's wrong?" Kord asked. "We got out."

"We got out," she echoed. "But the Hand. All that work."

Kord watched the swamp water drain. The scriptorium was gone, nothing left but broken stones and mud and bodies. No one lived there now; even Murdis's gigantic figure was gone from the sky. Kord no longer had his soul-shard, but he was convinced the old man was dead.

He shifted his position on the slope, and his pouch banged against his hip. He brought his hand to it, squeezed it. Opened it, and took out its contents.

"This Hand?" he said.

Elin sat up, and her eyes went wide. "You have it?"

"So it seems," he said. He held the crystal up. It was no longer clear, but blackened on the inside, as if something within it had burned, scorching its inner surfaces. It was cold to the touch. "But not its contents, I'd wager. Murdis used up the soul, defeating Antrem. Saving us."

"So it's, what? Worthless?"

"A trinket," Kord said. "Still, the soul was his in the first place, right?"

"Damn him!"

"You want it?" He tossed it to her. Elin snatched it from the air before it could fall. She peered into it, or through it. If she saw anything in there that he hadn't, she gave no indication of it.

"Maybe I can find a buyer," she said. "As a novelty, if nothing else."

"Take it, then. You were promised a reward, and it means nothing to me now, regardless."

She turned it in her hands, then tucked it into a pocket or a pouch Kord couldn't see. "There's a collector of antiquities, in Xarinthia," she said. "He might offer a coin or two."

"That's where you're bound, then? Xarinthia?" Kord tried to keep the disappointment from his voice.

"As good a place as any. There's that collector. And there's another there, an explorer. He claims to have found the resting place of Tuthlekel the Morbid. Last I heard, he was preparing an expedition. If he really has..."

"Could be treasure," Kord agreed, wondering if that had really been her goal in acquiring the Hand all along, to steal it and simply sell it for profit. And do what with the funds? He'd never asked her why she wanted it, and now the moment was long passed.

"And you?"

"My purse is empty," he said. "But there's still a war on. With Antrem and his Glory Squad gone, Celaeus will need more soldiers if he's ever to unseat Puell."

"You think he'd be a better emperor than Puell?" Elin asked, a bitterness he didn't understand in her voice.

He shrugged. "Not my concern."

She looked like she wanted to say something more. Her head was thrust forward slightly, toward him, her lips parted, eyes bright. But then she seemed to think better of it. She lowered her gaze, let her mouth close. She was ragged from the fight and the chase, bruised, her hair a wild tangle.

And yet, she was the most beautiful creature he had ever seen. He wanted to tell her so. Moved his hand closer to hers. She, seemingly unaware, took hers away.

"So you'll hire out again?"

"If anyone will have me."

"Xarinthia's in the wrong direction, then," she said softly. "For you, anyway."

"No fighting there that I've heard about."

"Right."

Kord eyed the rubble below, the scriptorium where he had grown up, learned to read, to think, really. Where he had found family, in Murdis and Kenaris. Where he had, all these years later, met Elinore, and seen what a single intact soul could do.

Movement caught his attention. He looked back, and Elin was on her feet. "You're going, then?" he asked. "So soon?"

"Sun's rising," she said. "I've all day to travel. If I can make it clear of the swamplands before night, so much the better."

She stood, looking at him. Did she want him to say something? To beg her to stay?

Perhaps, if he'd had the scriptorium to offer, or so much as two coins, he could. But she had a plan, and he had, at best, a vague notion.

"Well," he said. He pushed himself to his feet, every muscle aching, his head pounding and his gut still queasy. He held out his hands, crossed at the wrist. She crossed hers and took his, gave them a squeeze. "Safe travels, then."

"And to you," she replied. Then she released his hands, turned away quickly, and started up the hill.

His destination lay in the other direction, back through the swamp. He watched her climb for a few minutes. Once, she looked back, and if she had so much as smiled, he knew he would break, run to her, beg her not to go or plead to go with her. But she simply gave a nod, then kept going.

When she had crested the hill and vanished from sight, he started down it, toward the swamp, wondering if he would ever see her again. But Elin had made her choice, he told himself. And he'd made his.

With every step he took, he wondered if he'd made the right one.

Probably not, he decided. But she was gone, and she hadn't asked him to go along. Not that he'd offered.

Anyway, he was getting used to wrong choices.

Story of his life...

— THE MACHINE —
by Kenny Soward

N IKSELPIK THE GNOME rummaged through his knapsack with tiny, shaking hands as the voices of ghosts blew through the ancient cavern, whispering accusations. Another voice, his own, berated him particularly hard, reminding him of how stupid he was to have come here, how small he was in comparison to the power he sought.

It also reminded him of how everyone around him always died.

How long will you continue to repeat the same mistakes? You are nothing but a silly, stubborn little gnome, once again in way over your head.

His inner voice balanced out the *others*—hurrah for self-loathing— reinforcing personal flaws he had already come to terms with, while the ghostly voices promised something more dark and eternal.

"*Poor girl,*" they said, sounding like wisps of silk drug across stone. "*You got her killed. You can atone by joining us…forever.*"

"I'll pay for her death in my own time," he mumbled. "She came of her own accord. If I'm to be blamed for *her* death then I might as well be blamed for every other death in the world."

"*But you let her go first. You practically* pushed *her to it, and the machine ate her.*"

"No!" Nikselpik shouted, slamming his fist into his knapsack. The gnome's cry was so emphatic that the battle-weary mercenaries looked up from where they tended wounds or simply rested.

"Are you well, my tiny friend?" Priest Louh approached, taking a pull from his wine skin and offering it to the gnome. Considering the priest's pallid appearance, Nikselpik could ask him the same question.

"No thanks, priest. And yes, I'm fine." Nikselpik averted his eyes. He pulled a heavy bracer of what appeared to be chitinous material from his knapsack. At his touch, the dark bangle came to life, twisting its body and wiggling hundreds of copper-tipped legs.

Nikselpik glanced at his ragtag group of four hirelings, caught a glimpse of their haunted eyes, and wondered if they heard the ghosts, too.

The living stood in a great cavern vault plucked from the real world and placed into the nether by the ancient *Rapur*. It was a place filled with tempting secrets, great artifacts of power, and promises of death. The mechanical, rune-covered portal they'd just come through still whirred next to them. The towering farmer's son, Jorsh, gazed at it, leaning on his sword. "Maybe we should turn back," he said. "We lost Malten already. We could cut our losses and be back at the Broken Dog within an hour, a pint in each hand."

Jancy, a quiet, waif of a girl dressed in what amounted to a burlap sack, agreed. "It's death ahead."

"No! There is no turning back." Nikselpik clenched his teeth, focusing on the heavy, iron door embedded in the wall across the chamber. The machine's gate. "I'm getting the stones, and if you want to earn your silver then you'll quit your whining and loosen your blades."

"And who is *she*?" growled Glanois, the armored dwarf. He glowered at a young woman who had suddenly appeared between them and the machine's gate, and he gripped his bloodied axe tighter.

The woman watched them, her hands clasped at her waist. Bright orange hair lay soft and vibrant against her shoulders, a vivid contrast to the spotless white tunic she wore. Her brilliant, warm smile was directed toward Nikselpik.

The gnome blinked and then gritted his teeth, "She's no one. Just another ghost." He slapped the wiggling bracer onto his wrist, where its needle-like legs entered his flesh, taking blood and returning a potion far richer. His misgivings melted away, replaced by a head-pounding rush of power. He strode through a sea of mist and howled at the machine's gate until blood seeped from his nose and ears, and the world spun into darkness.

"Here, let me help you." Words with no meaning, filtered through ears that buzzed and rang. Hands helped him to sit. A battle raged before him, although he was too shaken to make any sense of it, like a dizzying dream filled with mysterious yet familiar characters.

A small group of fighters faced a horde of terrible creatures pouring from the warped iron doors of the once-mighty gate. They were led by a stout dwarf—*Glanois?*—his back laden with a tarnished steel tank covered with oleaginous leakage. A tall warrior by the name of Jorsh fought beside the dwarf, their weapons tethered to the tank by hoses. They danced beautifully, like brothers born for battle. The two worked triggers and handles on their weapons, causing liquid fire to coat their blades. The warrior struck downward into the wave of shadowed figures. The shorter dwarf spun around the legs of the tall warrior, striking with deadly precision and power, cutting great swaths of fire, filling the cavern with dark, sooty grime.

"How does he do that?" Nikselpik slurred, feeling pained and drunk, his throat raw and filled with phlegm. "That tank seems so heavy. Such a weight to bear."

"Let me get the blood off your face." The voice again, a young woman's. The sound sent a pang of regret through his chest. A cool, wet cloth patted his cheek and neck, and he almost passed out from the pleasure. "You blew the door wide open, but you paid a price."

In the fray, Jancy bounded around with wide-eyed ferocity, climbing up some spindly-limbed monstrosity and locking her legs around its shoulders. Her murderous knives stabbed down like pistons, spraying gouts of ichor. She leapt clear before the beast could rend her to bits. Behind the mercenaries, Priest Louh moved like a strange, stiff dancer, dipping at the knee and waving his right hand above a large cup of steaming liquid held in his off hand. Whenever the darkness threatened to pour around their flanks, he would dip his hand into the cup and fling droplets in that direction. The tiny beads spun like fireworks, sizzling with thaumaturgic energy, and ripped through the enemy like a thousand slivers of glass.

"Beautiful," Nikselpik murmured. The fuzziness faded, and he recalled his purpose. The plan. He would tear the machine's gate from its hinges, and his mercenaries would clean up the mess. Then he would have the stones.

He struggled to his feet, helped by gentle hands. "The stones are near. I can feel them." He tore the bracer from his wrist, dead now that its purpose was fulfilled, and stumbled forward, nearly tripping over his robe.

"Why don't you wait?"

"There is no waiting," he snapped, anger and greed and anger contorting his face.

He shook his finger at her. "You want the stones for yourself. You always wanted them. I worked for decades to find them, and you rode on the coattails of my labor. You *deserve* what happened—"

The woman slapped him across the face, filling his nose with light, sweet perfume. His head lolled, and the sounds of battle faded for a moment. When his senses returned, he found himself nose-to-nose with her. He wilted beneath her white-gray eyes. She seemed amused except for a single tear running down her cheek. *My beautiful Jezzi.*

"I'm sorry for calling you a ghost," he said.

"Why would you be sorry?" Jezzi replied. "It's what I am. As for the other part though, I accept your apology. I never coveted your artifacts. I only wished to learn."

The mercenaries struggled to hold the line for a while before finally giving ground in a slow retreat. The darkness rolled in waves, and wicked figures sliced and cut from beneath the shadows. A slender appendage caught Glanois around the neck, its hook sinking into his flesh and pulling the dwarf forward as if to pitch him to the ground. Glanois put a boot into the mewing face and drew upward, extending the limb and then cutting through it with a one-handed swing of his fiery axe.

Nikselpik closed his eyes and meditated into his *wellspring*, his cache of power. His head hurt, and the tendrils of energy that normally writhed and churned for him gave no immediate response. The stones would change all that, but not until they sat in the palms of his hands.

He clenched his teeth. "We're finished. *I'm* finished."

Jezzi tsked. "You knew this path would be difficult. You should have tried a connective tendril again. With the right *mindthread* you would have gotten closer to the machine without going through all of this."

She was right, but too late now. Nikselpik shuddered, remembering his last venture into the machine's gate. Faces of dead friends flashed through his mind, followed by a spike of self-loathing. He hated his ambition.

Have I fallen so low, to think of life this way? To have to argue with myself about what is more important?

Deflated and sour, the gnome's eyes burned with tears. He rubbed them, which only managed to grind in more dirt and sweat, and watched his latest batch of mercenary fodder fall back, fighting desperately now. He made a surprisingly easy decision. The side of him that drove relentlessly for power fell away in the face of something purer.

"I was a fool to have brought us this way. I'm not going to abandon them. Not this time. We'll all die together if that's what it comes to."

The woman caressed his cheek with the back of her hand and stood to her full height, tall even for a human, towering over him. "No. Not this time. Not in either case." She left Nikselpik teetering and walked toward the raging battle.

When she raised her hand, a soft, quiet glow emanated from her palm. It grew more brilliant, spreading through the darkened chamber, splitting the sooty air with razor light. Her dark brothers and sisters, those vengeful spirits and creatures who made up the foul darkness, wailed and drew away until they too were divided into pieces.

The woman strode past Jancy, who fell to her knees and dropped her wet blades, flexing her hands in pain. The two warriors stopped swinging and leaned over, gorging on air, and Priest Louh quit his dance and gaped at the passing lady.

Up the chiseled stairs she went, striding confidently within her own cleansing light. At the top, she turned and smiled at Nikselpik, tilting her head to one side. Tiny flames burst around the bottom of her tunic, crawling upward, devouring her entire form, breaking it apart into smoldering ash that floated away like fireflies. The woman disappeared in a soft puff of smoke.

Her thoughts reached him. *Enter by the machine's gate.*

Nikselpik nodded, tears streaming down his face, hands balled into fists, as if he might bring her back.

"Just a ghost, huh?" Priest Louh asked.

"Jezzine. That was her name. She was a student of mine."

And she forgives me.

The machine seethed with reckless purpose, a monstrous puzzle of gears, sprockets and pistons propelling a conglomeration of spinning arms tipped with deadly implements; spikes, twirling blades, and other dangerous-looking devices. Rods dispersed thaumaturgic and electric charges into the air, hinting at vast power flowing through the system.

Corpses rotted between the machine's teeth, the fates of adventurers who had failed to best it. Many other bodies lay beneath the machine like drained husks expelled from a spider's web.

Nikselpik once again wondered at the madness of the machine's creator, and where that mind might have gotten off to.

"This fucking thing makes my head hurt," complained Glanois, putting a gore-slick hand to his forehead.

"That's because of the energy. Can you feel it?" Nikselpik put his hands out as if feeling the heat from a hearth.

"I feel the need to find the only stool at the Broken Dog that doesn't wobble, and have a pint," the dwarf growled, clearly nearing the end of his patience on this particular quest.

Nikselpik glanced with burning eyes at the dwarf. The gnome hoped the obtuse warrior felt his disdain. "You wouldn't know true power if it slapped you on your fattened rear end."

Glanois only grunted and limped away, favoring an injured leg.

"I'll hear what you have to say, my friend," said Jorsh. His blade rested on his shoulder, his voice and posture belying his appearance, which was a messy aspect to say the least.

Nikselpik approached the machine as near as he dared, gazing reverently at its smooth, deadly power. "The machines are the ultimate guardians, impassable to all but those with the proper key. The ancient Rapur placed their greatest secrets within them. They could have hidden the machines on our world, but they went a step further. They spread them across several worlds. Easy to understand why."

"I understand exactly why," Priest Louh interjected, crossing his arms. "They, this *thing*, should have been destroyed centuries ago. It is an abomination. If this power were to find a way into our world..."

"There is that." Nikselpik sighed. No one ever appreciated anything he did. No one ever understood the skill and effort required to discover miracles like this. Oh well. He no longer cared what any of them thought. He only wanted one thing, and then they could all rot. "In any case, we need to extract the stones."

"We need our pay," the dwarf called out.

"Yes, yes. Always demanding payment, you dwarves. There are other things in life more important than *payment*."

"When you find out what those are, you let me know. Until then, pay us."

"As you wish."

The gnome reached into his knapsack and pulled out two ropes fastened to small grappling hooks. "Let's get to work."

He made the first toss, targeting a bag of bones impaled upon a spike, held together by dry-rotted armor and various leather packs and straps. He hooked the armor and pulled hard, bringing loose bones scattering across the stones. The gnome dragged the rest of the remains clear of the dangerous machine and began rifling through them.

Jorsh and Glanois looked at one another, shrugged, and picked up a rope each.

"A gold, two silver, some coppers," said Nikselpik. He held up a tattered piece of paper and grinned. "And a rather lewd drawing of a man and woman performing coitus over a tree stump. Not bad for a first haul."

"I'll take the drawing, if you don't mind." Priest Louh plucked the parchment out of the gnome's hand.

They went on like that, pulling the deceased from their resting places and finding more than enough gold, silver and gems to be paid twenty times over. They even found three bottles of wine that had been resting on their sides, aged quite nicely.

Nikselpik and Jancy sat cross-legged before the machine, meditating on its structure. Beads of sweat ran down Nikselpik's face. His eyes focused on a pedestal deep within the machine's center.

Priest Louh sat down on the other side of the gnome and took a pull from one of the bottles. "And where is your key?"

The gnome snatched the wine from the priest and turned to Jancy, offering her a drink. She took a few long draws from the bottle.

"Do not look at the machine," Nikselpik said to her. "Look *into* it. See beyond its gears and cogs, beyond its sheer power. See only purpose. What do you see?"

"I see a pattern within a pattern. I see…a *path* through the chaos. Yes, it's there!"

"Turn it off, Jancy," Nikselpik said, inclining his head at the machine. "Turn the big bastard off."

"She was the key? The whole time?" Priest Louh scratched at the stubble on his face and grinned. "Lucky for us she's still alive then."

"A reasonable risk," replied the gnome. "We needed her blades, too. Jancy is a special girl."

Jancy no longer paid attention to either of them. She walked toward the machine, her eyes transfixed. Everyone watched as she leapt up and forward, arms extended, and clutched a metal pipe affixed to a scaffold. She swung up, and before anyone could shout a warning, jumped upon the hub of a great gear, narrowly avoiding being chopped in half by a swinging blade. The machine quickened, seeming to sense her presence, but Jancy made her way toward the center, leaping and landing gracefully in precarious places, spinning in circles to avoid flying darts, ducking between blades.

Glanois looked away, embarrassed, as some of the maneuvers exposed very private areas of Jancy's young body. But to everyone else, it was a graceful dance that filled them with a new respect for the girl. At last, Jancy dove toward the machine's center, thin legs springing her high into the air where she flipped and landed lightly on the wooden pedestal. She put both hands on a large lever above her head, pulled down, and flashed Nikselpik a mischievous grin.

Yes, Jancy. You are my new number one.

Nikselpik applauded, pacing back and forth as the *whirring* of the machine slowed and finally ground to a halt. He proceeded eagerly into the guts of the thing, picking his way past the deathly implements, ducking and hastening forward until he stood next to the pedestal.

The others followed with caution, curious but not eager to have an accident along the way.

Nikselpik placed his hands on the engraved wooden box and flipped the lid open. He inhaled sharply and lifted two milky, oblong stones from their padded resting places. He held them tightly in his hands and tucked them with great relief into his pack. Once the stones were secure, the fire in his head dimmed and his shoulders slumped. He was tired to the bone.

He looked over his bedraggled group.

Only one soul lost this time. My odds are getting better.

"I've got the first round at the Broken Dog for anyone who can walk, hobble, or crawl there."

"Wait, here's another for the picking." Jorsh knelt down next to a corpse in the shadows, previously hidden from view on a walkway to the rear of the pedestal chamber. It rested on its side against a block of stone, the legs and hips smashed and twisted, the arms outstretched in the direction of the pedestal.

"Almost made it," Priest Louh said, touching his forehead two times with his thumb and index finger in a gesture of respect.

"No, don't touch that one." Nikselpik pushed past Jorsh and knelt down next to the body. The clothing, while ruggedly made, was unmistakably female. The gnome gently moved her into a sitting position as a thick crop of dusty orange hair fell to her shoulders. He arranged her hands so they rested in her lap, positioning her hair in a more respectable fashion, pulling the strands down reverently over her rotted, sunken cheeks. Nikselpik stayed there a moment, his eyes closed as he spoke silent words of thanks to his former student. He was happy the others kept silent, for another affront from the dwarf would have forced him to test the stones' power.

You were too good for me, Jezzi.

He clutched his knapsack to his chest and slunk away.

— SEASON OF THE SOULLESS —
by Betsy Dornbusch

ACOW LOWED IN THE night. The Norvern Region air was sharp and cold even in newseason, but the first of the bright moons had risen and another had breached the horizon, the gods' promise of warmer days and brighter nights, even for the faraway war. Faint smoke still lingered in the air from field-burn.

Erryna leaned out the windowsill. Calves were born every night, but she hadn't had the chance to see one yet this season. Climbing down the stone wall of the manse and running for the pasture wouldn't take long. She'd done it loads of times before, albeit not in a proper nightgown as her parents insisted she wear. The only risk was Phelan slipping in as he sometimes did. Even as a toddler, he'd realized he could get her in trouble by tattling, while he, the little lordling, could do as he well pleased.

That thought clinched it. Erryna pulled on her boots, salvaged during the maturation of her wardrobe, and climbed out.

She'd misjudged the hindrance her nightgown would be. She glanced back into her room, considered getting into real clothes. But it would be much easier to hide a stained or ripped nightgown than an embroidered gown made for courting.

As she touched the ground outside her Father's study window, the twinned scents of sweet garleaf and roanweed smoke drifted from his dual-bowl pipe through the open shutters.

"Will you take a walk about, Captain? Check on the guards. I'd rest easier. Aychus' news has me nervous."

"Of course I will, my lord."

Erryna smiled at Captain Roran's raspy voice, familiar from his storytelling. She wondered at the news. Captain Roran's son, Aychus had returned injured from the war when the final snow dusted the ground two sevennight before. She hadn't seen him yet. Not for lack of trying, but Father said it wasn't proper for her to go. So very *much* wasn't proper now that she was grown.

Out in the field, the herd shifted as one, restless. She picked up her nightgown and ran toward the copse of gartrees and tinewoods where cows liked to calve. There. A lump under a tree, dark against the shadows cast by the rising moons. It shouldn't be on its side though. A breech birth? That could kill both animals. Cold sweat prickled Erryna's back under her cloak, and she ran faster. But a twanging thud stopped her—*a bow!* Something fell from the gartree and hit the ground hard.

Erryna stared into the darkness, clutching her cloak around her. The cow didn't move, nor did the smaller, new lump. Erryna edged forward, silent but for her boots brushing the damp, newseason grass. The gartree leaves trapped the scents of rain and cowcakes and a sickening, rusty smell. Erryna's stomach flipped. Her mouth tasted sour. The herd rustled behind her. The moongod Khellian eased upward, his cold light piercing the shadows under the tree.

Erryna gasped. The cow was dead, but from an arrow to the eye. The stiff legs of a calf jutted from her back end like two bent sticks. And beyond... Erryna closed her eyes tight. When she opened them it—*no, he, Ramean*—still sprawled on the ground. Khellian kept rising, revealing relentless details as if coldly hostile to Ramean's death. His quiver still strapped to his thigh. His strung bow had bounced a few steps away to rest against the back of the cow. A single arrow stuck from his chest. Roran had called that a deadheart shot when he'd taught her about shooting.

Erryna dropped to her hands and knees as supper followed the bile climbing her throat. Her nightgown soaked through from the bottom and cold seeped under her cloak.

When she finished, she sat back on her heels and wiped her arm over her mouth. Who had done such a thing? Thieves? Wilders? She weighed the unpleasantness of getting in trouble for being outside at night against warning her father someone had killed a cow and one of his soldiers. She had to go back, though. He'd said he was worried—

The ground thudded beneath her wet knees. She looked up and saw a shadowy mass galloping through the moonlight. Another herd? *No. I'm a fool. Not cows.* She ran around the rear of the tree and pressed her back to it. Horses thundered by, but their riders made no sound. In a moment they didn't have to. The herd started lowing and running, their lumbering strides thudding through the ground. Some screamed, making noises of terror she'd never heard before. It took a moment for her to realize they were death cries. A group this size, and killing cattle, could only mean a wilder tribe was attacking.

With a tremendous force of will, she forced herself to look. Every window in the house glared at the night. She gasped. *Fire!* A shrill scream cut the night. A vague wordless voice warned her against going to the house. But the house was safety. Father. Home. She stumbled toward the gate, staring. The household staff was being dragged out. Some limp, some screaming and fighting. Wilders, with braided hair and beards, swarmed them with bared steel.

Erryna stumbled closer, through the open gate. Her father sprawled on the flagstones in front of the house, his head...all wrong...*separate*. A tall wilder was strapping on her father's sword, fixing the baldric over his shoulder with a grin, which died when his gaze found her.

Erryna muffled a cry behind her hand and turned to run. Back. To the dead man's bow. *I will kill them all.* She had been a fool to leave a weapon. In Captain Roran's stories, no one would leave a weapon.

"Get her." A guttural command.

Erryna's legs pumped, she tried to gather up her voluminous nightgown, but her boot caught the hem. She hit the ground as if Khellian had reached down from the sky and thrown her.

A sturdy arm caught Erryna around the middle and lifted her. Her legs pumped, trying to catch the ground as she was dragged backwards. A voice as tight as the grip: "Enough, pretty girl, or I slap some obedience into you."

The wilder threw her to the flagstones. Erryna flung her hands out to catch herself but was too late; her forehead knocked the stone. For a blessed moment blackness offered its embrace, but pain won out. She groaned and pushed to her hands and knees.

Nearby her father's face stared past her at nothing. She could reach out and touch him if she tried, but he wouldn't know, wouldn't feel it. Erryna's lips parted but nothing came out, not even air.

Deep voices with rough wilder accents surrounded her.

"Pretty prize, that."

"Girl of the manse, wager by the lace."

She tore her gaze from her father to look up. The wilders all had arrow-shaped marks on their cheek. *They're Arrowhenge...* The world seemed to sway.

"I'll take her, Lyorn," someone offered, as if he was doing a favor. "She's past ready to breed."

A firmer tone. "No, you won't. We'll buy peace from Bonehaven with her."

"Bonehaven is eager enough for war. What does some girl buy us?"

"This isn't just some girl. She's the landed's daughter."

Someone strode closer and pulled her to her feet. A rough hand grabbed her chin, forcing her to meet sharp blue eyes in a pale face smeared with blood. The arrow wasn't painted or inked into his skin; it had been *burned* in to his cheek. This close she could see the indentation, the stained, mottled flesh. Stories of Arrowhenge told true.

He turned her chin and pulled her lip down with his thumb, examining her face and teeth as if she were a horse.

"Do you know what I am, girl?"

She tried to twist free, but his grip bruised her cheeks. Arrowhenge, the most feared tribe, wilders who branded themselves and magicked away their souls to make them invisible to the Seven Gods. Captain Roran had said there were few stories of them because they rarely left any of their victims alive. Truly, a party of Kings' Soldiers had over-nighted at the mance before trekking into the Norvern Wildes to destroy the Arrowhenge last Hoarfrost. They had never returned.

Erryna gave a mute nod.

"I am Lyorn." He wound scratchy rope around her wrists tight enough to make her fingers tingle.

"Why are you here?" The words burst from her in a hoarse torrent.

He just tipped his head and raised his brows. "War." He said it like he was worshiping Khellian Himself, except the soulless did not worship the Seven Eyes. "What other reason is there for killing, girl?"

"Cruelty. Hatred." No tears stung her eyes, thank the gods. "Revenge." A wry, lopsided grin tugged at the corner of his mouth. "Let us see to your dead."

What fresh torture was this? She protested, wanted to fight, but the words never reached her lips, and the ropes were thick and rough on her wrists.

Lyorn shoved her toward the house. She almost tripped on her nightgown again but managed to stay upright. Smoke made her cough. They walked her around the bodies sprawled on the flagstones and on the little road in front of the cottages. The dead lay pale and still. Blood ran in thick, glossy pools. Roran lay on his stomach, looking smaller than in life. So many faces.

Bile rose but did nothing but sting her throat. She had nothing left to bring up.

Back at her manse, the fire was so hot they couldn't draw near, hot enough to consume her parents' bodies. The edges of the very stone had softened, as if it melted. Black streaks ran down each window like sooty tears. The whole villa looked like a blackened, blurry memory, a ghost in the fallen night.

How did they make stone burn? Magicks?

"Who is missing?" Lyorn asked.

Her lips parted. No sound came. She swallowed hard. "My little brother."

"Dead in his trundle," someone said cheerfully.

Phelan! She stared at her father's baldric, the worn buckle crossing Lyorn's broad chest. His big, meaty hand rested on the sword hilt.

"Anyone else?"

So many faces. She couldn't think, couldn't rectify the dead with the living she'd known... Aychus! Roran's son. But surely he was dead, trapped by his injury in his bed.

"No." She swallowed. "No one else. You killed them all."

At the camp, she realized there were far fewer Arrowhenge wilders than she had thought. They had seemed a massive horde; in truth, they'd destroyed her father's manse and all their people, over a hundred, with fewer than two dozen warriors.

Lyorn handed her down off the horse and gave her a little shove toward a fire. "Go. Sit."

She stumbled over to it, trying to arch her back enough to keep the front bloodstained hem of her nightgown from catching under her boots, and she sank down by the firepit. One of the wilders tossed some black powder in and scratched a stick on the stone. Fire burst up and he yanked his hand back with a rueful grin.

She sat on her cloak on the bare dirt, though it wouldn't take long for the damp to soak through. She was utterly conscious of being bare under her sheer nightgown and, without her hands free, she couldn't close the cloak about her properly.

Every noise dug the knife of terror deeper into her bones. Two wilders sat nearby to examine spoils from the house. She blinked at the delicate necklaces, rings, wedding torques, and anniversary bracelets in their rough hands. Others cooked over a fire, some small game and birds on clever folding spits. Her stomach twisted at the thought of food. All around her warriors set up small oilcloth shelters. They stank when unfurled, rotted fat, smoke, the salt sea, sweat.

Maybe I'm asleep in my bed. She tried with all her might to wake up.

"Pretty thing," one of the men sorting the spoils—*Mama's jewelry*—grunted, eyeing her.

"Saving her for the Bonehaven truce," the other said. "Can't touch her."

The first lifted his gaze and stared hard. "What would Bonehaven care so long as she's not broke between the legs?"

Lyorn was abruptly *there*, striding from behind Erryna on silent, soft boots. His hand lashed out and caught the back of the wilder's head. The wilder snarled back but dropped his chin.

She hadn't noticed his boots before. Soft, pliant, stained black around the edges, a stiff, thick coating. *Blood.*

Our blood.

Captain Roran never said anything about stained boots and wet nightgowns in his stories. He never told her how much blood was in people. Her teeth clenched and her shoulders tightened.

In short order, a rough bowl was set on her lap. She looked up at Lyorn, eyes narrowed.

"Eat. You're no good to me half starved."

She reached forward with her bound hands and picked up a piece of marinated meat that dripped down her chin and onto her nightgown. She rubbed it from her chin with her arm. It left a watery red-brown stain on the snowy sleeve. "What are you going to do with me? What is Bonehaven?"

He eyed her. "Got any family at all left? Soldier brothers or bastard sisters, eh?"

She lifted her chin. "Answer mine first."

A muscle twitched above his braided beard. Amusement? "I'll trade you to stop a war with the Bonehaven tribe. More noble than a rich girl tatting lace, eh? Think of the lives you'll save."

"You already took all the lives I care about."

His open hand flashed out and cracked against her face. The blow whipped her head to the side, her neck muscles seized, and a whimper escaped her before she could stop it. She raised her bound hands to her flaming cheek.

"Until we treat with Bonehaven, you will carry the water from the river to the campfire as needed. That you can do with your hands bound."

As the camp settled into sleep, Lyorn bound her hands to at tree with the end of the long rope, pinning it in place on the other side of the thick trunk with a thick spike. Erryna sank to the cold ground, put her back to the rough bark, and did not sleep.

Two mornings later, she staggered with the heavy bucket of water toward the camp. The river had swelled overnight with newseason snowmelt, and she had to wade in deep to get a clean bucket full. Her legs and feet were still wet and cold. A snake on the bank startled her and made her splash water on herself. Her heart was still galloping. For a moment she let herself think about this same water running through the wheels at the army outpost downriver. Roran had once told a story about a babe in a basket that floated to a new family on a river.

The long tail of rope binding her wrists dragged the ground. Her wrists bled from constant chafing. Her palms blistered from carrying the bucket. Her hair hung in ropy tangles around her face. She stank, two days of living in the woods in the same nightgown left her sweating during the day and shivering at night. Her cloak dragged in the damp undergrowth; the wilders sometimes stepped on it to stop her progress.

A scowling young wilder walked alongside her, apparently there to do nothing but keep Erryna from running. She never offered to help scoop the water or carry it, nor did she say anything at all. She wore a braid woven with red reeds down her back, and her face would have been pretty without the arrow brand.

Erryna slouched, her back stiff and sore, and shuffled her boots to keep from stepping on her nightgown. Her boot still caught the root of a nearby gartree. She slammed to her knees with a little cry, and the water sloshed all over the ground, running in little rivulets between shoots of new green growth.

The guard grunted in disgust. She reached out and yanked Erryna to her feet. Erryna bent to get the bucket but the Arrowhenge stopped her and drew a blade from her belt. She knelt and grabbed her nightgown. Cold shot through Erryna's bones as the cool morning air hit her legs. The Arrowhenge stabbed the blade into the nightgown and ripped it, then kept stabbing and tearing the fabric, all the way around, until it bared her ankles and calves. Then she handed Erryna the bucket and gave her a shove back toward the river.

Erryna drew a shuddering breath in relief and went.

Instead of going back with her, the guard leaned back against a boulder, legs crossed, the shreds of the hem of Erryna's nightgown strewn like torn body wrappings at her feet, and started to clean her fingernails with her knife.

Erryna walked back to the river, the air itchy on her legs. She thought about the bucket. The wilder's knife. She filled the bucket, but not so full this time, and walked back to her guard. She thought about how they were still were a little distance from camp. She thought about the outpost of the King's army downriver.

She walked carefully, wondering exactly how to do it. She'd have to knock her on the head somehow. Or strangle her with the ropes. She wasn't all that much bigger than Erryna.

Slitting her throat would be quickest.

Erryna's stomach twisted at the thought.

"You have to," she muttered.

She walked brisker than usual, chin up. The Arrowhenge guard was right about one thing, the nightgown had been tripping her up far too often and shuffling her boots made her noisy. Now Erryna could walk more carefully, quieter. The guard didn't even look up at Erryna's approach, her gaze focused where her blade met her finger-nail. Abruptly Erryna knew what to do. She strode close and swung the heavy bucket at the elbow of the Arrowhenge's blade hand. The knife sliced deep into her finger and she blurted a strange, shapeless cry. Erryna realized with horror that her tongue had been cut out.

In that instant she heard bootsteps rustle the ground behind her. Before she could turn, a solid, square hand grabbed the Arrowhenge's arm, spun her, and a fist cracked her jaw. Her head snapped back and she crumpled to the ground.

Erryna gaped at the man who owned the fist.

Aychus Roran shook his hand loose, winced, and looked at Erryna. "We must go."

She stared. "Aychus! But—"

He grabbed her by the wrist and pulled her along, back toward the river. "You've got terrible timing, you know that? I almost had her until you threw that bucket."

"I was trying to escape!"

His limp made a distinct, uneven rustle through the grasses. "Yes, well, I'm trying to rescue you so keep your voice down. They'll be quick on our tail. Did you happen to pick up the knife?"

"You dragged me out of there too fast."

Aychus sighed, his jaw tight, eyes darting from tree to tree.

"You didn't either," she added.

He hushed her again, holding up his hand to stop her walking. He hissed a curse, grabbed her rope, and yanked her into a lopsided run. In an instant she heard why; voices behind them, shouting out directions to each other. Aychus dragged her toward the river and into its muddy, swollen flow. It caught at the remains of her nightgown, which wound wetly around her legs. The mud sucked at her boots, ripping through blisters on top of blisters. She tried to pull free of Aychus' grip, but it was like iron on her rope. "I can't… I can't do this. I can't run in the river!"

"Water kills our trail," he said.

The Arrowhenge were entering the water, hooves churning up the muddy bottom, gaining on them. Erryna tried to pull her boots free and fell to one knee with a curse; was she always destined to stumble back into her enemy's arms? Aychus pulled her up with some difficulty.

Lyorn raced past them on the hard bank and spun his horse. It reared and Erryna had a sudden terrified vision of giant hooves crashing down on them. But Lyorn drew the horse to a prancing stop. "And you said all your friends were dead."

"Soon will be." A bow creaked behind them.

"No!" Erryna cried. "It's not his fault. It's mine. I tried to escape and—"

"And we don't kill him, why?" But Lyorn raised a hand to stop the archer.

"Because he—he could be useful."

Lyorn looked down at Aychus, standing in the mud. "What use are you?"

Aychus straightened his back. Standing behind him as she was, Erryna noticed for the first time how broad he'd become, and tall. Far taller than her, which wasn't saying much. She'd always wanted to be tall, but never more than this moment. Long legs made quick work of running.

"I can fight and hunt," he said. "Sword and bow."

"Sounds dangerous." Lyorn grinned and rough laughter broke out all around them. "You're also lame."

"I got around well enough to kill Erryna's guard."

"No!" An idea was taking shape. "It was my idea. I killed her."

"*Stop* helping," Aychus muttered.

"He just did what I told him to. He's good at taking orders."

Aychus turned his head and glared at her.

"He's a strapping lad, I'll give you that." Lyorn narrowed his eyes. "Right, then. We'll see what he's made of. See what he's ready to spend to live."

One of the Arrowhenge started to speak but Lyorn cut him off. "Tribes are built, not born."

Whatever it meant, it silenced the protest.

"Take him back," Lyorn said. "Hand me up the girl. I'll have to see to her myself, I suppose."

Someone sloshed through the water behind Erryna and, before she could duck out of the way, he snaked an arm tight under her ribs, carried her to Lyorn's horse, and shoved her up. Lyorn grabbed her, arm around her, and put her in front of him. Her nightgown slipped up shamefully and the saddle pressed the tender skin of her inner thighs. She tried to shift a little, but Lyorn's arm was too firm, leaving her wedged between the saddle and his big body.

Back at camp, Lyorn dismounted and hauled her down, his fingers rough and painful. Erryna bit back a cry of frustration at being handled like a child. He bound her to a tree and pinned her rope with the spike and mallet again. Aychus had been made to walk, hobbled at wrist and ankle, a noose around his neck that jerked tighter every time he fell behind. He bore it all with no more than a few frustrated grunts. At camp, they strapped him to a tree nearby to Erryna, ropes digging into his skin high under the chin, shoulder, ribs, hips, thighs, and ankles. He struggled but couldn't move.

"If he breaks, he'll be useful," Lyorn said to Erryna.

"What are you going to do to him?"

"Same as us all. Tribes are built, not born, girl."

She stared at him, mystified.

He made a noise of disdain. "We mark him and see where he lands, eh?"

One of the Arrowhenge laid something in the hot coals, stirring them up. His back blocked Erryna's view.

Erryna's stomach twisted in to a tight, sick knot. "Why did you come here?" she hissed to Aychus. "You were free."

"For you," he whispered. Air rasped in his chest. *"My lady."*

She blinked.

Lyorn wasted no time. Aychus snarled but Lyorn grasped his chin and stuffed his mouth full of a wad of fabric. He strode back to the fire, pulled something out with tongs, and grasped it with a thick rag. Another warrior laid his hand on Aychus' forehead and turned his head so one cheek pressed hard against the rough bark. Aychus made wordless noises.

"Tell him to be still, if he answers to you, girl," Lyorn said. "It'll go easier on him."

Erryna swallowed and forced herself to look at Aychus. He tried to twist his head from the meaty hand holding it in place.

"Aychus. Just. Please be still."

His wild eyes met hers. He blinked and quieted his struggle, though she could see his trembles.

Lyorn drew in close and pressed the hot arrowhead against Aychus' cheek, holding it in place. Aychus made muffled cries of pain and terror; *gods, it sounds like the cry from that muted wretch.* The smell of flesh burning turned Erryna's stomach and she fought down her disgust. She would not throw up again. She would not falter, not when Aychus was at stake, when his eyes were locked on hers for courage. She forced herself to stare at him, even when his gaze slid away.

At last Lyorn released him. Aychus sagged in his ropes and spat out his gag, which crumbled from his mouth in a wet, bloody mess. He must have bitten his own tongue. The arrow burned in his cheek was red as new-spilled blood.

"Loosen the lad's ropes. I wager he won't try to escape for a bit."

Aychus let his head fall forward. His hand strained to get to his face, but it was still bound to his side. Erryna's eyes heated and her throat tightened. She turned her face away, unable to keep watching. But a sick, twisting fury built inside her.

After spending a day tied to the tree and then given a bath in the river "to wash away the stink of nobility" as Lyorn put it, Aychus passed the day limping silently around camp, doing odd jobs as the Arrowhenge bid him. Lyorn looked pleased, Aychus kept his marred face downcast, and anger festered in Erryna like the burn on Aychus' cheek. Surely if he was so compliant, the brand had robbed him of his soul.

That night, Lyorn took Erryna into his tent. She slept rolled in her filthy cloak on the cold damp ground, her rope tied around his brawny arm. He was a light sleeper; he opened his eyes at her every motion. There was no escaping him.

"Tomorrow, Bonehaven comes," he said the next evening near nightfall. "Tonight, you bathe."

"There's no bath, no soap, no—"

Lyorn laughed. "There's a river." He unpinned her rope from her tree and gestured to Aychus. "You, lad. Bring her *ladyship* soap and a cloth to dry with." He tossed Aychus a bulky, soft bag.

Aychus limped behind them in silent obedience. Erryna wondered if there was some magicks at work within the mark they'd given him.

She wondered if he would ever stop limping, if the war injury caused him much pain, how badly his cheek stung. She wondered if he still had his soul.

Aychus stopped at the river's edge with the items in his arms. Lyorn settled on a rock close to the bank and went to work striking a fire in a two-bowl pipe.

Erryna's breath froze in her chest. *Father's pipe.*

Lyorn eyed Erryna when she didn't move. "Get to it."

"Aren't I to have any privacy?"

Lyorn just looked at her.

She turned to the river with a wince, putting her back to him, and pulled the cloak from her shoulders. It fell to the ground in a crusted heap. Then, nothing for it, she undid the lacing on the stained nightgown and let it slide down her body. The cool air made her shiver, but she was glad for whatever darkness the gods had granted in the pre-moonlit evening. She stepped from her boots and walked carefully over the slick rocks. Icy water rushed over it, chilling her feet to the ankles and then up her calves. She shivered. The water was so cold it felt as if it burned her legs.

She thought of Aychus and his burned cheek. Her back straightened.

"Hair, too. You stink," Lyorn called. "Toss her the soap, lad."

She crossed her arm over her breasts and turned a little. Aychus tossed the soap, a misshapen bar of grey, without looking at her. It splashed upstream. She slipped going for it. The hard stones, while rubbed smooth from the river, still hurt her backside. She sat, stunned by pain lancing up her spine, freezing river rushing by. The soap floated out of reach. She snatched at it, missed. Something brushed by her back and she shrieked.

Lyorn barked laughter. "Just a redcarne snake. They're good for supper." He rested her father's pipe on his knee and wiped his eyes, bent over with the strain of mirth.

A snake!? She rose out of the water and started back to shore. A moon was rising. So much for the gods granting privacy of darkness. Brightest, tiny Zozia's light had spilled over the river and onto the bank.

For the first time since Aychus had been branded, he looked right in Erryna's eyes. Then, quick as that snake had gone by, he was on Lyorn. She didn't even see him limp. Every strike was neat, well placed. The thud of fist against bone went right through her. But Lyorn was bigger, stronger. He roared and came back on Aychus. The two grappled and rolled.

Erryna stared, naked in the frigid water, clutching the soap to her belly. Took a step forward and tripped. Again she went down, forward this time, battering her knees and palms. Fury consumed her. She slapped the water, cursing. She cut her hand on the sharp edge of a big, jagged rock. She wanted to throw something, scream, destroy. Hitting water wasn't enough. She scrabbled at the rock, dislodging it from the sucking mud of the river bottom, though it wasn't too heavy for her to lift once she pried it free. She climbed to her feet.

Lyorn slammed Aychus to the ground and hit his face. The fragile, new burn on his cheek tore. Aychus moaned as blood splattered. Lyorn raised up enough to drag him to the water and shove his head in, twisting his head so the water flowed over his nose and mouth. Aychus' moans turned to sputtering. His whole body struggled but he couldn't fight it. His whole body shuddered and struggled. Lyorn threw his whole weight on the younger man with a growl.

The rock bounced off Lyorn's head from the impact. He collapsed on top of Aychus, who tried to lift his head. Erryna splashed closer, reached down and grasped Lyorn by her father's baldric, slipping in the wet mud as she hauled him off Aychus. He was a limp, dead weight. She kept tugging until Lyorn was face down in the water, wishing she could hit him again, but the rock was on the bank. She twisted her fingers into his braid and shoved down as hard as she could, pressing Lyorn's face against the rocks in the bottom, water streaming from her naked body, leaning over him, putting all her weight into it.

She didn't know how long it was before she felt a warm hand on her back. "Erryna." A cough.

She startled, stumbling back in the water. The hand steadied her.

"We must go. Now. Before we're expected back. Come." Aychus sounded rough but calm. He kept his gaze steady on her face. Blood streamed down his cheek from the torn brand. His hair curled into tight gold ringlets.

His mother had curly hair. She'd seen it on the sprawling dead woman, ringlets floating in blood.

"Did they take your soul?" she whispered.

"Erryna. We must go now." He tugged on her arm.

Her heart lurched into a painful sprint. She blinked at him and sucked air. Caught the scent of blended pipesmoke. She stumbled from the water to the bank and found it, unbroken among the reeds. Grasped it and drew in more familiar scent.

"Boots. Go. Across the river." Aychus shoved the lumpy bag and her boots into the water, and strode into the water to Lyorn. He rolled Lyorn over, fumbled with the buckles on the baldric and belt, and pulled the sword from the body. "Go!"

It was easier to do as he bid rather than think. She slipped her muddy feet into her boots, clutched the bag to her chest with one hand, the pipe in the other, and splashed across the river. The air chilled her bare wet skin but she shoved off the thought and kept running, weaving between trees. She heard nothing behind her and turned to look. Aychus ghosted behind her in his limping, silent lope.

In the night, she sat against a tree, running her thumb over the smooth bowls of the pipe, every so often lifting it to catch the scent. The dress in the bag was warm, a serviceable gown. Aychus frowned at the crimson fabric, but told her he'd get her decent clothes later.

"I also need to teach you to move quietly through the woods," he said.

"Your father taught me when I was a child."

"You must learn again."

Her own father, the lord, had taught her nothing. Fine. She would learn to survive on her own, then. A rough plan was already taking shape in her mind, something that terrified and thrilled her all at once.

Aychus ripped up the bag for bandages. She'd taken her feet out of her boots to dry more fully and to ease the hurt of their rubbing. He *tsked* as he wrapped them. "This will help the blistering. I'm sorry we've no salve."

"You'd need it for your face worse. Will the army take you back like that?" With a wilder scar on his face? Would they even believe he was loyal anymore?

"It doesn't matter. The king is dead, Erryna."

She blinked at him.

"It's why the tribes are fighting, why Arrowhenge dared attack the manse. It's why I came back. I had to warn your father and mine."

"But—"

"You're a lord's daughter, the last of your line with a claim to the throne. Some lord would as soon kill you as let you be a problem."

A lord's daughter. It's what Lyorn had called her; the measure of her worth. And now maybe her death. Her back straightened. "And Arrowhenge? They killed my family."

"They killed mine, as well."

She lifted the pipe to her nose for a moment, then lowered it again. The damp, fresh scents of the woods smelled foreign. Her fingers closed tight around the pipe and she tucked it into a pocket in her skirts.

Faint fieldburn smoke rode the air that first night, before the wilders came. And then her stone manse had burned. Stone, molten like iron thrown on a fire...

"Father had started burning the fields," she said slowly. "How do they do that, make damp ground burn?"

He gave her a look. "Burn powder."

"Where does he keep the powder?"

"In the dugout by the creek. It'll start anything."

She stared at her father's leather baldric crossing his chest. "You speak like you will stay with me. You carry my father's sword."

"My family is liege to yours," he said, "and you don't know how to use a sword."

"Are you soulless?" It came out harsher than she meant.

His hand went to his burned cheek. He dropped it. "Would you turn me away if I was?"

She should. The soulless could be dangerous. "I'm going to kill the Arrowhenge. If you remain liege to me, you will follow. If not, I release you." She pulled on her boots and ignored her sore feet. "I won't turn you away unless you wish to go."

His jaw tightened. "How? You don't know how to fight, Erryna."

Not like him. Not like her father. But swords weren't the only weapon in the world.

Zozia was nearly gone and no other moons had dared the horizon. Night was safest, especially a godless night such as this. Fitting. The Seven Eyes had watched their families die and done nothing. They'd be too cowardly to watch them seek justice, and they couldn't see Aychus anyway.

The night was so silent they barely dared to whisper. Fortunately, spreading powder on the ground in a thick circle around the camp didn't make much noise. The dampness of the soil cloaked their footfalls.

"This is madness," Aychus hissed.

She shook her head. At least she could make sure the Arrowhenge didn't survive to kill anyone else. Still, her belly was in knots as she trailed the powder from the awkward bag toward the low fire flickering at the center of camp. Aychus stayed behind, as she ordered. No sense in both of them getting caught.

Two wilders sat on the other side of the fire. The coals were crimson and hot; perfect. She'd have to run quick in and quick out to escape. No small trick in a gown. She'd fallen before, but no gods were present to trip her up this time.

She drew a breath and ran at the campfire, trailing the powder in a thick black line from the heavy bag. The wilders leapt to their feet and came at her, shouting. She tossed the bag onto the flames, turning to run back in the same motion. She stumbled over the front of her gown but caught it up in her fist and kept on. The fire burst, hot on her back, and flashed all along the powder trail, turning shouts into panicked screams.

The first thing the Arrowhenge would do was try to put out the fire. With luck, it would also be their last.

She met Aychus at the river and they crossed without talking. Screams pierced the night air and all the other noises died but for birds on the wing overhead. When she glanced back, she saw the night around the camp had grown bright despite the missing moons. The woods echoed with the dying cries of the soulless.

— FIRE WALKER —
by Keith Gouveia

I GNIS WATCHED FROM THE SHADOWS as his mother and father performed for the gathering crowd. Light from the pyres refracted off the polished steel of his father's daggers as he tossed them into the air with grace, catching them and returning them to the air with skilled precision. His mother, dressed in a red gown that glowed in the firelight, gradually added another blade to the collective until his father juggled six.

The rain had come and gone earlier in the day, but the clouds remained. Their presence almost blocked out the light of the red moon entirely, allowing the fires to burn brighter in their shadows. Though he preferred not to be this close to the savage land of the Oscura, he could not deny the brilliance of his father.

Not a bad turnout, he thought as the crowd settled around the performance square. Even the drunkards from the tavern had abandoned their ale to see. *You were right, Father, they are indeed happy for the distraction.*

Life in Cruor was tough enough without worrying about Oscura raiding parties, and what possessed these good people to claim their right to live so close to the cannibals' borders was beyond Ignis's reasoning.

His father tossed one of the blades toward the crowd. Screams of shock and surprise echoed as the blade harmlessly penetrated the soil at their feet. The panic quickly turned to laughter and applauds as, one by one, the daggers his father juggled hurled toward other sections of the crowd. Two young boys who had been sitting side-by-side scurried away from each other as the last dagger landed in the small opening between them. With their eyes wide and mouths agape, they stared at the pommel of the weapon, obviously fantasizing about the possibility of it killing either of them.

Soon Ignis would be introduced and then it would be his turn to perform. With his staves in hand, he dipped the wicking ends in the bowls of nujol oil and waited for his mother to ignite his entrance. All he need do is to not make a mistake, else face the harsh sting of his father's whip. Even if the crowd failed to notice his left foot an inch off its mark, an erroneous error as that would not escape the critical eye of Darshawn.

"And now," Darshawn said with his hands raised high, "good people of Fanguard, I introduce you to Ignis. My son. The fire walker!"

With a smile and a twirl, Ignis's mother lit a torch in the nearest pyre and then bent at the knees to ignite a path of rocks that had been soaked in nujol oil. As the flames spread along the path leading to the back of his parents' wagon, Ignis took a deep breath and waited for the cue.

A wall of flame burst forth as the fire reached the end of the trail where a heavy saturation of fuel lay dormant. The fire's roar caused several of the on-lookers to lean back, and before the fire died down, Ignis jumped through. His staves instantly catching fire as he passed through the flames.

As his feet touched the hot rocks, his arms and hands went to work twirling the staves, surrounding his torso in an orange glow. He stood in place for a moment, circling his body with the fire, the heat intense enough to evaporate the sweat from his body as it formed. With fluidity in his movements, Ignis performed the routine his father had taught him. He'd been doing it half of his life now.

In the crowd, he saw the young boys watching him. Their eyes wide and lower lips drooped open in wonderment. Ignis wondered if they were ever going to blink.

I'll show them something they'll never forget.

He twirled the staff in his left hand horizontally, the flames kissing his cheek as he prepared for his next trick. Once ready, he tossed the staff into the air, then quickly jumped forward into a one-armed handstand. The crowd erupted into applause as the airborne staff came to rest on the soles of his feet. As he felt his balance waver, he kicked his feet upward. The staff hurled into the air as he righted himself in a flip, he then caught the falling staff and entered a new series of twirls.

The applause continued as he danced down the stone path. The flames licked his ankles and relayed the urgency that he needed to pick up the pace. Once off the flame-covered path and on soft, cooling soil, he tilted his head back and swallowed an ignited tip of his staff, extinguishing the flame.

As his mother took the first staff from his right hand, Ignis rotated the second staff in his left hand and proceeded to swallow the other lit end. He could feel his throat widen as the wick material passed over his uvula. His stomach tightened, but he overcame the instinct to gag and withdrew the now extinguished staff end. The second one always gave him trouble; he figured it was due to the irritation caused by the first. Fortunately, his father never asked him to do more than the two ends.

While his mother dipped the first staff into a bucket of water, his father coated one of his daggers with nujol oil.

"For our finale, my son requires complete silence from the audience. One distraction, one second of doubt, and my son's life will be forfeit."

Every time he heard the speech, Ignis found the words amusing. He didn't need silence; he just needed to keep his eyes on the prize.

Ignis steeled his nerves as his father ignited the blade in fire. An eerie silence befell the crowd as Ignis's father stepped in line with him and took aim. The blazing dagger drew back and slowly sliced through the air as his father determined the proper attack point. He aligned the blade up once more and let it fly from his hand. The crowd gasped as one. Ignis's mother screamed — all part of the show — as the blade came toward his face with precise accuracy.

With his hands pointing upward, he caught the blade between his palms — the sharp tip a hair's length from the bridge of his nose. The crowd stood and erupted in thunderous applause.

"Ladies and gentleman...my son!" Ignis's father started to clap, then bowed before the cheering crowd. Ignis followed his lead as, too, his mother.

"Bravo! Bravo!" said a man as he stood, his portly belly reverberating as he clapped. "Excellent show. What extraordinary feats."

"Thank you, my lord is too kind," Ignis's father replied.

"Your son, how does he do it?" asked the bulbous man.

Ignis took that as his cue to return to the wagon. Without his gloves, the dragon scales sewn into his palms were visible. More often than not, the crowd demanded the opportunity to shake his hand and to share drink and food as part of the payment for the entertainment. He needed to mask his secret, else face his father's wrath.

"Now, my lord, surely you know it is not befitting of a performer to reveal his secrets."

"Ah." The man waved his hand as if to dismiss the notion, but pressed no further.

Upon entering the wagon, all further conversations were out of Ignis's earshot. He closed the door behind him to discourage any of the children from following him, and he took a moment to breathe and relax.

He rubbed the hard, course scale embedded in his right palm. When he was just an adolescent, he and his father came upon the decaying remains of a dragon on a plateau while foraging in the mountains neighboring the town of Mossdeep. Fearful of entering the accursed town and being afflicted with the black moss, his father refused to put on a show and trade for much needed supplies. Instead, his mother remained with the wagon as Ignis and his father climbed the steep rock face in search of rostrum eggs or malikboar to take with them on their journey to the next town.

The dragon had been long dead, its meat rotten and festering with insects. However, scattered across the ground, its blood-red scales were perfectly intact. At first, his father was more concerned with finding a rostrum nest, certain the carcass would have attracted a flock or two. But as Ignis explored the once majestic beast, and no rostrums were found, his father's thoughts turned to profit, rather than food. After picking up a scale and feeling its rough texture, his father figured the dragon's hide was too thick for the rostrums' beaks to open and that they most likely sought more suitable food while hoping a larger scavenger would come along and penetrate the scales.

"Amazing, isn't it?" his father had asked.

"What Father?"

"That even in death, these scales protect the beast. I can't tell you when I heard of the last dragon sighting. It's been so long, and this creature must have been atop this mountain for many darkenings."

There was an unmistakable look in his father's eyes that day — wide and glossy. One Ignis would never forget. He had looked upon Ignis not as his son, but rather another piece of his show. A commodity he could manipulate to his benefit. Father collected scales and moved on.

When they had reached the bottom of the mountain, to their surprise, a malikboar lay at his mother's feet. A pool of blood gathered around its head and Ignis took notice of the dagger plunged in its neck. The silver quills on its back twittered as the wild-beast expelled its last breath. Ignis caught sight of the blood on the beast's tusks before realizing his mother clutched her left arm. The flesh of her bicep spread apart in a crimson crevice, exposing ligaments and globules of fat.

His father rushed her into the wagon and Ignis had watched him tend to the deep gash. He gave her something to drink and she lay peaceful in sleep as the wound was sewn closed. Ignis still cursed himself for not inquiring how or what the concoction was, but he was just a boy stricken with guilt for leaving his own mother unguarded.

When his father was finished dressing the wound, his attention returned to Ignis. After pouring him something to drink, his father explained the significance of the dragon scales and the theory running inside his mind.

After the conversation, his memory was blank. That was the last thing he remembered before waking up with the scales stitched into his palms and soles of his feet. Even now, as a young man, he would often find himself scratching the scales out of habit. How they itched and irritated him. When his father had caught him trying to pull the scales from his flesh, his arms were tied to his sides until the outer-lining skin fused with the scales. While healing, he was fed by his mother as if he were a babe again.

Though he performed at his mother's request, he still harbored a hatred for what his father had done. Not just at the deed, but the man as well. A hatred so strong, he felt as though he would carry it on, and it would keep his fire burning even in the next world.

It was selfish of you, Father, Ignis thought as he scratched at the edge of the scale.

"Ignis," his mother called for him. "What's taking you so long, dear?"

Ignis's mind returned to the task at hand. His gloves and boots were by the door, right where he left them and he quickly slid them on.

"What were you doing in there?" his father asked as Ignis stepped out of the wagon. "Our host is waiting."

"Sorry… I couldn't find my gloves," he whispered so as not to be overheard by the surrounding crowd. After what his father had put him through and the threats made against him should his secret be revealed, he had no problem lying to the man.

"But I thought I saw… ah, never mind." His father put his arm around Ignis. "You did good today, Son. I'm proud of you."

"Hear hear!" several of the men in the crowd roared.

Fools, Ignis thought. He knew better than to believe the farce. *Just another part of the show.*

"Come," said the portly man, "we have prepared a great feast in your honor."

They followed him to a large banquet table set up outside with a variety of foods from one end to the other. At the center, a large malikboar sat proudly — its fur draped over the cooked meat to make it look as if it were still alive. Potatoes, onions, and carrots circled the dead animal. Dozens of game birds were displayed much the same way; their colorful feathers lay atop them like a morbid garnish. Piles of bread, pitchers of ale, salted meats. Tonight, Ignis would eat like a king.

"Pinguis, you honor us," said Ignis's father as he slapped the fat man on the shoulder.

The man laughed, hands upon his reverberating belly. "I only wish it was more. Your performance has lifted our spirits."

"And that is all the payment we desire."

Ignis shook his head at his father's lie.

The town folk gathered around the large table, but the food remained untouched.

"Please," Pinguis said, extending his right arm, "guests first. Enjoy."

Ignis's father bowed, then approached the table. One of the town's women pulled off the malikboar's hide to reveal the evenly cooked meat lying in wait. While his mother and father grabbed a loaf of bread and ripped it in half, Ignis approached the once wild beast and plucked a piece off its shoulder.

He breathed in the meat's aroma, then passed it over his lips and lay it upon his tongue. *Delicious*, he thought.

"Here honey," his mother passed him the half a loaf of bread, "use this to gather what you want so the others can partake."

The bread was partially scooped out, creating a trench so he could pile on what he wished and carry it away. While his mother made another trench for herself, Ignis ripped off a leg quarter from a game hen, grabbed a potato and onion, then tore off another strip of meat from the malikboar's hind leg. As he left the table, he grabbed a smaller loaf of bread — a small, rounder loaf with a darker crust.

As he walked away from the table he noticed the wide grin on Pinguis's face. He nodded as he passed the man.

"Enjoy lad, perhaps later you can teach me a trick or two."

Ignis simply smiled and continued on his way. There was no way his father would allow him to tell anyone of their secret. He had refused a bag of gold coins once offered; a hearty meal and a warm smile would not be enough to persuade the stubborn man.

As the night carried on, the townspeople ate, laughed and forgot about the constant threat of living so close to the Oscura border.

"Now Ignis, I hope you don't mind my pestering, but I have seen enough to know that your skills are the greatest in the land. I have studied the art..."

Great, he thought as the portly man continued.

"...and I know that the time of contact along with the thermal retention of the coals is the secret. Yet, you remain in one spot longer than anyone I've ever seen. How do you do it?"

"Sir," interrupted a petite woman wrapped in a black shawl. She was carrying two trenches of food. "I'd like to bring the men stationed in the towers something to eat, but I need help. It's only right they get to partake."

Ignis stood, seizing the opportunity to get away from the interrogation. "I'd be happy to do it."

"Pignuis, are you pestering my boy again?" Ignis's father asked as he approached.

"Not at all," the man lied.

"I was just going to bring some food to the guards," Ignis said.

"Well hurry back," his father ordered.

"Yes sir."

With that, Ignis excused himself, taking one of the trenches filled with meat and potatoes from the young woman. She smiled and led the way. He followed her away from the cacophony toward the edge of town, and then broke away when she pointed him toward the right side tower. As he walked, he looked over his shoulder to see her approach the left side tower.

The towers were made from long, slender tree limbs with a lookout perched high above the homes. When he grabbed hold of the ladder leading up, Ignis knew it was not going to be easy with one hand. The whole structure seemed to sway with his added weight.

Once at the top, the stationed guard placed his hands under Ignis's arms and helped him inside the wooden basket.

"Thank you so much," said the guard as he accepted Ignis's offer. "I was watching you perform, you were remarkable."

Ignis smiled. "Thank you. I'm glad you got to— " Out of his peripheral vision, movement caught his attention. He focused his eyes and watched the ground with unblinking eyes. The tall stalks of grass swayed in an unfelt breeze.

"What's wrong?" asked the guard.

"Something's out there."

Wasting no time to verify Ignis's words, the guard ignited the tip of an arrow and launched the flaming spear into the air. The arrow stuck in the ground and the small flame ignited several stalks of grass upon impact. The sudden light exposed dozens of pale men — wearing nothing but scaly loincloths — crawling across the ground on their bellies as if they were serpents, heading straight for the town.

"Oscura!" said the guard.

A horn blew and Ignis knew then the guard in the other tower had seen the imminent threat as well. The guard beside Ignis lit and launched several more arrows in order to reveal the savages' true numbers. However, with their position exposed, the Oscura warriors stood and charged, making it near impossible to count the odds.

"There's too many of them," said the guard as he took aim on an enemy warrior. He released his arrow and caught his target in the chest, just above the heart. The Oscura warrior screamed as he toppled over, driving the arrowhead deeper into his chest.

"Should have known they'd take advantage of the cloud cover. Man your posts!" Pignuis commanded as he unsheathed two short swords from their scabbards. "And whatever you do, protect the dead to the best of your ability. Do not allow them to take a single one of us. I'll die before I allow them to feast on your bones and I hope you'll do the same for me."

Seeing the townsfolk of Fanguard take up arms and create a line to meet the threat, and with a newfound respect for the bulbous man in charge, Ignis joined the battle. As quick as he could, he climbed down the rickety ladder and headed toward his family's wagon for his staves. Though he was efficient with a sword, he preferred the staves. The rock hard material could easily bash a skull in on itself, and quite often the staves instilled arrogance in his opponents that he could capitalize on.

"Ignis, let's go!" His father waved him toward the wagon.

The coward is fleeing? he thought as he ran to him.

"We have to go."

"We can't leave these people, we can help," Ignis said.

"It's not our fight," his father said.

"Ignis, don't argue," added his mother.

"We have to help them. How far do you think we could actually get if they fail to hold them back?"

"They'll be too busy skinning them to worry about us."

The sound of metal clanging was followed by screams as the Oscura warriors reached the town's limits.

"They need us, Father. Can't you see that?"

"Look out!" His father grabbed him by the arm and pulled him forward.

An Oscura warrior had penetrated the line and flanked Ignis. He felt the sudden whoosh of air against the back of his neck and realized then how close he was to death. The sound of steel smacking the wagon's wood echoed in his ear, followed by scraping metal as his father withdrew his sword.

"Savage!" his father announced, lunging with his sword.

The Oscura warrior deflected the blow and quickly parried, but Ignis's father easily recovered. As the two dueled with neither gaining the upper hand, the ground shook. Ignis's legs wobbled as he searched for the cause. The fire outside the town's limits from the arrows slowly faded, but there was a soft orange light illuminating the darkness beyond.

"Whoa," he whispered as the shadows at the outskirts of town receded to reveal a great beast approaching. He ran closer.

"Ignis! Wait!" The command was followed by a scream of agony and Ignis knew the savage had fallen to his father's blade.

He disobeyed his father, and forgot to grab his staves in the process.

Dragging a long, slender tale across the green pasture on four short legs that barely bent at the joints, a creature unlike any Ignis had seen in his travels. Its belly hung low, scraping the ground. The orange skin seemed to glow in the darkness and revealed dark, black spots. If not for the massive body, the rounded face with a short nose and beady eyes would not inspire fear within him. Flames danced at the edges of its wide grin, and Ignis knew then it posed a great threat to the people of Fanguard.

He looked around to see the townspeople locked in battle. Behind him, his father approached, slaying any Oscura warriors foolish enough to cross his path. "We have to get these people out of here," he said to his father, but the man had his hands full with protecting his unarmed son.

"Leave our homes to these savages? Never!" said Pignuis as he deflected a strike from an Oscura warrior with one of his short swords and ran his other across the man's abdomen. Entrails spilled, and the warrior dropped his twisted blade to catch the tubular tissue.

As Ignis watched Pignuis plant his boot into the Oscura warrior, he felt a strange heat baring down on him. He turned around in time to see a large fireball hurl toward him. Without panic, he quickly rolled to his left, narrowly dodging the large ball of flame. He looked over his shoulder to make sure no one else was in danger. Plumes of flames and dirt launched into the air as it struck the ground just behind him.

The beast continued its approach. Ignis looked around in hopes of finding someone to aide him in taking down the great beast, but there was no one. Even his mother was too preoccupied to help him stand against this monstrosity. He stepped toward it. The beast's head tilted back and when it lowered it, another ball of flames shot forth.

Not wanting the ball of flames to harm anyone, Ignis forced all of his strength to his legs and braced himself. Palms out, nerves steeled, he received the fireball. Though the dragon scales protected his hands, the immense heat caused boils to form on his forearm almost instantly.

I've got to get rid of this, he thought.

Ignis tilted his hands back, then shoved forward with all his might. The fireball flew back toward the dragon-like creature and struck the beast on its left side. Its rider screamed and fell to the ground and was trampled underneath the beast's clawed foot.

He looked at the white swelling orbs on his skin and realized he could not afford to do that again. Even without its rider, the beast continued its march into Fanguard.

I've got to stop it.

"Ignis!"

He turned toward Pignuis.

The man tossed one of his short swords toward him. "Take it down!"

The weapon clanged against the ground at his feet. He bent at the knees and scooped it up without hesitation.

With the short sword in hand, he charged the lumbering beast.

As he drew close, it swiped its massive claws. He ducked and saw the mount's reigns dangling at the beast's neck. He changed direction and took his chances. Ignis lunged and grabbed hold of the leather straps and planted his feet against the beast's leg. Heat radiated from the creature's neck and he quickly climbed up toward the mount, hewing at its flesh the entire way. Molten blood flowed from the wounds. The beast thrashed its body, but Ignis held the straps steadfast.

When he reached the mount, Ignis plunged his sword all the way to the hilt into the back of the creature's neck. A deafening roar echoed on the air as he pulled the blade out and delivered another blow. The beast's flat head reared up, flames spilled over its bottom jaw as it bellowed in pain.

"Die!" Ignis pulled the blade out once more and with all his strength, drove it into the back of its skull.

A shockwave trembled across the lizard's body as its legs no longer had the strength to hold it up. It toppled over to the right, Ignis falling with it. The beast crashed to the ground and succumbed to Ignis's blade and pinned the boy's foot under its weight.

"Ignis!" his father shouted as he ran toward him.

He struggled to roll the spongy flesh off of him, the heat radiating from the creature searing his unprotected skin. Movement at his left caused him to take his eyes off the task at hand. An Oscura warrior charged toward him, a twisted blade raised over his head.

Ignis closed his eyes as the savage came within striking distance.

"No!"

Father?

Steel clanged. He opened his eyes to see his father's blade locked against the savage's just above the bridge of his nose.

He saved me.

Another Oscura warrior charged. With his father vulnerable to attack, Ignis pushed with all his might to free his foot.

With both hands on the grip of his sword, Ignis's father finally achieved the upper hand in the clash and shoved his opponent away. Without missing a beat, and with an uncanny fluidity in his movements, he arced his blade and sliced the savage's throat. The warrior dropped his sword and clutched his wound. Blood seeped through his fingers and spilled to the ground, the viscous fluid in his throat turning his final breaths into an incoherent gargle.

"Father, lookout!"

The second warrior capitalized on the distraction and thrust his sword into Ignis's father's back. His father winced and exhaled a painful gasp as the tip of the sword protruded from the right side of his abdomen. He then turned around to face his assailant, pulling the sword free from the surprised warrior's hand.

"Vile beast!" His father swung his sword, running the blade across the warrior's chest. Without a tunic or chain mail, flesh parted to steel and both Ignis's father and the Oscura warrior fell to their knees.

Finally freed, Ignis inspected his father's wound. Given the sword's angle, Ignis doubted it would be fatal. He braced one hand against his father's back and the other on the sword's handle.

"Don't," his father said.

"But—"

"If you pull it out, I'll surely bleed to death before I reach the wagon."

For the first time in his life, Ignis experienced the fear of losing his father. All that time spent hating the man for what he had done was wasted. He knew that now. "What do I do, Father?"

"Nothing. They'll pick me off if I try to walk. You must go. Save yourself and protect your mother. The two of you are all that matters."

Tears pooled at the thought. "I can't leave you."

"Behind you!"

Ignis turned around at his father's command. An Oscura warrior charged toward him, his twisted blade perched high above his head ready to slice through his skull. His blood boiled at the sight of the pale man and he stepped forward to meet his adversary.

As the blade descended, Ignis caught the man's wrists and kicked the savage underneath the scrap of lizard skin around his waist. The warrior fell to the ground in a heap, clutching the tender organ. Ignis picked up the twisted blade and plunged it into the savage's chest, just above his heart.

"Come on," he said to his father as he grabbed hold of his left arm and draped it over his shoulders.

"You're being foolish, boy. We'll never make it," his father said as he was hoisted onto his feet.

"Then we'll die together." He stepped forward, forcing his father to step in time with him.

"Well in case we do...I love you, Son."

Ignis's knees buckled and he wasn't certain if it was his father's added weight or the weight of his father's words that caused the slight stumble. "Don't talk like that," he finally said after several steps.

All around them, Oscura warriors were locked in battle with the residents of Fanguard. Men and women fought side-by-side to combat the threat. What he once thought of as a terrible place to live revealed its appeal to him. There was a camaraderie unlike any other in Cruor and he realized, though it pained him to admit it, he was still young and naïve to the world.

"Their numbers are thinning. We're going to make it."

"Ignis!" He heard his mother's voice.

"Julianna, stay where you are!"

Ignis's mother ran to them — a bloodstained dagger in each hand. His gaze traveled over her body, searching for signs of injury and seeing her healthy and disobeying his father, forced a smile upon his face.

Now I know where I get it, he thought.

"Stay away from them!" Julianna stopped long enough to toss one of her daggers.

Ignis's gaze followed the trajectory of the small, jewel encrusted blade and watched as it landed with precise accuracy in the throat of a nearby Oscura warrior. He stumbled forward, fell, and lay in a lump.

"Julianna, you—"

"Oh, hush up, Darshawn," Ignis's mother said as she crouched low and tucked herself against his father's side.

With the burden of his father's weight eased, Ignis picked up the pace. Their path was clear, but he knew at any moment an Oscura warrior could strike and take them down. By the time they were a mere ten paces from the family wagon, cheers echoed in the night.

"They're retreating!" someone shouted.

"Roku and Keagan, pick off as many as you can," Pignuis yelled to the two sentry towers. "Don't let them drag anyone away!"

"Is it over?" Ignis's mother asked as they reached the wagon.

"I think so," he said, looking over his shoulder to see townsfolk catching their breath.

"Good. Let's get your father inside. We need to remove this sword."

"And I'm going to need some mead," added his father.

"What are you lazy dogs lounging for?" Pignuis yelled to the crowd. "You can rest when the wounded have been moved to the infirmary and the dead have been collected. I want guards stationed on the outskirts of town in case any of those vermin are brazen enough to try that again. Let's put some hustle into it!"

When the wagon's rear door closed, Ignis could no longer hear Pignuis's bullish voice barking orders. He had to admit, after seeing the man in battle and the way he commanded his people, the man deserved respect.

"All right, Darshawn, we're going to lay you down on your side. Try not to move."

"What can I do?" Ignis asked, wanting to help his father the way he had helped him.

"We'll need some clean water and rags," his mother said.

"Right." Ignis exited the wagon and grabbed the bucket that dangled on a hook underneath the rear end. He remembered seeing the well over by the tavern and headed in that direction.

Wails of pain and suffering filled the air as the townsfolk dragged or carried the injured to safety. He wished he could help, but vowed to after his father was taken care of. Once at the well, he had to wait his turn as two women were already ahead of him, filling their buckets. He could only assume they were taking them to the infirmary.

With his bucket full, he returned to the wagon to find his mother had cut away his father's shirt and two daggers were placed over the open flame of a lantern.

He looks like a skewered malikboar, Ignis thought.

"Good," his mother said at his return, "I need you to hold him down while I pull the sword free."

"Are you sure?" he asked, not wanting to cause harm.

"Just push your weight down on him, but keep your hands away from the wound."

Ignis nodded, then followed her command.

"Make sure you pull the blade out straight," his father said when Julianna reached for the hilt.

She shoved a wooden spoon into his mouth. "Darshawn, I know what to do. Just try to relax and bite down if you need to."

His father looked so helpless with his wide, teary-eyed gaze. Ignis watched with unblinking eyes as his mother's hand slowly gripped the sword's handle. She hesitated and eyed him, obviously checking to see if he was ready. She nodded and he braced himself against his father. With a quick yank, his father's back straightened as he screamed. The sword clanged against the wood floor when his mother dropped it to quickly soak a rag in the water bucket.

"Here," she handed him a wet rag, "wash the edges of the wound while I clean this one."

As Ignis pressed the cloth against his father's wound, Darshawn grunted in pain and squeezed his eyes shut. With both wounds cleaned, his mother removed the daggers from the lanterns flame and handed him one.

"We have to try to do this at the same time," she said. "We don't want to prolong the pain."

Ignis nodded.

"Quickly, before the steel cools."

He followed her lead and placed the red-hot steel against the wound. The wooden spoon slipped from his father's lips as he screamed in agony. Flesh sizzled as a ribbon of smoke snaked into the air.

When the blades were finally removed from his skin, his father was left panting. Sweat beaded his brow and Julianna quickly patted him down with a fresh, wet rag.

"It's over," she whispered as she stroked his cheek with a loving hand.

Darshawn took a deep breath, closed his eyes, and succumbed to the overwhelming pain.

"Is he—?"

"No, Ignis, he's just resting."

He breathed a sigh of relief, then asked: "Do you need me anymore?"

"Why?"

"I want to go outside and help the others."

She nodded in understanding. "All right. But be careful!"

"I will." He kissed her forehead and headed out the door. When he turned around to catch the door in order to stop it from slamming and disturbing his father, someone grabbed hold of his left hand and twisted his palm up.

The door closed and Ignis turned his body to see who dare touch him.

"I knew it!"

Ignis stared down at the exposed dragon scale in the palm of his hand, his protective gloves incinerated and barely clinging together. He yanked his hand free from Pignuis's pudgy hands.

"Easy lad, you're secret's safe with me."

"What?" he said, shocked by the man's response.

"I saw what you did, I'm grateful to you. As far as I'm concerned, the reason Fanguard is still standing is thanks to you."

"Thank you."

"Did you do this to yourself?"

"No. My father did it when I was very little."

"Genius," Pignuis replied.

"You think?" he asked, staring at the crimson scale. For the first time he realized they represented something more than a man's greed.

"Oh yes. Wish I had thought of it myself. Is your father...?"

"He's fine. He's resting. I want to help the others."

"Then come," Pignuis put his large arm around Ignis's shoulders and pulled him close, "there is much to do before the 'morrow and the threat still looms over us."

Ignis allowed the man to lead the way, willing to do anything asked of him.

— THE HEIGHT OF OUR FATHERS —
by Jeff Salyards

MY SISTER HAD LONG DARK LASHES that would often hook together to form a net in front of her eyes, and she would blink furiously to free them, eyes rolling white like a frightened horse. And this seemed to happen more frequently when she was excited, as she was when we stood before the tomb. I was looking around the mound, into the woods, trying to see if anything was coming upon us. This wasn't the first time we'd broken into graves, but it would be our last. Together at least.

The Vorlu believe that each of us goes on a journey in the afterlife, that everyone should be outfitted according to our deeds and station. A babe is buried with a wooden toy in the hollow of a young tree, tarred in, so the two might grow strong and old together. A priest is laid in the earth with his bones and runes, staff and oils. A warrior, his war gear: spear, axe, shield, what have you. But a warlord—a leader of men, a pillager, a great man—he's either burned in a pyre or buried in an underground vault in his helm and mail, armed with his finest sword, often accompanied by his horse, and his crypt is filled with fruit and meat, milk and mead, furs, coin, hunting horn, drinking horn, bow, glass, musical instruments, perhaps even a slave or two. Everything he would need in the afterlife to pass the time in comfort. A rich grave, indeed. And just the kind we stood in front of.

My sister, Soffjan, looked at me, eyes dark and alert, the cromlech of our ancestors leaning this way and that in the dying light, our breath beginning to show in the air. She looked at me, at the tomb, and then laughed. "Grandfather never did much like company." I had misgivings, but I deferred to her that night, as I did regularly when we were growing up. She suggested our first robbery two summers before. It had always been graves from villages far off, but we couldn't go much farther without our absence being noticed, and if someone from another tribe caught us at our business, the punishment would be death. If someone from our own tribe caught us, we figured we'd be publicly flogged or made to clean smegma for a year. And while scraping the prick of an unwilling stallion was deterrent enough for most, it wasn't quite enough to put us off.

We stood in front of the mound, a pebble cairn as tall as a man with a layer of white quartz around the entrance shining bright as snow, and seeing nothing in the darkening woods, we moved the carved slab blocking the entrance. It wasn't overly heavy—presumably fear of hobgoblins or spirits kept intruders at bay—and after looking at each other briefly, my sister and I entered the grave and waited for our eyes to adjust. The outlines of things would be enough—most of the tombs are constructed the same way, so we knew what to expect. We passed through the antechamber, crept into a corbelled passageway that led down to the burial chamber and all the goods contained therein.

There, we were completely blind. Most cats would have thought better and retreated at this point. I moved slowly, but I couldn't help bumping into some jars and a bowl. Soffjan hissed, but it was hard to tell from where. And then I heard her stop moving and draw in breath. I asked what happened. She didn't answer. I tried again. "What, what is it? Tell me!"

She said, "He's here."

"Of course he is. It's his tomb."

"No. I found him."

I shuffled toward the sound of her voice, and bumped into her back. She was tall for a girl, even for a boy, and I hated her for it, sure I would never catch up. She reached out, fumbled for my wrist, and drew my hand forward. When it touched bone, I stopped breathing. We were both silent for a time, my grandfather's knucklebones laid before us like misshapen die, and Soffjan asked, "What do you remember about him, Bray?"

I thought about it before answering. "He was big. Tall. A gray beard, but nothing on his top lip. Or the top of his head. He had a scar that ran the length of his jaw, breaking up his beard. He was mean. You?"

Even though she was older than me and surely remembered more, she said, "Nothing."

"Do you remember how he died?"

"I think he choked on a chicken bone."

That was her. Mocking the dead and living with equal vigor.

And with that we started looting. We shuffled about and began to catalog the items around the room, whispering what we found, sometimes examining them together, weighing the rot against the price we imagined they would fetch with the merchant. Wooden gameboards with painted pieces, a comb carved out of antler, both discarded. A harp, considered briefly, but the wood too warped. I found a spear with an engraved winged head—my people are prone to naming their favorite weapons, often believing them imbued with magic or power, and I traced the etched name of the spear, "Skybiter," amid many runes. The ash staff was bent and felt like it might not withstand more than a thrust or two, but the head would barter well so I laid the spear on the ground in front of the table.

My sister did the same with a large round shield. The wooden planks were beginning to separate and warp, but the umbo had fared well enough. And so it went, this to steal, that to stay, the pile in front of the table growing, the rest of the chamber strewn with everything else. Having finished searching the goods around the dead, we began to go through the items on his person. We moved to the head of the table. Soffjan unbuckled the helmet and tried to pull it free without disturbing where his bones lay—we might have been graverobbers, but we had no intention of being desecrators if we could help it. But we couldn't. His skull slid away from the other bones and fell free as she hoisted the helmet, clattering on the dusty floor.

The padded lining was soiled and rotten, no doubt the meeting hall of a legion of beetles and spiders, and the metal was tarnished and rusty, but the helm was ceremonial, with gold fittings and elaborate silver engravings, never having been worn in battle, and it was certainly worth keeping. I found a brass torc resting on his neck bones and slipped it into my tunic, ice cold against my skin. Soffjan undid the round clasp holding a beaver skin cloak, dropped it in a pouch at her hip. Beneath the cloak was a shirt of mail, so rusty it hurt to touch, the links all but forged together.

Then we found what we were really looking for. A buckskin belt across what remained of his hips, and a sword in a scabbard. We both jumped for it at the same time, nearly knocking the sword, ourselves, and the boneworks to the floor. We stopped wrestling. I felt for the buckle, undid it. My sister said, "*This... this I remember.*"

Our hands moved up the scabbard. Wood covered in leather, the inside lined with wool, no doubt yellow as piss now. Soffjan got to the hilt quicker and slid the blade free. She stepped away and I heard the sword rush through the air. "Stop. Let me see it, too," I said. I didn't hear any more swings but didn't trust her. "And don't stab me—I'm on your right, I think. Let me come to you." I did and we held it together. It was a broadsword, both the pommel and the ends of the guard carved with the heads of boars. The fuller was wide and long, and the blade was beautifully balanced. Even in absolute darkness I could tell it was a wonderful sword. I hit my sister on the arm with the scabbard and handed it to her. "Put it back, Soff. We have more to claim yet."

She slid it home, reluctantly, and laid the sword against the wall. We were examining his boots when Soffjan grabbed the sleeve of my tunic. "Did you hear that?"

I listened but there was only our heavy breathing. "What? What did you hear?"

She paused. "I don't know. I thought—" And then we both heard it, a scrape, at the entrance from the sounds of it. It could've been a dog sniffing about, a mountain cat looking for moles, a large mountain cat looking for dogs. But it also could've been someone who didn't share our disregard for tradition, sanctity, and ancestors.

Soffjan let go of me and moved away. "Wait. Where are you going? Wait," I whispered, and I might have done too good a job because she didn't respond. She picked something up and moved again, no doubt toward the entrance. "Wait!" But it was no good. It was rarely any good with her. She did as she chose. And she chose the sword.

Phantoms didn't frighten me, but something scraping in the beginning of night is usually armed with blade or tooth. And both scared me quite a bit just then.

I felt my way through the pile in front of the table, grabbed the shaky spear, and hurried to catch up, nearly stabbing my sister in the stomach. Her eyes had adjusted more than mine and she dodged me, pushing me against the wall with her forearm. "Careful," she said. "And be quiet. Listen."

I did, but heard nothing but our breathing and the wind. I waited and began to make out the entrance ahead of us, the outline of my sister, the outline of myself. "I don't hear anything. Do you? Do you hear—"

She snapped, "You. I hear you. Shut up."

We waited together. Nothing. I volunteered, half-hoping, half-believing, "Maybe it was a squirrel. Or a deer. Maybe—"

"Shut. Up."

I did. And we waited some more. Just as I was about to speak again we heard a few pebbles fall down the stairs. We moved toward the entrance together. Soff held the sword before her with both hands and I followed close behind, looking quickly to our left. Nothing there, and as I turned back to the right there was a blur of movement. A crouching figure sprang up, smashing my sister in the head with a shield and sending her sprawling to the grass.

I thrust the spear forward but the shield came whipping back down and almost wrenched the spear out of my hands. Thanks to my useless father, I wasn't as familiar with spear fighting as I should've been at my age, but I knew you couldn't possibly beat a swordsman with a shield if you stayed in his range, so I took a few steps back.

The swordsman was wearing a helm with a leather aventail covering everything of his face save his eyes. He was rangy and familiar, but I didn't have time to think about it as he advanced. I thrust again, this time at his exposed left leg, but he parried it easily. I retreated, sending out thrusts, and he kept closing, almost lazily, swatting them aside.

My opponent moved like a veteran of a hundred battles while I wasn't the veteran of one, and spears work best with other spears in a shield-wall, or from horseback. So, martial inequalities being what they were, I threw the spear at my opponent's foot and ran the other way. Does that sound cowardly? It should. It was. But just then my sister wasn't my concern. My skin was. So I sprinted as if my grandfather's wraith was behind me.

But I only took three steps before pain exploded across my shoulder and then the backs of my legs. I collapsed in the grass, rolled to my side, reached behind me to feel for blood when a boot caught me in the stomach. I closed my eyes, struggling to breathe. When I finally opened them again, my assailant was resting on one knee beside me, helm off, beard in braids, but his upper lip bare like his father before him. "Be glad it's the flat of the blade, boy," My uncle Sirk said. And with a flash of silver he smacked me again.

Once Soff had been roused, my uncle led us back like cattle. If we had an inclination to run, neither of us acted on it. There was nowhere we could go on the island that Sirk couldn't follow, and if he had to capture us twice, the second would have been even less gentle.

Our grandfather's tomb wasn't far from the settlement. Still, it felt like an eternity before we finally left the woods and approached our village—it was small, situated in the foothills of a broad mountain. There were a dozen or so turf longhouses positioned around a large firepit. As was the case on most nights before the snows fell hard, a group of men and women were gathered around the fire, drinking, glassy-eyed, and listening to the skald recite epic poems they'd all heard a thousand times before.

Our uncle told us to stay where we were and walked over to our parents. He threw his helmet down and though we couldn't hear him, we didn't have to. Our parents both stood up and looked in our direction, shaking their heads. Sirk spat again and threw the sword point first into the dirt, where it stuck, quivering, reflecting firelight.

Sirk continued raging and our father looked at him the way a man looks at someone speaking a foreign tongue in a threatening tone, uncomprehending and afraid. When a Vorlu chieftain dies, his holdings are split equally between the children, in this instance, three sons. And as might be expected in such a backwards system, fratricide often results. Age doesn't matter, only strength. And my father was a weak man who preferred his beehives to the battlefield. So his brothers fought it out, and my uncle Drunik drove Sirk and my father from his lands, to the fringe. Sirk had been skirmishing with Drunik on and off ever since, with mixed results. But my father, well… when he died my sister and I would split a handful of underfed goats, a meager flock of sheep, and far too many beehives.

Which, besides her innate perversion, was why Soff was so willing to crack open tombs and dig up the dead, and why I was so willing to follow her. War is the primary means of accumulating wealth in my homeland, graverobbing a distant second. Even if it was reserved for graves outside the tribe.

Our father was a short, jowly man who moved slowly, talked slowly, and always looked as if he drank too much despite not drinking at all, and he made his way around the fire with even less speed than usual, each step seemingly more weighty than the last. Our mother had no such hesitation. She all but sprinted, shouldering onlookers aside until she stood before us, the veins in her arms and throat full to bursting. She looked at my sister, looked at me, nostrils flaring, fists clenched, trying to determine who deserved the greater portion of bile.

And then she slapped me as hard as I've ever been slapped—and I've been slapped viciously on a number of occasions—and I bit my tongue and spit blood. The men in the circle laughed at this, slapped each other in the face too, and drank some more.

Our father reached us and stood there, cheeks billowing, eyes teary as if he'd just been the one slapped. Sirk was with him, and said, "Your children must answer for this. Now."

My father looked at us, obviously wanting to ask if we'd done this thing, hoping we could assure him somehow we hadn't. But he knew his brother wouldn't lie about something as grave as graverobbing, and he looked ambushed, defeated, his thick lips moving slowly and soundlessly in the middle of his thin beard. If I hadn't been so afraid, I might've felt sorry for him. Looking back, I wish I'd shown remorse, penitence, something. But I'm sure all he saw in my face was regret

I'd been caught and terror of punishment. Soff gave him even less, stonefaced.

He turned his back on us, saying only, "Come," and walked toward our longhouse.

My uncle let him go alone for a bit and then smacked me on the back where the blade had landed earlier, and I yelped, again to the amusement of the drunkards around us. My mother grabbed a handful of Soff's hair, twisted it in her long fingers, and pushed her forward as well, but Soff was silent. I wish I could've been half as stoic, but the best I could muster was not crying or pissing down my leg.

Our father was waiting for us in the longhouse, having lit some rushlights, his back toward the door, arms at his sides as if he were holding heavy invisible stones. He heard us enter but didn't turn around. Sirk pulled the deerskin flap shut behind us and our father took a deep breath, sighed, shoulders falling.

Finally, still not turning around, and in a voice so quiet it seemed he was talking to his weak shadow on the wall, my father said, "You didn't know him well. Your grandfather. You were young when he died, and few knew him well. I'm unsure I did. You probably heard stories, though. He was a fierce fighter, a man feared and respected by enemies and allies alike. A bold warchief, embarking on raids others would have balked at. The few defeats he suffered he avenged quickly, viciously. For these and many other reasons, everyone was in awe of him."

Our father turned around then, face flushed as if he'd been leaning too close to a fire. "You should ask your uncle about your grandfather's exploits some time. Sirk fought for him far more than I did, that's a fact. Your uncle knows a great deal about the glories of war. But there are other sides, too. Your grandfather was bold, brave, crafty, all true enough, but he was also cruel and unforgiving. He did things to his enemies that were… unspeakable."

Sirk snorted. "Get on with it, brother."

Our father kept his eyes on us. "War demands a strong stomach and a weak memory. But not all warleaders flay their prisoners alive, or gut them while the remaining prisoners watch. Not all warleaders carry a bag on their hips filled with the heads of their foes. Or burn eyes out with firebrands, or drive victims off cliffs, even while they beg for mercy.

"All this to his sworn enemies. But do you know when he was cruelest? Do you know when he was most vengeful? To those who lied to him, betrayed him. Stole from him. Just as you stole from him today."

He reached up with both hands, put his palms on each of our cheeks. "I don't want to know who planned this. I don't want to know why you didn't choose a different grave. All I want to know is... knowing what you do of the dead man you stole from, what do you think your thievery deserves, children?"

Unless it was some sort of trap to make our punishment even worse, our father was giving us a means of escape. But while I groped for an answer, Soff didn't. "Break our hands, father. Not both. I mean both of us, but not both our hands. Just our off-hands. That way we can still be useful."

If I was stunned by the question I was even more stunned by the answer. Break our hands? Was the girl mad? I wanted to hit her, tackle her, choke her. But then my father turned to me. "And what of you, Bray? Do you agree with your sister?"

I felt like I was swallowing hot sand, like the distances in the room shifted and my father and his question were very far away. It wasn't him who trapped us, but my sister, the one who initiated the idea, the one who planned out each robbery, who challenged my manhood, goading me into going each time. And here she was challenging me again. If I suggested a lesser punishment, I would be less than a girl, a cretin, the lowest of the low.

Hating her, I sucked down the sand and nodded once. My father nodded too, as did my mother, and for the briefest second I thought I saw the corners of her lips lift, but then it was gone. My uncle, however, didn't nod, and certainly didn't smile. He glared at my father, and though he didn't spit, I'm sure he wanted to. "No. It isn't enough. They broke into our father's grave, brother. A chieftain. It isn't enough."

Our father patted our cheeks and dropped his hands to his sides. "They understand what they've done. They understand how they must pay."

Sirk opened his belt pouch and pulled out the torc and cloak clasp he'd seized from us. "They stole for profit, Findarr. Profit. Bad enough if they were just jealous of his accomplishments, his possessions. Few don't covet from a chieftain. But they wanted only coin."

Our father looked at us and asked, "Is this true, children? Did you steal these things to sell them?"

Before Soff could make it worse, I replied, "No, father."

My father crossed his arms in front of his chest and looked at our uncle. "The punishment matches the crime, Sirk. I've made my decision."

Sirk's lip curled. "They lie. But it doesn't matter. This isn't your decision to make. It's ours, Findarr. Ours. All descendants must agree on the punishment, and I don't."

"They are my children," my father said. "And I've spoken on this matter. If you had children, you might understand. But—" Sirk gave my father a withering look, slid the sword in his belt, and then disappeared through the deerflap.

Our mother tucked a strand of hair behind her ear, looked at my sister's face and then mine. She opened her mouth, shut it, and opened it again, "I'm ashamed of what you've done. But proud you didn't run from it. Now go to bed." And so we did, heading to our pallets for a sleepless night.

The hours passed slowly, and despite the chill in the air, my pallet was a mess of fur, sweat, and spindly limbs. I changed positions a hundred times, each worse than the last. I was finally closing in on exhausted sleep when I saw Soff sit upright on her pallet, arms braced behind her. I was happy to see her tunic as sweat-stained as mine, but nervous about her expression.

"What's going on?"

She didn't look back at me. "It's Sirk. He's come back."

I listened. Voices, angry from the sound of it, although they were some distance from the longhouse.

Soff stood, slipped into her trousers, threw a belt around her waist, pulled her hair out of her eyes and knotted it behind her head. "Get up and get dressed."

"What? Why? I don't—"

"Just do it," she said. "They'll be back in a few minutes. It's impossible to be strong crouched and naked. Now get up."

"For what? Strong for what? Are they..." I had difficulty saying it. "Are they going to do it, now? Break our hands?"

Soff walked over and pulled me to my feet. "Worse."

"Worse? Than breaking our hands? How worse? What's—?"

"They're taking us to the grove, Bray."

I stepped into my trousers, cringed as they slid across the welts on the back of my legs. My words felt small and so did I. "I don't understand."

Soff wrapped a belt around my waist and buckled it. "Of course you do. Uncle called for a Reckoning. And unless I mislistened or someone was lying, it's about to start."

I would've fallen back on the pallet if she hadn't been holding my shoulders. "But last night, father said he decided, you were there—"

"The priests don't see it that way. Now splash some water on your face and comb the hair out of your eyes." She gave me one of her rare smiles. "It's also easier to be strong when you can see who your enemies and allies are."

And so I readied myself as best I could and sat at our table. Soff brought me a hunk of dry bread, a small bowl of honey, and a clay jug of goat milk. I protested, but she pushed the food on me. "Eat."

It wasn't long before we heard our parents enter the adjoining room. My sister had time to wipe some milk off my face and tell me to stand tall, and then the flap opened and they stepped through. My father looked at us both, looking weary. "Your uncle Sirk, he—"

"We know," Soff said. "We heard you outside. Or I did. We know about the Reckoning."

Under any normal circumstances, my mother would've berated Soff for interrupting. Instead, she said, flatly, "Do you?"

"Yes," Soff said. "And we're ready."

My father nodded again. "Good. Because the priests are ready for you. But before we go, I want you to know something—your uncle is no less fierce than his father before him. Fierce in love, fierce in vengeance. And it's only his fierce love of his father prompting this. Nothing else. Remember that."

Our father led us out of the longhouse, into the cold gray daylight. The village was deserted, as we expected. Everyone was at the grove, waiting. Our parents leading, we walked over small wooded hills, oak trees rising high above us, an ageless trail and our breath before us. Autumn and winter fought for possession of the land and leaves crunched beneath our feet. The Reckoning site wasn't far, a clearing carved out of a grove of birch alongside a small river, and it wasn't long before we could hear the gurgle of rushing water.

The site had been used as far back as any skald could remember, and had never changed. Or hadn't, until the summer before the graverobbing. As we made our way through the tall, peely birch, the change wasn't immediately obvious. First one tree, toppled, as if blown over by wind, its white bark flaking off in huge ragged chunks. And then another, much further along on the path, on the opposite side. Nothing truly peculiar. Trees die, and fall when they do. But the closer we got to the river, the more trees we saw on the ground. Two dead birch laying across each other on the right, trunks rotted, and more on the left, increasing until the dead outnumbered the living. What had once been a small clearing in a tightly knit forest was now a vast opening, littered with trees poisoned by some unseen thing.

Stones and logs served as seats at the outskirts of the clearing, all occupied. Our uncle was standing with the river at his back, flanked by our three priests garbed in furs and the drab colors of the deep forest. Grubarr, the Earth Priest, was a short, hairy man, head as bald as a stone, big-bellied, big bearded, his mustache covering all but the bottom of his bottom lip. Another, taller and of middling weight, but pale, beardless, and ill-looking, a Moon Priest, called Throp to his face, Milkthrop behind his back. And last, Sun Priest Hrodomin. Impossibly tall, impossibly severe Hrodomin. Though Grubarr was the grayest of the three, Hrodomin's bark face and rooty hands attested to his years. But he still had a voice like a slide down a gravel pit, deeper and rougher with each word, and a legendary temper.

Hrodomin saw us at the edge of the grove and with one clap of his gnarled hands conversation ceased. People began looking over their shoulders and spinning on the stones to find us.

Hrodomin waited for us to enter the circle and then spoke to all attending, "A Reckoning has been called, a Reckoning must be had." The other priests echoed him and he continued. "We're here today to decide the punishment of Soffjan and Braylar, children of Findarr and Morlen. Though they were caught in the middle of their crime, their punishment is in dispute. It will be settled today. So says the tribe, so say the priests." Again he was echoed.

Hrodomin raised a hand, his sleeve falling down his sinewy arm. "Soffjan, Braylar, step forward." All eyes were on us, a mixture of scorn, disapproval, and curiosity.

As we came closer, I wanted to look away, at the ground, the dying birch, the sunless sky, but a Reckoning is a tricky business—to stare defiantly at the priests was to risk their wrath, but to avoid their gaze entirely was to show disrespect and cowardice. I looked at Soff and sure enough, her head was high and she was staring directly at them, the only sign of discomfort a few blinks to free her long lashes. It seemed she was determined to make this as bad for us as possible. I thought if I looked at my shoes penitently we might balance out, but when Hrodomin cleared his throat to speak I found myself looking up anyway, into a face craggier than our mountains.

He said, "You swear upon the gods you'll speak nothing but the truth, today and forever."

We nodded. Hrodomin didn't continue. It was Soff who remembered the next part, saying, "Today and forever." It took me a second before realizing I was required to say it as well and did.

Hrodomin said, "Last night you were discovered disturbing the grave of your grandfather. Is this true?"

Soff replied, "This is true," and after a moment I parroted.

"Your uncle Sirk was the one who discovered you. Is this true?"

A duet of "This is true."

"Sirk claims you were not vandalizing, but opened the grave to loot it. Is this true?" Neither of us spoke. "Let me remind you, Soffjan and Braylar, you swore before your priests, your kin, your ancestors, and the gods. Let me also remind you that refusing to reply is the same as a lie. Now, do you freely admit you broke into the tomb to loot it?"

Before I could stop myself I said, "Not freely."

Soff elbowed me in the ribs and there were a few laughs behind me but Hrodomin clapped twice, demanded silence, and got it.

He took a step towards me, towering even more. "What did you say?"

I licked my lips but held my tongue. Hrodomin bent at the waist, his mixed beard of white and black dangling in front of my face, his breath like the air in a dark, dank place a dying animal might choose to hide in. "Speak, son of Findarr."

"I said... I said not freely."

He raised a hoary eyebrow. "Meaning?"

"Well... " I looked at my sister and then at my uncle standing alongside the other priests. He still had our grandfather's sword in his belt, one hand resting on the pommel. "You said to speak the truth, and that's the truth. We don't admit to looting. Freely. If we had a choice I'm sure we wouldn't be here at all."

"Ah. I see." Hrodomin rose back up, turned and walked back to the center. "Let it be known Hrodomin, Sun Priest of the Tribe Vorlu, misspoke in asking the question." There were some chuckles around the grove. He faced us once more. "Let me try again. You broke into the tomb to loot it, to sell what you found. Is this true?"

I was afraid my mouth might betray me again, so I kept it shut, but Soff had no such reservations. "Yes. I mean, this is true. We did."

"But you told your family something different last night." He paused and then looked directly at me. "Is this true?"

Soff looked at me too, along with everyone else. Afraid my voice might squeak, I simply nodded.

Hrodomin waited, apparently dissatisfied. Very quietly, I said, "This is true," and immediately began wondering why my sister insisted on telling the truth when it clearly wasn't helping us.

Hrodomin continued, "So, it seems you're liars as well as thieves." Soff started to object but Hrodomin overrode her, hand raised, palm out. "That wasn't a question." She shut her mouth more quickly than I believed possible. "Liars and thieves prove to be very poor witnesses. Especially in their own trials. Which leads me to believe asking more questions of you is a waste of this council's time, oath or no oath." He crossed his arms in front of his chest. "Before I'm done with you though, I have one final question: you could've chosen any grave to rob, and yet you chose not only kin, but one who was a respected chieftain as well. Why?"

I looked at Soff, since the plan was hers, but she was silent. Hrodomin approached us again, but this time addressed her. "Your brother is better at 'this-is-true' questions, but seeing as how he's younger, I'm sure he looks to you for guidance. There are many tombs in these hills, and you could have chosen any of them, yet you picked your grandfather's." He stood directly in front of her. "You would be wise to tell me why."

I was afraid she might be possessed by another fit of damning honesty, admitting to the previous graverobbings, but she didn't. Instead, she said, "His was the finest tomb we knew of. I thought so long as we were going to steal, we might as well steal big."

Hrodomin's wrinkled face somehow grew more wrinkled with anger. "Do you have anything further to add before I dismiss you, daughter of Morlen?"

I hoped she wouldn't. Foolishly. "I understand what we did is considered wrong," she said. "I'm sorry for having been caught, but I'm more sorry for any pain I've caused my kin." She looked at our father briefly and then back to Hrodomin. Never one to know when to bite her tongue, she added, "But I'm also sorry to see such fine things left in the ground to rot. Seems a shame to bury it all, tradition or no. That's it. That's all."

Hrodomin waved his hand in dismissal to both of us, but it was evident on his face that wasn't quite the sentiment he has expecting to hear. He stepped back and rejoined the other priests; they conferred quietly for a moment and then gray Grubarr spoke, "Come forward, Findarr, son of Drogan."

Our father walked a few steps closer to the trio of priests. I wondered if he was relieved. Where Hrodomin embodied menace and intimidation, Grubarr was a study in detachment. Amused detachment. Disconcerting in its own way, but still better than Hrodomin.

Grubarr blew on his hands and rubbed them together. "Findarr, your brother tells us you decided upon a punishment for your misbehaving brood, but he...disagreed with you. Tell me more of this."

Though it was cold, my father was sweating, but he still managed to smile as he glanced in our direction. "After explaining the severity of the crime, I asked my children what they thought would be a proper punishment. I was satisfied with their answer."

Grubarr seemed interested, although only mildly. "Their answer?"

"Soffjan suggested we break one of their hands. Braylar agreed."

Grubarr looked at us briefly, quizzically perhaps, then back to our father. "Hmm. A moment ago, this daughter of yours didn't sound so...penitent. Most impenitent, in fact. What do you make of this?"

Our father replied, "She's a headstrong girl, stubborn to a fault. Braylar is little better. But when confronted last night they showed more courage than I would have at their age. Maybe any age. I would have suggested a less harsh punishment than what they came up with themselves."

Grubarr didn't appear wholly convinced or unconvinced, still looking at us curiously. "Hmm." He licked his fingers, played with his mustache, and said, "But your brother, he felt... differently?"

"Yes. He did."

Grubarr tapped his chin, licked his finger, and then said, "Very good, Findarr, father of strange thieves. Thank you."

Our father rejoined our mother, Grubarr rejoined Hrodomin, and then it was Throp's turn to speak. Though Milkthrop often had the pale face and shaky demeanor of someone who just vomited, he took his office seriously and intoned with a great deal of vigor. "Sirk, son of Drogan, step forward and be recognized."

Sirk stepped forward, one hand on the hilt of his father's sword. Milkthrop pointed at our father as if Sirk might have forgotten his identity in the last few minutes, and said, "You have heard your brother on this matter. Do his words sound ill-forged to you?"

The season's first snowfall began with his words, heavy, wet flakes falling straight down. Sirk replied, "Not ill-forged, Moon Priest. But there's strong metal and there's weak."

"Meaning?"

"All here know how he responded when our father died. He didn't side with Drunik. He didn't side with me. Fine. But he didn't even side with himself. He stayed out of the conflict. That's his way. Avoid a problem, avoid a fight, avoid anything demanding something of him. Weak."

My father's face tightened with these words, but his turn to speak had come and gone, and he couldn't really offer any evidence to the contrary.

Sirk continued. "The same holds true with his children. Over-indulgent. If he could avoid punishing them at all in this matter he would. A few stiff words would be all. But he can't. I won't let him. And you won't let him."

"Don't presume to know the mind of this council, Sirk."

Had these words come from Hrodomin, he might have let them go, but Sirk replied, "We're here to see justice done, are we not?"

Milkthrop raised a finger, as if admonishing a child. "We are indeed. And we will see it done. We. Your purpose here is solely to supply information. In calling for this Reckoning you relinquished your right to determine punishment. You would do well to remember that."

Sirk looked ready to choke but slowly forced himself to reply, "As you say."

Milkthrop said, "You believe your brother weak and indulgent. This much you've said. And this council might be inclined to agree if he hadn't suggested such a punishment. But—"

"He didn't suggest it, his children did."

"Fine. But does the origin make it any less substantial or appropriate?"

Sirk pulled his father's blade from his belt and Milkthrop took two quick steps back, nearly tripping over himself. "Need I remind this council who this belongs to? Alive it was his; dead, just the same." He spun around and addressed the crowd. "He's ten years in the ground, but there isn't a person among you," he looked directly at us, "save stupid children, who don't remember him well. My father was a hard and powerful man, respected if not always loved, but he did what no one has done since Hrolan. Unified the mountain tribes. I challenge any of you to name a more revered chieftain in living memory."

He waited, looked at the priests to see if they had anything to offer, but Milkthrop looked as pale as dead birch and the other two remained silent. Sirk went on, "And how do we repay him? We let children rob from him." He pointed the sword at us. "They broke into his tomb, they stole, and for what? To keep the loot for themselves, to admire? No. It's no coincidence the merchant will be riding through here soon."

Whatever else I could say about my whoreson uncle Sirk, he was no fool. "They stole objects belonging to the greatest chieftain the Vorlu have ever known and they stole them for profit. And when caught, they lied, and when confronted today, they mocked the council, and would have lied again if they thought they could get away with it." He addressed the three priests. "So you ask me if I'm satisfied with the punishment? No, I'm not. It's a start, but not near enough. Their hands must be broken, but there must be more."

Milkthrop's assurance had vanished when the blade was drawn, and he'd regained some of it in the interim, if only a little. "And what do you propose, Sirk?"

Our uncle looked at us, and though his eyes were angry, his words were flat. "When the next tribal dies in this village, part of him will be burned into ash, and these ashes will be mixed with broth, made into soup. The rest of him will be entombed in a vault. These two thieves will be entombed with him for one week, with nothing to live on but the soup of the dead. One week, in the dark, with the rotting dead, living on the broth of his body." He turned back to Milkthrop, "Maybe when we dig them up they'll be in less of a hurry to disturb the dead again."

I didn't believe it possible, but Milkthrop looked even more ill than usual. "I see. Do you have anything else to add before we pass judgment?"

"No. That's all."

"Then we will convene—"

My father spoke up. I'm not exactly sure what prompted him. But he said, "Third priest, may I be allowed to speak? One last time?"

Milkthrop started to answer but Hrodomin overrode him. "All here have been heard, Findarr. You've spoken already."

I expected my father to back down. That's what he was best at. But this day, snow melting in his hair, face splotchy, hands plump and red, he did not. "I know this is irregular, Sun Priest Hrodomin. But I have one more thing I'd like to add before you make your decision. I will be brief."

Hrodomin looked ready to deny the request, but Grubarr touched Hrodomin's elbow and said something in his ear. Then Hrodomin looked at Sirk. "Will you allow your brother to speak?"

Sirk slid the blade in his belt again, regarded his brother with a look I couldn't quite measure. "He wants to prattle, let him prattle."

"Very well, Findarr. But be brief. My bones do not like this cold."

My father nodded. "As you wish, Sun Priest. Sirk is right about one thing. I am not a strong man. And I probably am too lenient as a father. Given he has no children of his own, I'm not sure if he's the best one to judge." Sirk looked like he wanted to spit but held it in. "But it is true, nonetheless. Most days, I bend too easily. But this isn't one of those days. I want to share one thing with you now, one last thing, and then I'll be silent and stand by your judgment in this matter."

Hrodomin waved him on. "Proceed."

"My father was a strong man. Sometimes a brutal man. This much is known. But there was more to him than that. One day, many, many summers ago, our brother Drunik, the eldest, told us it was our time to become men. We were about the same age as these two," he pointed at us and continued, "maybe younger. Drunik said we were going to steal some sheep from the Brunzi. Of course, children can't raid unless accompanied by elders, but that was Drunik's point. If we could return with sheep without being caught, we'd be deemed men, and having proved ourselves, we'd be asked to go on the next raid, and every raid after that. I was uncertain, frightened, but my brothers went, so I went.

"But things did not go as Drunik hoped. An alarm was raised. We managed to get a few sheep between us and tried to flee into the woods. But pursuit was fast and we were stupid. And worse still—and I am sure Sirk remembers this well—I was shot in my rump by an arrow as we ran through the woods."

Sirk's face didn't change, but there was something in his eyes that said he now understood where this was going and he didn't like it one bit. "My legs went numb, so my brothers carried me home. I had lost blood and was very dizzy, but I still remember the look on our father's face when we were brought before him. Here was a man who had already become celebrated for his raids and daring, his cleverness and brutality, and his sons return from an unsupervised raid, sheepless, and with one of their own injured in a most unmanly fashion. I am sure you can imagine his reaction."

There were some small laughs at this. "For those of you who cannot, he was furious. He wanted to put arrows in all our rumps." This was greeted with larger laughs. He let them rise and fall before continuing. "We had disobeyed him and broken the law. Surely, not in the same way my children did last night. Do not mistake my meaning;

I'm not comparing the offenses. Still, a broken law, a damaged son, and the seriously wounded pride of a man who already had the reputation as being one of the most feared and ferocious fighters in our tribe. And do you know how he punished us, this enraged man so gifted in violence?"

Ordinarily my father would have preferred eating live eels to public speaking, but this was a rare occasion and he rose to the task, pausing for effect before saying, "He didn't shoot us with arrows. Didn't even beat us. Our father made us take a handful of our own sheep to the Brunzi, me hobbling the entire way, and once there, he presented us to the chieftain, and told us to offer him the sheep and publicly apologize for being such incompetent thieves, and then our father made us swear if we were ever allowed to accompany him on a raid, we would reclaim our own sheep as well as several of their lambs. The Brunzi erupted in laughter. And I suppose that was our father's intent. A humiliation we would never forget.

"That is how he punished us. Appropriate to the crime." My father bowed. "That is all. Thank you."

I saw Grubarr try to hide a smile with a cough and then Hrodomin clapped his hands again. "That was less than brief, Findarr. We convene. Our decision will be forthcoming soon. Stay or go as you wish." The three priests walked towards the stream. Several people stood to stretch or shake their cold limbs, but no one left.

The priests talked far longer than I expected, and my legs began to ache as I stood there, both from the cold and the welts, and the glade was quiet for the most part, only a few low murmurs here and there, so the time stretched indefinitely.

The priests returned. Hrodomin raised his arms and said, "We have reached our decision. Step forward, Braylar and Soffjan."

Soff didn't hesitate, but I felt rooted to the spot. I looked around the glade, at our tribe, and something struck me, disturbed me, a detail I will never forget. Everyone's breath was visible in front of them, but where I expected everyone to be breathing differently, shallow and deep, fast and slow, puffs here and there and everywhere with no rhythm or pattern, the breath I saw was almost collective. Uniform. Everyone seemed to be inhaling and exhaling together. Except me. I wasn't mirroring their breath—they were spectators while I was the spectacle. And I had never felt so miserable and alone.

My father touched my back and pushed me forward. I looked up at him, and he swallowed and nodded then gave me another push. I didn't see his breath at all.

I took a few steps and stopped beside Soff. Hrodomin said, "You've committed a heinous deed, and you're too old to blame your crime on youth. If we don't respect the sanctity of the dead, we can't respect the sanctity of the living. It's been noted you lied when caught and I believe you would lie again today if you thought it would do any good. Truly, these actions must be punished severely. Your hands will be broken. But your uncle is right—there must be more."

I nearly vomited.

"However, your father is right as well. You did conceive of the first part of the punishment and the second need not be brutal to be effective. You won't be buried with the dead, but you'll be made to serve them. For the next three years you shall aid Grubarr in all burial rites. You shall prepare the bodies of the dead, dress them in their deadclothes, dig the graves and prepare the pyres. You shall ensure the sanctity of the dead is both arranged and protected. If any kin are dissatisfied with your service, you shall answer to me. If any graves are looted, you'll be held responsible. For three years hence. So ends our judgment."

Hrodomin turned to Sirk, "You'll break their hands and begin their punishment. Step forward."

Sirk said, "Gravedigging? Dressing up the dead?" He laughed, something as rare as Soff's and far more ugly. "This is your judgment?"

"It is. Step forward, son of Drogan, and complete this Reckoning. I have need of a fire, and—"

"It isn't enough," Sirk said, and the collective breathing stopped.

Hrodomin wasn't a man accustomed to being interrupted, less accustomed to having his authority challenged. His face, possessing little enough color on the best of days, turned to ash. He said, "It's the ruling of this tribunal and it is final."

"I don't agree with this. It's not enough—"

Hrodomin brought his hands together and the clap echoed in the silence. "You're wrong, son of Drogan. You do agree. You called for this Reckoning and by doing so you agreed to our judgment, regardless of what it might be. Now break these whelps' hands and be done with it or you'll find yourself on trial today, and I swear to you I won't be so impartial or patient a second time around."

Both men were shaking with rage, and all waited to see what Sirk was going to do. Finally, he complied, though without replying to Hrodomin. He marched over to us, grabbed Soff's arm, and started to drag her towards the nearest stone seat.

I ran after them and grabbed Sirk's other hand. He stopped and looked down at me.

"Break mine first," I said. Both of them looked surprised and confused, but I continued before anyone could stop me. "For lying. Break mine first." I was terrified if I saw my sister cry out or wail I wouldn't accept my punishment willingly, would try to run or beg. There are few shames greater.

Sirk released Soff's arm and grabbed mine, roughly guiding me to the first row of seats. He told old Urgus to move and she didn't argue, though he had to tell her twice, she being nearly deaf. Sirk put his hand on my shoulder, pushed me to my knees. And then he pulled his father's sword from his belt and I cried out, sure this was how he planned on answering Hrodomin's threat, by cutting off my hand. But he grabbed my right hand, laid it on the stone, and brought the pommel of the sword down on top of it, hard enough that I heard several bones snap.

I screamed and pulled my shattered hand away, covered it with the other one, and fell forward, my forehead landing in the snowy grass. I heard Soff shouting, something about how it was supposed to be our off-hands, and then there was another crunch, and then everything was silent. I felt nauseous, and looked over at Soff. Between the tears and the snow I only saw her blurry silhouette, but while she was holding her hand the same way I was, she hadn't fallen over. She was sitting on her calves, back straight, shoulders rigid, and though crying quietly, her head was up, staring straight ahead.

Soffjian never stole from another grave. That was the end. That day changed her somehow. I wish I could say I never looted again, but that would be a lie. If anything, the Reckoning only inflamed my irreverence and anger.

But I was changed in a different way.

The Vorlu is a warrior culture. A man is judged on how well he wields a sword or a spear, how many raids he has been on. A man who does these things well is glorified in song and poem, his exploits recorded and celebrated, and a man who does them exceptionally well is remembered in songs sung for eternity. A man who fights poorly might still be valued in the tribe for his husbandry, crafts-manship, knowledge of the law, what have you. But he'll never be glorified, and even if he's gifted beyond measure at what he strives at, he'll be forgotten. Quickly.

By that rubric, I'd always considered my non-martial father a weak man, a frightened man, an embarrassing man.

I don't know if any of us know our fathers well. We often see them as less or more than they truly are. But that day in the grove, when the first snow fell and my uncle broke our hands as viciously as he could, for the first time in my life, I looked at my father and saw him the way he was.

I will always remember the crunch of bone. And the interminable sentence of preparing and serving the dead that followed. But more sharply, I will remember my father's quiet show of strength, standing up to his brother, the priests, all to protect his children that didn't deserve it.

Misguided? Yes. But I loved him for it.

— THE LAST MAGICIAN —
by William Meikle

THERE AIN'T NO MAGIC any more, boy," the old man said. "It went away to the west with the trains and the wagons and what was left of our dignity."
Tom kicked at the dirt at his feet in frustration.
"But the stories said..."
"Them's just stories, lad. That's all them is."
The old man looked so sad that Tom couldn't bring himself to say any more. He'd come in search of the old man for two reasons, the first of which was to find out where to find the magic he'd read so much about in his books. Now that hope had been quashed, he kept the second reason to himself.

It would be his secret, just between him and his newest friends.

He'd found them by accident, in the creek that bounded the north edge of the farm. When they first spoke to him, he thought he might be going daft.

"Soft in the head," his Pa said, and that didn't sound like a good idea at all to Tom, having your skull all squishy and the like. So that first time, he'd just stuck his fingers in his ears and ran, fast as spit, back to the kitchen.

But the voices were insistent. He woke in the night to hear them, singing and dancing out there at the big pond. He got up, crept to the window, and watched the lights, blue and silver and emerald green, spinning and dancing and having a high old time.

He didn't go out. Not that time. His Pa told him it was just a dream, a bad dream, and although it hadn't seemed bad at all, Tom knew better than to argue with his Pa during harvest season.

It was three days before he went out to the pond.

They were there, waiting.

"Tell us a story, Tom," the blue one said. "An old story."
"We love old stories," the green one replied.
The silver one merely danced a bit faster.

Tom sat with them for the longest time, telling them of bears that talk, grandmothers with big eyes and wizened little men that spun gold.

They liked that one a lot.

At the end of the day they thanked him profusely.

"We have given you a gift," they said in unison, their voices mingling in a most pleasant chorus. "Something to remember this day by." They vanished with a *pop* that made Tom's ears hurt.

He looked everywhere for his gift, but there was nothing to be found, even after a thorough search of all his pockets. He went home feeling slightly sad that his new friends had deceived him.

Ma was in the scullery, frying ham on the big skillet. She turned when he came through the door and her hand hit the skillet handle. The heavy pan tipped over. Tom saw it all happen in his mind; the hot fat was going to spray everywhere and scorch his Ma's arm.

He did it without thinking. He reached out and although he was on the opposite side of the room, he felt the weight of the skillet, felt it shift under his hand as he pushed it away to one side so that the fat skittered on the stove and not on Ma's skin.

"Did you see that?" he whispered.

Ma was too busy cleaning up spilled grease.

"Dashed near did myself an injury," she said. "Don't you be going scaring me again like that, you hear me?"

"But Ma...I saved you."

"Near had me in the infirmary you mean? Now away with you and wash yourself. You can't come to dinner with muck all over you."

And that was that.

In the washroom he tried to make Pa's shaving brush move just by looking at it, but nothing happened except that he developed a headache that lasted until bedtime.

The next morning he went into town, looking for the oldest man he knew of, one that might know where the magic had all gone.

Now he was trudging home, having failed in his quest.

Them's just stories, lad. That's all them is.

He had to cross the creek to get back to the farm. They were there, under the footbridge.

"Who's that walking on my bridge?" a gruff voice said, quickly followed by three singsong voices laughing in unison. "Tell us a story, Tom. Tell us an old story."

He told them about the girl with the ugly sisters, the seven dwarfs, and the princess who couldn't be woken. They liked that one too. But the stories took a while in the telling, and the sun was going down in the west before Tom was finished.

"Look what you made me do," Tom wailed. "Pa's going to take the belt to me again for sure."

The silver one danced and swirled around Tom's head.

"Do you believe, Tom? Do you really believe?"

Tom nodded, remembering the weight of the skillet as he'd pushed it away, the feel of it in his head.

"Then here is our second gift to you," the blue one said. "Use it wisely."

And away they *popped*.

Once again Tom checked his pockets. His fingers found only old dirt and lint. The second gift was as elusive as the first, but Tom felt excitement growing as he headed for home.

Pa was indeed furious.

"Where in heck have you been all day, boy? There's work needs doing, and I ain't about to do it all on my lonesome. That's a lesson you ain't learned yet. Fetch the belt."

The leather strap felt cold and stiff in Tom's hands as he lifted it down from its hook. Tom didn't need any reminding how it would feel against his skin, or how the memory of it would linger long after the pain itself subsided. Pa had only ever taken the belt to him once before, and Tom had surely deserved that one, having nearly burned down the barn when playing with matches.

But I ain't done nothing wrong this time. I just want to find the magic.

He kept quiet. That wasn't anything Pa wanted to hear. Tom assumed his position as Pa swung the belt. And right at that point, an anger he never knew he had in him flared.

"I ain't done nothing wrong," he shouted. "Stop."

Pa stopped.

So did everything else.

The farm was quiet and still; no wind blew, no kettles whistled, no burning wood cracked and split in the range. Tom looked up. Pa loomed above him, belt raised. The leather hung in a sigmoid curve high above. Pa's face was contorted in rage and, something else, something Tom was seeing for the first time; Pa looked like administering the punishment was going to hurt him somewhere deep down. It was only now that he was perfectly still that Tom could see it; a single tear glistened in Pa's right eye.

"Pa?" Tom whispered.

Pa didn't move. Tom slid away from underneath the belt and walked round the big man, studying what had happened. Pa was as still as the statue that stood above the Crawford grave in the churchyard, and looked nearly as dead.

"Pa?" Tom said, almost a shout this time. He pushed at Pa's arm. There was no give in it; it was as solid as cold stone.

"Ma!" Tom wailed, and headed for the kitchen. Ma was there at the stove again. But like Pa, she was perfectly still, unmoving. She'd been caught stoking the fire under the plates. Tom bent and looked in. The flames were as still and cold as his parents. He reached out gingerly and touched at what should have been the hottest part. It felt more like ice than fire.

"Ma?" he whispered, but there was no response.

He was at a loss as to what to do next. He went and stood in the doorway, looking out over the farm towards the creek. It was as if the whole world had stopped. A moth had been caught mid-beat, hovering at the porch lantern. Tom took it in his palm and studied it. It looked like a perfectly carved miniature statue.

Something giggled out in the dark by the creek, and now there was movement, blue and green and silver, dancing.

"Tell us a story, Tom," they sang. "Tell us an old story and you'll have your third gift."

"Bring my Ma and Pa back," Tom shouted, almost crying in fear and frustration. "Bring them back right now."

The green light flew, faster than thought, to stop right in front of Tom's nose.

"Only you can do that, Tom. It's your gift, after all."

"Well if you can't help, just go away."

It went away.

One second it was there in front of his nose, the next, with only a *pop* to show for it, it was gone. There was nothing but dark and silence out over the creek.

But Tom had started thinking.

It's my gift.

And they gave me two of them.

He reached with his thoughts, feeling his Ma's warm embrace, the heat and weight of her as she held him. He pushed, hard.

"Start," he whispered. "Please start."

A confused moth fluttered away from the porch, Ma swore under her breath as she nearly burned herself at the stove, and Pa's shout echoed through the farmhouse.

"Tom Miller. You get back here right now. I ain't finished with you, boy."

Tom went. He knew the belting was coming, but it was something familiar, something he could feel on firm ground with. He had tears in his eyes as the belt finally came down, but it wasn't pain he felt.

He forgot about magic for a while after that, caught up in the daily routine of schooling and harvest. Some afternoons he'd stop at the bridge and wait, but nothing spoke to him; nobody wanted his stories. Besides, Tom had taken a bad scare, and wasn't right sure he wanted another in the near future.

So he worked; he bailed, he shucked, he cleaned out the stables and he played the dutiful son.

Pa was happy.

"One day, lad, it'll all be worthwhile. One day all of this will be yours."

Tom was appalled at the thought.

And while sitting through the Reverend Martin's impenetrable droning at the Harvest festival service, he started to dream again, of dancing lights and gifts, of stories and of magic. He took to lingering at the bridge for longer stretches of time, and often could be seen there as the sun went down in the west.

But still nobody spoke to him, and he started to fear that the magic had gone as quickly as it had come.

I could try something?

That thought was the merest whisper in his head, and it was kept down by fear. But it was growing louder all the time.

And finally, harvest season was over and done. Tom had been waiting impatiently for this day for a long time. The carnival arrived in town, bringing sideshows and circus, stalls and as much candy as a boy could eat without being sick. And Pa was so pleased with Tom's diligence over the previous weeks that he allowed the boy a looser rein than in previous years.

"You're nearly a man now, Tom," Pa said, and handed over two dollars. "Have some fun while you're still a boy. Just be home by nine, or your Ma will fret."

The things under the bridge were still quiet, but there was a different kind of magic in the air; the carnival was just getting going as the sun set. Tom was soon dazzled by the colors and music, the feats of strength, the bearded lady and the Carolinas Ape Man. His two dollars seemed to vanish all too quickly on a succession of games of chance and food that looked too good to ignore. He only had a dime left by eight o'clock; it was still far too early to leave. He strolled around, looking for one last thrill.

His heart almost stopped when he saw the tent.

The Great Suprendo. The Last Magician.

He spent his last dime and followed a small group of people inside. A small stage was set up at the far end, the only thing on it being a table draped with a velvet cloth that hung to the floor. A thin man, younger than Pa but not much, stood to one side. He was dressed like a city gent, in the black wool suit, stiff white collared shirt, black cape and a tall hat that sat slightly askew making him look lopsided. Tom was disappointed even before the act started.

He ain't no real magician.

Tom's suspicions were confirmed over the next twenty minutes. The man went through a perfunctory series of card tricks, pulled a bored looking rabbit from his hat, and joined up three iron rings into one as if it was the best thing in the world. He looked as bored as his audience was the whole time. Tom considered leaving, but just as he turned away the man announced his last trick.

"All the way from the west, where the magic is still real."

That was enough to get Tom's attention, for at least a minute until he saw it was only going to be another bored piece of sleight of hand. Finally Tom could no longer stop himself. When the man brought a rather bedraggled dove out of his jacket sleeve and sent it fluttering into the air, Tom whispered.

"Stop it. Just stop it, right now."

Everything went deathly still, the dove caught in mid-flutter just out of the magician's reach, the crowd all staring forward, mostly with bored, disinterested expressions on their frozen faces. Tom pushed his way to the front. The man – Tom couldn't bring himself to give him the title he had taken with so little ability to back it up – had his gaze following the flight of the dove. Tom had to stand on tiptoe to reach it, and when he did it felt heavy, like a rock in his hands as he pulled it close to his chest. He climbed up onto the table and sat cross-legged, facing the crowd, the bird nestled in his arms.

"Start," he whispered.

He saw the faces of the crowd change from bored stares to astonishment in less than a second.

And why not? It must seem as if I've popped in out of nowhere.

The applause started just as Tom released the dove. With a startled *caw* it flew off overhead, depositing a streaky white lucky gift on the so-called magician's head and completing Tom's enjoyment of the moment.

It didn't last nearly long enough. The crowd filtered away and Tom was left, still sitting on the table.

I did real magic. Can't they see that?

The man behind him touched his shoulder, gently, as if afraid something might happen.

"How did you do that?" he asked softly.

"You're the magician, why don't you tell me?" Tom said, getting down from the table and starting to move away.

"Please, tell me how it's done?" the man said. He was pleading now, almost begging. "I need something new, something to bring back the spark."

"Then use some real magic," Tom said. "Not this pretend stuff."

"There is no real magic," the man replied. "It all went away, into the West, long ago,"

Tom reached out a hand and pushed with his mind. The table lifted a foot off the stage and started to head for the tent entrance before he let it down. The man was astonished.

"How did you do that? You're just a boy."

Just a boy.

"I just want to bring the magic back," Tom said.

"So do we all," the man muttered under his breath. He looked at Tom, his eyes suddenly filled with something that looked like hope. "Can you show me where you learned this?"

Tom backed away again.

"Can you bring the magic back?" he asked.

The man nodded eagerly.

"If I can learn what you did, I can."

Tom came to a quick decision.

"Come on then. I have to be home by nine, but there should be enough time for what's needed."

A full moon hung over the footbridge, the reflection dancing happily in the creek as they approached.

"What are we doing way out here" the man asked. He'd got increasingly agitated as they got further from town, as if he was afraid to be so far away from the lights and sounds and comfort of the carnival.

He ain't no real magician at all.

The blue light came to meet them.

"Tell us a story, Tom," it said.

The green joined it.

"Tell us an old story, Tom, and we'll give you what you most desire."

The silver danced around the startled man's head.

"Tell us an old story, sir, and we'll give you what you most desire."

"What is this?" the man whispered. His eyes went wide, his mouth slack. He stepped backwards, as if meaning to flee. Tom put out a hand.

"Stop," he whispered.

Everything went still apart from the three dancing lights.

"He's not a real magician," Tom said. "But he wants to be."

"Not a real magician," the blue said.

"Not like Tom," the green added.

"But he wants to be," said the silver.

"So you'll help?" Tom asked. "Help him find the magic?"

"If he tells us a story, we will give him what he wants," the three of them replied in unison. "And Tom shall have his last gift."

"Promise?"

The lights danced and whirled.

"A last gift for a story, that is all we ask."

"Deal," Tom said. He would have spat on his hand to seal it, but there was no answering hand to shake.

He turned back to the magician.

"Start."

The man shook his head, as if waking from a dream. His eyes went wide again when he saw the three lights hovering in front of his face.

"Tell us a story, magician," the blue said.

"Tell us an old story," the green added.

"Tell us a story and you shall have what you want," the silver said.

"A story?"

"They like the old tales," Tom said, trying to be helpful. "Goldilocks, Red Riding Hood, that sort of stuff…"

Just then a voice rang out over the farmland.

"Tom? Is that you?"

"I'll be right there, Ma," he shouted, then turned back to the magician. "Best be quick about it. Pa ain't forgotten how to use the belt."

The man hunkered down on the bridge and, self-consciously at first, then with more fluency, told the tale of the gingerbread house and the trail of breadcrumbs.

The dancing lights liked that one, and hummed and sang and danced ever faster as the story came to an end. The man stood and stretched.

"What now?" he said.

"A gift for a gift," the blue said.

"Whatever you both desire," the green said, and bounced against Tom's nose.

"Just like Tom," the silver said, and bounced against the magician's nose.

Tom blinked, and looked down to see a tousled haired boy look up at him.

"I'm young again," the boy said, and smiled.

Tom lifted his arms, marveling at the feel of the wool suit, the swish of the cape.

"I can do real magic."

Pa shouted from across the farm.

"Tom Miller, get in here right now, or there'll be words spoken."

The boy looked up.

"I'd best be going," he said.

The magician nodded.

"He ain't a bad Pa. But it's best to stay on his good side."

The boy spat on his hand and put it out. The magician shook on it. The lights danced and capered, and followed the boy back to the farm. The magician could still hear them as he turned away.

"Tell us a story, boy."

"Tell us an old story."

He smiled, set his gaze on the distant lights of the carnival and started walking.

The Great Suprendo, the last magician, had magic to give back to the world.

— RESTORING THE MAGIC —
by Ian Creasey

WHEN I HAD CLIMBED HIGH enough that my breath came in great panting gasps and the sheep in the valleys looked like tiny flecks of fallen cloud, I heaved off my backpack and looked for the best spot to plant the final sapling. Birch and goat-willow dotted the exposed slopes, hardy species that withstood the storms and chills of the High Tatras. My oak required a more sheltered home. I saw a south-facing escarpment, and scrambled across to investigate. The gray rock felt warm under my hand, retaining the heat of the autumn sun. Behind an outcrop, in a small gully, the wind dropped to a light breeze. I pulled up tussocks of grass to inspect the soil, and found it damp but not sodden, thin but not barren. An earthworm crawled away into the moss and leaf-litter. Instinctively, I felt that a dryad would thrive here.

I fetched my pack, took out the trowel, and began to dig. Soon I had a hole big enough to receive the sapling's earth-encrusted root-ball. I threw a handful of compost into the bottom, then lowered the tree into the ground and trod down the soil.

I peered at the sapling to make sure that the tiny young dryad still clung to the stem. I was tempted to get out my magnifying glass for a good look, but I didn't want to risk scorching her in the sunlight like a small boy torching ants. There were hazards enough for a dryad, for a tree, without me being careless. I staked a large plastic tube around the sapling to protect it from sheep, rabbits, and other nibblers. The plastic looked nasty and artificial in the rugged Slovak countryside, but it would biodegrade in a few years.

Finally, I recorded the location in my logbook and tied a small metal tag to the tree. The reintroduction zone was secluded, but not secret. The tag contained a project code, a dryad number, and my initials: "BK". My parents christened me Jeremy Benedict Kemp, but at university I dropped the first name and began signing "Ben" to the emails and Christmas cards I sent home.

This was my fourth project since graduation, and my second outside England. I looked forward to tagging my initials across the world, as we strove to restore the magic it had lost. I just needed a permanent job with the Phoenix Foundation: I couldn't afford to keep doing voluntary placements.

My stint in Slovakia had gone well, although I was annoyed at spending so much time on the dryads. Above me, the peaks held dragons' lairs. Alzbeta, the local warden, was fiercely protective of the dragons. She hadn't let me anywhere near them; the closest I'd got was collecting a few scat samples. And I couldn't argue with Alzbeta, because I needed her to give me a good reference.

After eating my tuna sandwiches, I started back downhill, enjoying the stroll with my backpack now considerably lighter. I scratched my itchy new beard, irritated that it still hadn't grown in properly. All the conservationists on TV had luxuriant beards, as though providing vast hairy habitats for rare mammals. My straggly blond wisps wouldn't even harbor a small beetle.

I descended via the foothills of the nearest lair, looking for any scat to collect. Over the summer, I'd learned to spot the unobtrusive droppings of our young dragons in their new habitat. As my insect repellent wore off and midges feasted on my neck, I spied a squidgy lump of undigested fur and bone. It looked fresh, so I scooped it into a sample tube. By determining what the dragons ate, we could gauge the suitability of potential release sites.

On my way back to the car, I discovered some late blackberries ripening in the sun, so I filled a spare sample bag with fruit. They would make a cheap and tasty crumble, especially if I swung by the farmer's orchard to see if any crab-apples had fallen. Working for a conservation charity meant stretching the budget every possible way. Down in the villages they thought we were all rich foreigners, so they tried to overcharge us whenever they could.

The ancient Volvo started the first try, and I eased it down the track with a minimum of jolting over potholes and ancient rusted trash. When I reached the smoother paving of the farmyard, I sighed with relief that the suspension had held out once more. I glimpsed the farmer emerging from a barn, and I opened the passenger-side window to greet him.

Then I saw what he was carrying. The farmer rushed toward me and threw the carcass onto the bonnet, splattering blood and tufts of wool all over the windscreen. He leaned down and shouted through the open window, blasting me with pipe-tobacco breath fuggy enough to smoke bees from a hive.

"Bastards! Are you trying to ruin us? You ignorant donkey—"

I'd made an effort to learn some Slovak, but he spoke far too fast for me to pick it all up. I let him shout for a while, until he ran down and started coughing. Then, not without trepidation, I got out of the car.

"I'm sorry for your loss," I said, carefully repeating one of the first phrases I'd learned. "If this is dragon-kill, you may be entitled to compensation—"

"If?" He pointed to the mangled lamb. "You think my cat did this? You think it fell down the stairs?"

"It might have died naturally. There are other scavengers...." Under pressure, I ran out of words. I didn't want to provoke him, but we needed to educate the locals that very few losses were really due to predation. Our dragons, being young, mostly ate rabbits rather than livestock. This lamb wasn't much smaller than an adult sheep: I was surprised a dragon had tackled it.

I riffled through my folder and plucked out the appropriate form. The farmer shot me a disgusted look from beneath his vast eyebrows. "Is that a magic spell to bring sheep to life?" He crumpled the paper and tossed it aside.

If he didn't want compensation, that would stretch the budget further. A shrill voice came from a high window across the yard. I didn't catch the words, but the farmer sagged under their weight. He bent down and grabbed the form, smoothing it as best he could. While he used the car's roof to write down his details, I dumped the carcass into the back. At the lab, we'd examine the remaining skin for hemorrhages—only live animals hemorrhage when bitten.

The farmer handed me the completed form, which gave his name as Jozef squiggle-something, and said, "We have a right to protect our flocks. And we have plenty of guns."

A fierce protective urge rose inside me. "You can't possibly need to do that," I said. "How often do you lose stock? When was the last time?"

"The more creatures you let loose, the more sheep we'll lose."

"That won't happen. Our research shows—"

He shouted an obscene insult, and went on, "What do you know about farming, you soft-handed foreigner? You've never done a hard day's work in your life! I've already called my brother. Our hunters will go up the mountains, through the towns, into the Belianska Cave if they have to." He paused to glare at me and relight his pipe. "Wherever the monsters live, we'll find them and shoot them."

I wanted to tell him that was illegal. I wanted to convince him that iconic predators created far more tourist income than they destroyed in livestock. I wanted to talk to him about restoring ecosystems, and our responsibility to put a little magic back to replace all that we'd lost. But I looked at the blood on the farmer's shirt, and realized this wasn't the time.

"Jozef, I hope you'll think again before you do that," I said, getting into the car. "Once more, I'm sorry about this. The office will be in touch about any compensation."

I decided not to ask for any apples as I left.

The smell of the carcass filled the car, making me queasy, and I couldn't open the windows without attracting flies. I drove faster than normal, even though I still wasn't fully accustomed to driving on the right-hand side of the road. When I reached Tatranske Matliare, I saw lights in our building. Alzbeta must have returned; I hadn't seen her for a couple of days.

I picked up the carcass, hardly flinching at all, and carried it into the lab. It was lighter than I'd expected. I took a few photos, and a blood sample just in case. As I labeled the sample, Alzbeta came in from the office.

She pulled down her glasses from their perch high on her elder-berry-dark hair. Watching her examine the sheep, I envied her aura of competence. She was about a decade older than me; she'd been the local warden for five years, after arriving from the Czech Republic. For my benefit, she usually spoke English.

"Definitely a live kill," she said. "Claws first, and then a bite. You can see hemorrhaging on what's left of the neck."

She pointed. I lacked the expertise to confirm her diagnosis, as I hadn't yet seen enough livestock kills. Alzbeta always handled the few that occurred.

"Are there any more tests we can do?" I asked.

"No, there's no need," she replied. "Might as well put it out for the griffins."

I hauled the carcass into the yard, where it was greeted by delighted squawks. Then I changed into clean clothes, washed my hands, and returned to the car to pick up my logbook and the farmer's compensation form.

Back inside, Alzbeta practically grabbed the form out of my hand. "I'll deal with this. Did you get all of the dryads planted?"

"Yes, I just need to update the database."

"Great job!" She smiled at me. That didn't happen very often. Normally she looked sour, harassed and overworked. Today she seemed bright-eyed, full of nervous energy.

"Which dragon do you think made the kill?" I asked.

She gave me a blank stare, as if this was the most bizarre question in the world. Then she recovered herself, glanced at the form where the farmer had written his address, and said, "The nearest would be Penelope, so probably her, though it doesn't matter which. We only need to confirm that it was any of them, for the farmer to get his compensation."

"But we should know, shouldn't we? For the records, so we know which of them are moving onto bigger food?"

"Yes, of course. I said I'll deal with it," she said, in a tone that reminded me of my mother. "You still need to update the dryads, don't you?"

Frustrated, I sat at my computer and started entering the GPS coordinates of each sapling that I'd planted.

Every time I tried to get involved with the dragons, Alzbeta kept rebuffing me. I'd had plenty of other projects to occupy my time: not just the dryads, but reintroducing kobolds into abandoned mines, saving the two-headed amphisbaena, and so on. Yet I'd volunteered for this placement because I wanted to work with dragons in the wild. It was the logical next step: I'd previously worked at an ostrich farm in Israel, where the ostriches incubated dragons' eggs until they hatched, and the staff hand-fed the young dragonets until they could start catching their own food. I remembered the thrill of feeding scraps to a tiny dragon, no bigger than my foot. I used to imagine how it would look flying over the countryside, giving everyone a glimpse of awe-inspiring beauty. I remembered the pride I felt at contributing to the rewilding program, helping to restore magic and mystery to the world.

I'd handled dragons. I had experience—admittedly, only a few weeks of experience, but I wasn't some ignorant bungler who might accidentally break a dragon's delicate wing. Alzbeta had no right to keep them to herself. How would anyone else ever learn?

It had been a long day out in the hills, and it took me another hour to finish the dryads' records. To boost my chances of securing a permanent job, I needed to excel at bureaucracy as well as conservation. I painstakingly updated the database, cross-referencing permits from the Slovak authorities alongside European Union grant applications. Then I signed off the file. Alzbeta countersigned it before she left; she had some evening meeting to attend.

I yawned, and thought about going home, to the hostel that I shared with various students and gap-year travelers. On an ordinary day, I would have gone. But my placement was coming to an end, and I needed to squeeze as much experience out of it as possible. I was determined to expand the "dragons" entry on my CV.

And I remembered that I still had the scat sample in the car, the one I'd collected before all the business with the sheep carcass.

I'd brought in samples before, but Alzbeta had always done the analytics. Still, I'd watched her a couple of times, and the equipment hadn't looked very difficult to use. Why shouldn't I try it myself?

As I returned to the car to retrieve the sample, I heard the griffins in the yard squabbling over roosts as they settled down for the night. Back at the lab, I fired up the sequencer. This impressive piece of kit had presumably swallowed most of the budget. Just turning it on made me feel like I was starring in one of those TV shows where scientists and detectives make important discoveries using shiny machines.

The screen asked me for an authorization code, which I supplied after ferreting out Alzbeta's emergency Post-It note of passwords. I placed the sample tube, still sealed, in the appropriate receptacle. Then I closed the lid and pressed the Go button. The machine itself would open the tube, extract the contents, and run the analysis.

In my eagerness, I'd forgotten that it was a slow process. Expensive as it was, the sequencer couldn't produce instant results. I would have to wait. What could I do in the interim?

Having just entered the dryads' locations into a database, I recalled that the dragons were all ringed with GPS transmitters. These enabled us to track their range. I logged in, and called up the records for the past few days. A map showed where our dragons had recently flown.

Zooming into the map, I found the farm where Jozef had dumped the sheep carcass on me. To my surprise, the flight paths disappeared. I frowned, and zoomed out. The dragons' tracks reappeared around the edge of the display, but they were nowhere near the farmhouse. Perhaps the farmer's land extended way up into the mountains; the map didn't show which land belonged to which farmer.

The lack of an obvious dragon-track meant that I couldn't determine the culprit. It might have been Penelope, or Chrysoprase, or the Prince of Wales, all of whom had flown in that area. I couldn't tell whether any of them had lingered to make a kill: the GPS fixes were only half-hourly, to conserve the transmitters' battery life.

I should have asked the farmer exactly where he'd found the carcass. Next time, I'd know to ask that question.

Except there wouldn't be a next time, because my placement was nearly finished. If I'd had training earlier, then I would have done better this time. It was Alzbeta's fault.

Annoyed, I stomped over to the sequencer to check its progress. The screen said, "Species analysis completed. Species detected: dragon, rabbit, hare, field vole, sparrow. Individual analysis pending."

The sequencer could swiftly detect "dragon", but it took longer to match individual characteristics against the profiles in our database, and determine exactly which dragon had left the scat.

But whichever dragon it was, it hadn't eaten any sheep.

On impulse, I began poking around in the sequencer's onscreen menus, looking for an Archive listing. As I'd hoped, the machine stored all the old analyses. It took me a little while to filter the dragon-scat entries from the other lab work. Yet the more of them I saw, the more my mouth widened in amazement. *None of the dragons had ever eaten sheep.* They'd only consumed smaller prey: rabbits, rodents, birds, insects.

So why did livestock keep getting killed? And why were dragons getting the blame?

Just to be sure, I logged back into the office computer and checked the older compensation claims. Alzbeta had indeed signed them off as dragon kills.

I scowled. Was it merely a scam, a money-making scheme? My fists clenched at the thought that I was volunteering to work for a tiny expenses allowance, while fraudsters were milking the budget.

Then I realized that it couldn't be a scam, because there wasn't enough profit—only a few sheep over several months, at a hundred euros per carcass. And Jozef had seemed genuinely angry at the death of his lamb. *Something* had killed it: "claws first, and then a bite," Alzbeta had said.

If not a dragon, then what? Was it something mundane, like a fox or a rogue dog? No, because Jozef wouldn't have blamed "monsters". And Alzbeta surely wouldn't authorize compensation for anything outside the Foundation's remit.

I racked my brain for about eleven seconds, until I remembered the master database of all the reintroduction programs. I called it up, and entered Slovakia in the regional filter. A list emerged: the dragons, dryads, kobolds, and the griffins, that never left our yard because they were too domesticated.

I already knew about every creature on the list. And none of them looked like a sheep-killer. Yet that made sense—if the real culprit had been in the database, then Alzbeta wouldn't have needed to blame the dragons.

This was definitely a cover-up.

Suddenly, the office felt colder and full of shadows. I was alone, and far from home. The moonlight shining through the windows reminded me that I'd spent hours in the office after a full day outdoors. Feeling the need for human company, I closed everything down and set off back to the hostel.

As I drove, I kept wondering what had killed those sheep. Whichever creature was responsible, there couldn't be very many of them. There'd only been half-a-dozen kills over the past six months.

A kill every month...I pulled over and stopped the car, because I couldn't focus on the road ahead. I was too busy trying to remember the dates on those compensation forms. Had they really been at monthly intervals?

I didn't dare return to the office to check. I drove on, into the moonlight.

The next day, I decided that I didn't need to go back to the office at all. My placement was almost over, and I'd completed the dryads project, so there would only be routine scut-work to do. And I felt disinclined to contribute any more of my labor in the service of a cover-up.

The sensible action would be to stick out the final days, and not say anything that might rock the boat. I would probably never return to Slovakia, so what did any local misdeeds matter?

But I wanted to find out what was going on, if only to validate the efforts I'd already made. I phoned Alzbeta and asked her to meet me at a café in town, ostensibly for a celebratory lunch to mark the end of my placement. Although I could have talked to her at the office, I felt safer meeting her in public.

During my stay I'd quickly learned that food was cheaper if you went somewhere less tourist-oriented. Of course, this meant a lack of English-language menus, and I'd spent weeks ordering adventurously until I figured out what everything meant. This particular café served lots of bryndza and oštiepok—sheep cheese—which I no longer felt like eating. I sighed, and tapped my fingers on the red tablecloth while I stared at the Warhol-imitation prints on the walls.

When she arrived, Alzbeta ordered onion soup and an egg sandwich. Like many conservationists, she was a vegetarian—a fact that now seemed hard to square with my wild surmise of the night before. I ordered a tuna salad. Before Alzbeta could distract me with any small-talk, I looked her in the eye and said, "I know the dragons haven't been eating sheep."

She flinched, but didn't speak.

"Something out there *is* eating sheep," I went on. "What is it? And why are we covering up for it?"

"If you don't know that, I'm not going to tell you," she said, sounding relieved. "You're right, there is a secret programme, but only a few senior people know about it. You haven't been with the organization for long enough."

"Why does it have to be secret?" I demanded.

Alzbeta gave me a frosty stare. "The same reason as always: protection. We don't publicize the location of the dragons' nests, because we don't want anyone hunting the dragons or stealing their eggs. You know that. And the principle is the same here."

"But I'm a volunteer!" I protested. "I'm not an egg thief or some idiot with a shotgun—"

"No, but you're only here temporarily. Soon you'll go home to England, or to another placement elsewhere. You don't need to know every detail of what's happening here in Slovakia. If you did know, then..." She shook her head. "Secrets are like viruses. They spread. Even when people don't mean to spread them."

"So you don't trust me?" I said bluntly.

"Not until you've proved yourself. Look, you seem like a nice guy, but I've only known you for three months. You've done a few placements, but they've been...what, less than a year altogether? If you stay with the Foundation, then gradually you'll acquire more responsibility, and you'll learn more about what we do." She paused and held my gaze. "You've done well here—you've worked hard, you've been reliable. I'll write you a good reference. You'll get another job, a permanent post. Just give it time."

Our food arrived, and she began lapping up her soup. I understood the implicit bribe that Alzbeta offered. If I stopped asking awkward questions, then she would smooth my path into a salaried role within the organization. She would give me what I wanted.

Yet I'd formed that ambition when I thought I understood what the Phoenix Foundation did. Should I still aspire to join it? How could anyone be confident that they supported the organization's goals, if some of them were secret? It wasn't just me. What about all the other volunteers, workers, donors?

"I understand your point about the dragons' nests," I said, "but we don't hide the fact that we're reintroducing dragons. Everyone knows they're out there somewhere. Yet if we run secret programs, then how can anyone agree or disagree with what we're doing?" I remembered the European Union grant applications in the database. "We take taxpayers' money. If we lie about what we do with it, that's fraud!"

Alzbeta was already shaking her head. "It's not fraud. Don't be silly. We're not spending it on unrelated fripperies. We're fulfilling our mission. If you go to our website, what's the slogan at the top of the home page?"

It took me a moment to remember: "'Restoring the Magic'."

"Exactly. But how magical is a dragon with a GPS transmitter on its leg and a CCTV camera in its lair? Real magic is mysterious. It's hidden. It's not labeled on a map, and it doesn't have technical specifications in a downloadable PDF file."

"But it does kill sheep, apparently."

Alzbeta shrugged. "A small number of sheep, for which full compensation is paid."

"And the dragons get the blame." I remembered Jozef's anger. "That farmer talked about shooting them."

She smiled. "Oh, it's all a big show to make sure they get their money. I bet you thought he was hard done by, huh? It's what they want us to think! But the compensation is actually more than the market value of those sheep. That's why—" She stopped mid-sentence, and instead concluded, "That's why you don't need to worry about the dragons."

I sighed and leaned back in my chair, wondering what she'd nearly said.

"Magic must have its secrets," she said firmly. "Without secrets, it isn't magic."

"But we live in an open society—a democracy. To reintroduce dragons, we had to educate politicians and voters, and get them on board. That's how it's supposed to work. We can't just secretly reintroduce anything on a whim, not without some kind of scrutiny. Not without licensing and all that." The idea of mysterious magic sounded alluring in principle, but rather more alarming as a blood-thirsty monster roaming the countryside.

She laughed. "Democracy? This is magic! You can't take a vote on transcendence. You can't flip-flop every five years over whether the world is mysterious or not."

"I take your point," I said—not because I agreed with it, but because I wanted the conversation to end.

Alzbeta clearly wouldn't come out and tell me what had really killed those sheep. Not until I'd been promoted within the organization—whatever that involved. Was it just a matter of paperwork and job titles, or was it something rather more visceral?

And if I confronted her with my suspicion, forcing her to respond, then would she simply nod and say, "Oh, how clever of you to guess?" Or would she take steps to preserve the secrecy that "real magic" depended upon? I imagined another version of the compensation form—instead of "Sheep: €100", it might read "Human: €1,000,000". The Phoenix Foundation surely had insurance policies to cover all sorts of accidents, dragon-related and otherwise.

Alzbeta paid for the meal. She thanked me for all my efforts over the past three months, and she promised me a good reference for any job applications. "I admire your scruples," she said. "That's what the Foundation needs: people who ask questions and care about the issues."

When I saw her drive away, my whole body sagged with the release of accumulated tension. I found a bench in the market square, and sat down to think. Pigeons swiftly approached on the off-chance of food, reminding me of the griffins in the yard; it made me nostalgic already.

I sympathized with Alzbeta. I understood her point about magic needing an elusive, esoteric side—the antithesis of today's form-filling bureaucratic culture. And I appreciated her efforts to arrange compensation for those affected.

But on the other hand...the arrogance! I shivered, recalling how she'd laughed at the notion of democracy. It's fashionable to denigrate politics: she probably thought she was on safe ground by sneering at it.

"Yet what's the alternative?" I asked myself. "Trusting in a secret, self-appointed cabal? That only sounds attractive when you're part of it."

Did I want to be part of it? I was tempted. I remembered the exhilaration of standing on the slopes of the High Tatras, surrounded by dryads and dragons, thinking of the beauty I'd helped restore to a gray, faded world. It would surely feel even more intoxicating to know all the secrets of the magic around me, to be responsible for the world's mysteries….

But Alzbeta had made it clear that becoming an insider would take years. And I hardly had a guarantee—she could simply have been fobbing me off, using an empty promise to keep me quiet. How could I trust her? How could I tell if Alzbeta was on the right side?

In the end, you can only judge people on what you know they've done. And the only thing I really knew about Alzbeta was that she'd lied.

I needed to learn more. I needed to stay with the Phoenix Foundation, and see what was happening around the world. Alzbeta's cabal might be the benign guardians of the world's secret magic. Or they might not—in which case, I needed to protect myself.

Looking around the square, I saw a jewelery shop. I walked inside, and I asked what they had in silver.

CHARLOTTE
AND THE DEMON WHO
— SWAM THROUGH THE GRASS —
by Mercedes M. Yardley

THERE ARE STORIES, and there are tales. And then there are fairytales, which are the most exquisite and precious of all. This is the fairytale of Charlotte, and the story of how she came to be.

Once upon a time, in a land that really wasn't so very far away, there was a little girl named Charlotte. Lotte was a sweet thing. An adventurous thing. A brave thing and a charming thing and all of this rolled into one small child, a girl with pigtails and wide eyes and a grand, exciting future.

But of course Lotte didn't know any of this yet.

She would wake up in the morning and rub her eyes. Get dressed into patchwork and sit almost still while her mother would tie her hair up in ribbons. Bolt a breakfast of toast and marmalade, and then scream out of the house and down the hill, into the meadow with her friends. And she would play. How she would play! She was a knight. She was a princess who rescued herself. She had tea parties and grand executions. Pretended she was the fiercest of dragons. Pretended she was visiting another planet. Pretended she owned the other planet. She shared all of this with her friends.

There was a beautiful boy with holes in his hands and the most glorious of white wings. A girl who used to be invisible, she said, but her bracelet of stars made her glow with light. A tiny star that chirped and whirred and snuggled, but mostly liked to ride inside of Lotte's pocket and peep out. Monsters. Demons. These were her friends.

"The Boy Who Hangs the Stars was terribly sad today," Lotte told her mother at lunch. She scarfed down her grilled cheese sandwich and tomato soup. Her hair had fallen out of its ribbons and her knee was scraped. She was exactly everything a little girl should be.

"Why was he sad?" Her mother tried to keep a neutral expression, a friendly expression, but it was getting more and more difficult as the days went on. "The demon tried to drag me into the pond, but

I got away," Lotte had told her the week before. She had tears in her clothing and scratches on her skin. "He's getting stronger."

"He's sad because the Invisible Girl has to go away for a while. She promised she'll come back, but he's afraid she won't." She leaned closer to her mother. "He loves her, you know?"

"Does he?"

Lotte nodded.

"Yep. She loves him, too, but she still has to go away. I think it might have something to do with the demons. The one that swims through the grass is getting scarier."

Charlotte's mother sat down at the table. Her fingers played with each other in a strange way, a way that said she was Worried, or Concerned, or the other words that her mom used sometimes when she talked in a low voice on the phone while discussing Charlotte.

"Lotte, sweetie, you know that this is all just pretend, right? These friends are somebody you made up. Friends from your imagination. They aren't real. Not the starry boy, or the invisible girl, or anybody else. Especially not the demon who swims through the grass."

Lotte drank her milk and wiped her lips with the back of her hand.

"Oh, don't say that, Mommy! It will hear you, and then it will get mad. It says it will do all sorts of things if it gets mad."

Her mother paled. "What sort of things, darling?"

"Bad things. Mean things. It doesn't want me to say."

"I don't want you pretending about the demon anymore."

"But Mommy—"

"Charlotte, stop!"

Of course her mother didn't understand. How could she? It had been so long since she had been a child herself. She, too, had worn pigtails and discussed life and dreams and fascinations with her own "imaginary" friends, but years had ground down the gears of her memory. Adults want to remember, they truly do, but some things just aren't possible after one reaches A Certain Age.

"I'll stop, Mommy."

"That's my good girl."

Demons don't care for good girls. They want scared little girls. Terrified little girls. Girls who run from them and have dreadful dreams. The demon who swims through the grass was angry at Charlotte for ignoring it, and especially angry at Charlotte's mother for disbelieving. It whispered its plans. It threatened. It promised to do the most poisonous of things to those who lived inside the house.

"I can't talk to you anymore," Lotte said. "I'm sorry. Mommy will get mad at me."

The demon would get angry, too, it hissed. Charlotte had better do what it says. The other friends, the boy and the star and a little ghost girl, pressed against Lotte, trying to keep her safe with the warmth of their bodies.

"Be careful," the Boy Who Hangs the Stars said. He took Lotte's hand in his own. His hands were soft and warm and the holes in his palms didn't bother Lotte at all. "The demon is getting more powerful. I'm afraid for you."

"I'll be okay," little Lotte reassured him, and smiled. He smiled back, and held her hand tighter, and everything seemed like it would be all right for a minute.

But it wouldn't. It wouldn't.

That was the night the demon set Charlotte's house on fire. Everything changed.

Charlotte had heard the saying several times. "You can't go home again." She was terrified to find out if it was really true.

"This your stop?" The bus driver asked her.

"Yes. Thank you."

"Somebody gonna to meet you?"

"I'll find out."

Indeed, somebody was there to meet our Charlotte, who went by Charlotte now. "Lotte" was a name for little girls in their frothy dresses, secure in the love of their family, their heads full of dreams.

Troubled women with cloudy pasts preferred to be called "Charlotte".

Charlotte brought one bag with her. It held everything she owned. She had grown quite adept at packing over the years, our poor girl. Moving from place to place. Escaping one situation for another. It is fair to say that Charlotte experienced very little magic.

But, as stated, somebody was there to pick her up. A woman she didn't know.

"Are you here to take me home?"

The woman sniffed at her.

"I'm here to take you to the house, yes."

The words were unmistakable. The house. Not her home. It will never be her home. Charlotte will never be welcomed back.

The ride was silent. Uncomfortable. The woman kept stealing glances at Charlotte, and Charlotte watched the road be devoured by the hungry wheels of the car.

"So much has changed," she said.

The woman didn't answer back.

The house came into sight. It had been rebuilt after the fire and was shaped strangely to Charlotte's mind. Rooms where there shouldn't be rooms. Spaces where there shouldn't be spaces.

"Looking at your handiwork, eh, firebug?" the woman said loudly.

"I didn't cause the fire."

"Sure you didn't. Maybe a pixie did it instead?"

"Stop it."

"Or faeries. You know how they are. So full of mischief. Wearing their little bluebell hats."

"I don't want to hear anymore!"

"Where were your friends then, huh? When the house went up in flames? When your mother was screaming with clothes and hair and hands on fire? She carried those burns until the day she died, afraid to leave the house because of the way she looked. She was nothing but stiffness and pain. But you? Found on the lawn in your pajamas, skin perfect as a peach. Not burnt at all, fancy that."

"Let me out of the car."

The woman ignored her. The house loomed, looking more and more sinister. Accusing. Charlotte's eyes filled with tears. She blinked angrily and one ran down her cheek.

"Oh, no you don't," the woman said, and her voice shook. "You don't get to cry. While you went to some fancy hospital for your delusions, I took care of your mother. She missed you, even after all that. I couldn't tell you why."

"I was j-just a little girl."

They were here. The woman slammed the car into park so quickly that Charlotte's seatbelt caught.

"Being young had nothing to do with it. Evil is evil. It starts at the root. And you're the worst of it."

Charlotte opened the car. Grabbed her bag. Cleared her throat before she asked because she was afraid her voice would sound weak, would sound afraid.

"Can you tell me exactly where my mother is buried?"

The woman's face went ugly. Changed into something horrible and voracious and mean. Charlotte nearly reached for the bottle of pills in her bag, but the woman's face calmed, returned to normal. It was anger, not delusion. Hatred that did this, not Charlotte's neurons firing in broken ways.

"At the cemetery near the bottom of the hill. Left side."

She reached over, slammed Charlotte's car door shut, and skidded out of the driveway, throwing gravel around her.

"Glad you're back," the Boy Who Hangs the Stars said. He put his broken hand on Charlotte's shoulder, and his large white wings fluttered.

"Great. I'm home for thirty seconds and I've already gone crazy."

This time she grabbed a bottle of pills from her bag. Shook two out and swallowed them dry. Took a deep breath and fit her key into the door of the house. Stepped inside.

The boy with wings watched her go.

Charlotte's room suffered little damage in the fire. Her mother, who still loved her little girl despite everything, had left the room exactly the same as it had been when Charlotte had left. "Left" wasn't exactly the word that Charlotte would have used. "When she was dragged kicking and screaming away from her mommy and into a hospital with tests and strangers and medicine in plastic cups and needles" is what Charlotte would have said, but of course, nobody asked her. So her mother simply chose to believe that her Lotte had left.

The room had blue walls with rainbows painted in the corner. It was full of dolls and board games and all of the things that makes a little girl happy.

Except her mother. Her mother wouldn't ever sit on the bed again. Wouldn't ever kiss Charlotte's cheek after tucking her in. She had seen her mother twice in the fifteen years since the fire. Two times. That was all. The hospital didn't want her to come, lest it interfere with Charlotte's treatment. And her mother wasn't physically well enough to make the trip to the other side of the country.

"Because of the fire, you know," a voice said next to her elbow. "Because of the tremendous pain she was in."

The voice came from a little shadow with white eyes and sharp teeth that stretched all the way around his face like a zipper. He started poking through Charlotte's bag. Pulling out a thin hoodie.

Pulling out a threadbare pair of shorts and pitching everything to the floor.

"You're not real," Charlotte told him, and then squeezed her eyes shut. Don't acknowledge the illusions. Don't give them any credence. Talk to them as if they're real and they might as well be.

"Good to have you back, by the way," the shadow said. His voice was dark and made of wind. "It was lonely here without you. Nobody to play with. Do you remember how we used to *play?*"

Charlotte closed her eyes, breathed through her nose. Thought calming thoughts. Repeated her mantra. Prayed to a god. Did all of the things that a woman who is on the edge of sanity does. When she opened her eyes, the shadowy creature was no longer there.

"Thank goodness!" Charlotte said, and fell onto her bed. She frowned. Felt something under the covers. She reached in, fished around, and came out with something sweet and tiny and very soft. A doll, with dark hair and blue eyes. She remembered it. A tiny Lotte doll. The doll of her, made with love by the invisible girl when Charlotte was only a few years old.

"I…thought this wasn't real," she said.

There was a snicker of laughter behind her.

Charlotte hid. That was the only word for it, poor dear. She holed up in her house, refusing to step outside, refusing to speak to the enchanted horde that deigned speak to her. She didn't want to face the town who blamed her for the fire. Neighbors who wondered if crazy was contagious.

She didn't want to stand by her mother's grave alone. That thought was too much for her.

"You won't be alone," said the invisible girl with the star bracelet. Her smile was soft and sincere, and Charlotte couldn't help but smile back, vision or no vision. "We'll be here with you. We loved your mother, too, you know."

Charlotte automatically looked for her bottle of pills, but the girl took her hand.

"You don't need medicine. You never did. We're real, Lotte. We always were."

Charlotte signed.

"I almost wish that were true."

The girl's smile grew even sunnier.

"It *is* true. Doesn't that make you happy?"

"It makes me crazy."

The invisible girl held Charlotte's hand tighter. Kissed her cheek. Dropped her hand and stood up.

"Are you the kind of daughter who starts her own house on fire? Who calmly walks outside and lets her mother burn?"

Charlotte was taken aback.

"What a terrible thing to say!" she said. Her chest hurt. Her eyes stung. She thought of her mother with her hair ablaze and feared she would vomit.

The glowing invisible girl watched her carefully.

"Of course not. You couldn't do it. You wouldn't dream of doing it, and it doesn't matter what the doctors say. But if you didn't, who did?"

The demon who swims through the grass, Charlotte thought, but didn't say it aloud.

The girl nodded.

"Yes. That's who. It's as real as we are."

Charlotte, sweet thing, didn't know what to say. Fifteen years of being told she was a decent person whose brain worked incorrectly. That visions are visions. That being insane isn't anything to be ashamed of, not really. Except when, of course, it's something to be ashamed of.

"I need to think about it," Charlotte said quietly. A tiny little star chimed and chirped and zipped over to her. It climbed into her lap and began to purr. Charlotte held it gently, feeling the warmth of the star in her cupped hands.

"Of course," said the girl. She patted the star on the head, and then did the same to Charlotte. "We're here. Take your time. And when you want to go visit your mother, I'll come with you, if you'd like. We all will."

The boy with wings stood in the doorway and nodded at the girl's words. He held his hand out to her, and the invisible girl took it. They both smiled. Charlotte smiled back. The star chimed.

"I think I like you," she told the star. "It would be so wonderful if you were real."

The star snuggled closer. Charlotte crawled under her covers and brought the star with her. For the first time in a long time, she was truly happy.

Several days later, she decided she was finished hiding. Crazy or not, she needed to see her mother.

She got dressed. Brushed her brown hair. Stared at herself in the mirror.

"I can do this."

The star jumped onto her shoulder and nuzzled her earlobe. Charlotte grinned.

"You make things easier, you darling thing. I think I can go if you come with me."

She stood on the porch, looking at the trees and grass and beautiful wonder outside. It had been so long. She had become used to white walls and carefully cultivated hospital grounds. But this? The wildness was stunning. The freedom intoxicating. She wanted to run down the hill, screaming with frustration and joy.

"Why don't you?" asked the Boy Who Hangs the Stars. He was smiling at her, his wings beating calmly. The star leaped from her shoulder to his and meowed.

"I don't know. I haven't..."

"Then come with me, Lotte," he said, and took her hand.

They ran. Ran through the grass, ran down the hill. Charlotte remembered the way her pigtails flew when she was Lotte, not Charlotte. She recalled screaming with joy and fierceness and delighted terror when she felt like her legs were outrunning the rest of her body. The boy laughed, his wild hair even wilder, and Charlotte realized she was laughing as well.

Laughter. Joy. This was real.

They reached the bottom of the hill and tumbled to the ground. Breathing heavily. Still laughing. Charlotte rolled onto her back and stared at the sky.

"We waited for you to come back," the boy said. "None of us thought it would take so long. But you're here, and we're happy."

"I'm still not sure if I believe in you," Charlotte said. "I'm sorry."

"It's all right." Another voice. A ghost girl with blonde hair. White Mary, if she remembered correctly. "Believe or don't believe. It doesn't matter." She smiled, and it was lovely.

"I'd like to see my mother," Charlotte said. She stood up and brushed the grass from her. "I'd also like all of you to come, if you don't mind?"

She looked at the ground, feeling shy. Feeling like she was asking too much.

Hands in hers. A chiming star in her hair.

"Of course we'll come," said the winged boy. White Mary nodded.

"Thank you," Charlotte said. "Thank you so, so much."

The cemetery was surrounded by tall apple trees in full bloom. Grasses swayed. Charlotte picked her way through the headstones until she found her mother's.

She dropped to her knees, the air knocked out of her, head and heart hurting.

"Mommy," she managed, and that's all she could say, because suddenly she was crying so hard that she could barely breathe. All of the sunny afternoons, the cold winter nights. All of the things about becoming a woman, about figuring out who she was, and her mother wasn't there to ask. So much time lost. So many empty arms for both of them. And why?

"Lotte," the Boy Who Hangs the Stars said, and his ethereal voice held warning. She looked up, wiping her eyes, and saw that the sky was darkening, the wind starting up. Far in the distance, the long grass parted like water.

"It's coming."

She didn't need to be told what. She knew. Knew deep in her bones, in that primal part of her that housed things like fear and regret and rage. The demon who swims through the grass.

The invisible girl who glowed like a star was on her knees beside Charlotte.

"If you run, maybe you can escape him. Maybe if you're fast enough, you can make it to the house."

"I can carry you," the Boy Who Hangs the Stars said. He spread his beautiful white wings, and they blotted out the sun. "I can get you home safely. Come on!"

"No," Charlotte said, and the word surprised all of them. She said it again, louder. With more force. It felt good. Felt like majesty.

"No. I'm not going to run. Not this time."

The demon swam closer. The invisible girl's glow diminished, seemed to pale. The boy reached out and held her hand tightly.

"We'll stay with you," he said, and Charlotte bit her lip and nodded. She stuffed her tremoring hands in her pockets and stood her ground, waiting for the demon to show.

It didn't disappoint.

"Charlotte," it breathed from deep inside the grass. Its voice was ancient and cold, stirring up primal feelings in Charlotte. She tasted horror. The fear of being chased, of being eaten. The things that she thought had evolved out of the human psyche long ago.

"Demon," she said curtly, and her voice was surprisingly strong. The boy and girl stood beside her. A team. A tribe.

The little grinning shadow demon with the zippered teeth danced nearby, watching the exchange. "Oh, goodie," it said with its hollow voice. "Just like old times. I'm ready to play, Lotte. Are you?"

"Back off," she told it. "I'm not talking to you. I'm talking to this one. You're the one that burned my house, right? Hurt my mother?"

The demon, still hidden in the grass, chuckled.

"I told you. I warned you not to ignore me. Your mother was filling your head with bad thoughts. *Untrue* thoughts. Telling you that I didn't exist. A mother shouldn't be telling a little girl things that are *untrue*, should she?"

Charlotte tasted something like blood on her lips. It was rage. It tasted good. Tasted wholesome. She could feast on it for weeks. For always.

"She was my mother, and you stole her from me. Stole my childhood from me."

She sounded dark herself, her own kind of demon. Fierce and powerful. She felt the support of her friends. The boy with wings and his star. The invisible girl. White Mary.

"There are more of us than you," she said, and her anger gave her strength. She took a step into the grass. It was long and tall and filled her with terror and mystery. She grit her teeth and took another step. Another.

"What are you doing, girl?"

The demon who swims through the grass sounded worried. Sounded like somebody who wasn't used to being challenged. This gave Charlotte new strength.

"Why, it's called revenge, demon. You took something precious from me. Now it's time I do the same to you."

The shadow demon who watched them stopped its chittering. Squeaked through its zippered teeth, and dove into the grass. Scrabbled away.

Charlotte grinned.

"Looks like your little pet took off. I suggest you do the same."

The demon laughed, but it sounded forced. Sounded afraid.

"What could you possible do to me, girl?"

Charlotte shrugged, but kept venturing into the grass. Each step felt like power. Each step felt like gain.

"I'm going to kill you. Maybe not at first. It might take me a few tries. But, oh, how I'm going to love the trying."

The demon who swims through the grass was her nightmare. It was everything she was afraid of, besides her own mind. But her mind wasn't broken. She was whole. This was real. It was all real, and the very reality of it took her fear away.

There was a sound. A strangled growl. The meadow swirled, and the demon who swims through the grass retreated. Whirled around and swam away, the grasses bending and flowing around it like filthy water, like fire.

"Come back here!" Charlotte shouted. "Get back here, you coward!"

"Lotte," said the invisible girl, and Charlotte calmed. Ran her hands over her face and took a deep breath.

"I'm sorry, you guys. I'm just…I'm angry…"

She couldn't say anything more because they had thrown their arms around her. The boy. The girls. The star slipped itself into her pocket and peeked out, just as it had when she was their dear Lotte, not Simply Charlotte.

"Welcome home, Lotte," White Mary said. Her hair blew around her face in a wind that nobody else could feel. "I'm so very glad you're back."

"Me too," Charlotte said, and she meant it. She was back where she belonged, with those who knew her best. It was time to make a new life for herself. The best kind of life.

They walked up to the house. There was so much conversation. So much talking and laughing. Recreations of Charlotte wading into the waist-deep grasses, going after the flustered demon. More laughter. Delicious, beautiful laughter.

At the foot of the hill, Charlotte's mother stood by her headstone, watching her little girl. Lotte had grown so much, become so strong. She had the gift to see things that few others saw, and this made the mother grateful. They could start anew. They could start right.

She disappeared into the evening. Soon she would visit her brave little Lotte, and this fairytale, like so many others, would indeed have a happy ending.

ON THE FAR SIDE
— OF THE APOCALYPSE —
by Peter Rawlik

DAWN IS ANNOUNCED BY a trio of Cherubim singing hosannas and hallelujahs as they dart between buildings and around street lamps and over underpasses. As I watch the sunrise, the three baby-faced, dove-winged angels stream by clad in chrome-spiked leather and sunglasses, their fingers and teeth stained yellow from fat, greasy cigars that trail smoke like streamers behind them. Today is Sunday, like yesterday and the day before and the day before that. According to the City Watch, every day is Sunday. Not a decree mind you, just an odd pattern established, perhaps by default, by Metatron, the Voice of God and Divine Governor of His City, the City of Angels.

Welcome to post-apocalyptic Los Angeles, a city finally both secular and divine. Walking through the streets (or what remains, for what need do Angels have of streets) are the homeless, the mad, and other residents who fight for space against the teeming throngs of refugees from Las Vegas and the pilgrims from Denver, Rome, and Mexico. L.A. has become Mecca, the final refuge, the new Babylon for those who remain. The official census lists the population at forty-two million, but pagans are not included in the polling. Private estimates place the coast's population at over a hundred million. The pagans, mostly Hindus, Buddhists, and New Wiccans are not recognized by, nor subject to the laws of the Inquisition and are therefore free to assume certain less than legitimate enterprises without fear of retribution. The Tao Tong controls the drug trade throughout the city, while prostitution is held in the velvet glove of the Ishtarian Sisterhood.

The press of humanity, whether forty-two or a hundred million, is almost intolerable. There isn't enough food, or water, or facilities to satisfy the need. Not that it matters much. The Angel of Death no longer walks the Earth. No one dies, only the plants and animals, creatures without souls retain that blessing. Starvation, dehydration, disease, and violence, all combine to drag the standard of living below any standard of acceptability. The atrocities of Germany, Eastern Europe, South-East Asia, and Africa were all just small-town, playhouse theater compared to the reality of California in the new millennium.

I gather my things for my walk across the city, a walking stick for defense, a hat to keep the sun off my head, and an umbrella for the rain. On the way out, I pause and gather apples from the tree on the patio. It is an old tree, old when my parents were young. Despite its age it is small, with small apples, no larger than a child's fist. When I gather the fruits, the guardian of the tree curls down around my arm, binding me to the tree with its scaled body.

The three heads that hiss in unison form a chorus of a voice, "Is it time Man-Killer? It has been a long time. I have almost forgotten. Is it time for my tree to grow?"

I take the time to stroke each of his heads. The flesh is soft and warm to the touch. I lift his body and whisper softly into his six ears, "Soon, old friend. Soon. I promise you."

The serpent draws itself up as if to strike. "I should have killed you when you stole the tree. I should have struck. I should have made your muscles knot, your bones break, and your brain burn. I should have made you shrivel and die."

"You know the law. You cannot touch me. No one can touch me. Not without fear of retribution." I hold the serpent's stare with my own.

"I know the law, Man-Killer," he concedes. "I also know the Lawmaker has abandoned your kind. I could strike you now and not fear His wrath." Like a cobra, the serpent sways before me, watching for my guard to drop.

"You could, old one. If you are sure that He is gone. Are you sure? Do you know something that all the Angels and humans do not? Feel free, serpent. Strike me down with your poison. Only be sure in your heart that He is gone. Be sure, because I myself hold no such belief."

The beast hisses in disgust, spitting acrid venom on the floor as he uncoils from my hand. He slithers back amongst the branches, leaving me to gather the last of the apples. By the time I finish my coat pockets are heavy with the dark, sweet fruit.

I stumble down the stairwell and into the open streets. Immediately, I am caught behind a tour group frozen in place, gazing awestruck at the sky. Above the masses, the countless Celestial Orders of Angels dance in a strange aerial ballet with scrolls of gold leaf, trumpets and rose petals trailing behind them. Their guide, a licensed civil servant of the Celestial Bureaucracy, supplies the spectators with names.

"There, ladies and gentlemen, there, just coming around the tower! In red and silver, that is Jehudiel, Archangel of the Spheres. His battle with the demon Marchosias tumbled down Chicago. And look behind him, Oertha whose valiant defense of Havana was all in vain."

I chuckle to as the crowd releases an audible "Oooohhhh." Jehudiel and Oertha, indeed. Those two are Farris and Hizarbin, minor angels, cogs in the wheel of the Angelic Politic, bureaucrats of no standing and no particular fame. Although Farris is known in some circles for his preference for young, Asian boys. Not all Angels are angels.

I push back the ignorant, misguided faithful and decide to take a shortcut through the Soukh. The marketplace reeks even worse than the rest of the city. It is a heavy acid and earth and rot smell, an odiferous mélange of what is sold in the Soukh. The first shops are clean and brightly lit and fully sanctioned by the administration. These are tourist shops, full of the usual flotsam and jetsam of human kitsch. The t-shirts are everywhere: I WAS JUDGED AND FOUND WANTING; MY PARENTS WENT TO HEAVEN AND ALL I GOT WAS THIS STUPID SHIRT; or my personal favorite, I SLEPT THROUGH THE APOCALYPSE. There are even some of those small water globes with cityscapes in them. When you shake them, millions of tiny angels and demons swirl in a maelstrom of imitation Armageddon.

Deeper in, the common gives way to the uncommon and you can find merchants offering the most unusual items for sale. Relics of Popes and Saints are common and, in most cases, fraudulent. Offers of heavenly swords and unearthly halos are not unheard of. These, too, are presumed fraudulent. You can, however, for the right price, buy a genuine heavenly relic. Items guaranteed to be Angelic in origin: Angelic feces, Angelic vomit, and Angelic urine. Angel piss has an unearthly color, and a sweet, burning cinnamon smell. The pilgrims buy it for twenty ounces of gold to the gallon, and more for the Higher Ordered Angels. A king's ransom for the waste of an Archangel. All sanctioned by the Hierarchy, and they get their cut. These days, Angels have need of gold.

At one of the more popular booths, six or seven merchants struggle behind the table trying to satisfy the souvenir needs of two-dozen devotees from Quebec. Around the crowd, a small mob of beggar boys have staked out the marks and have begun their routines. The youngest of them is six. There have been no children born since the Judgment, and there are no new souls. One of these young ones wanders toward me, looking for a handout. He is bright-eyed and full of life. I tempt him forward with an apple offered in my palm. He takes cautious and furtive steps. He is afraid of me, but he is also afraid of being noticed. If an older boy, a stronger boy, sees him with this prize, he won't keep it for long. His fingers, short, thin, and strong reach out for the apple. Another step, small but sure, and his palm reflects in the red skin of the fruit. He almost has it. A thin malicious grin grows on my face. Another second and the prize will be his.

In an instant, the child is jerked back. A look of surprise, fear and sudden shock fill the lad's face. An older boy, at the most twelve, perhaps the band's leader, perhaps the boy's brother, clutches the younger by the scruff of the neck. Like a kitten carried by its mother, the child dangles in the air almost immobile. The older boy whispers something furtive and esoteric into the young boy's ear. He knows something, this older boy. He knows I am a danger. I watch the child's eyes grow wide in understanding. I smile at the two of them. I smile sweetly, and the child shudders.

"Don't worry, boys, I don't want to kill you. You have nothing to fear from me, unless, of course, you're family".

The older boy takes a brave, cautious stand. He speaks with authority, clear and true, "Are we not all your family, uncle?" He spits at me. Not on me mind you, just at me. It is an old gesture, a desert custom, ripe with implications.

I turn and leave the boys to their begging. The apple I offered to them, I give to a pilgrim from New York still wearing his subway pass clipped to his hat. I stop suddenly in my tracks, stunned by the irony. I feel through my pockets checking the apples for size. I smile, secure in the fact that that was indeed the big apple. Behind me I hear the crisp bite of teeth in the flesh of the fruit. There is a chewing noise, and then something else. I hear the mob cry out. Like Lot, I don't look back as the marketplace is consumed.

I avoid making eye contact with the shoddy, unwashed priests gathered at the bridge, victims of the war and of the occupation. The clergy have fallen on hard times. Who needs those to interpret the Word when those who speak the Word walk among us? I shove apples into their greedy, hungry hands. They thank me. They bless me. They wish me peace and redemption. One grabs me by the shoulder and traces his other hand over my face. He asks me if I wish to confess, and I push him away. He pleads as I hurry over the bridge.

I pass over the bay, careful not to look down. In the shadows of the bridge, on both shores, members of the Penitente religious order hang, nailed to crosses—their flesh torn and rotting. Great clouds of flies swarm around them, impregnating the open wounds with countless eggs. The eggs hatch and billions of maggots slowly eat through the living flesh of those undying imitators of Christ. Some still offer up screaming prayers and pleading apologies.

"I am here, Father! I am Your Son made in Your image! Forgive me, Father! End my suffering! Release me from my earthly bond!"

Most, however, are beyond screaming or prayers. The pain, the hunger, and the thirst I suppose must be unbearable. It must drive them insane. Eventually, they end up slumped sideways with their eyes and mouth locked open in a sickening catatonia of drool and tears. The moist membranes are attractive morsels for the flies and their spawn, and the insects are quick to take advantage. The tongue and eyes are usually eaten first. The throat and the stomach are next to swell with the foul, crawling worms. The rest of the body is slowly devoured, leaving only the scarecrows of bone, cartilage, and ligament. The oldest of the Penitente are strewn as semi-mobile skeletons begging silently, without tongues, for death.

On the far side of the bridge, the line at the gate is like a slug, moving slowly and sweating vile fluids in the morning sun. Two Angels with flaming swords, Grigori, those who watch the gates, are collecting tolls. The cost is a gram of gold, a pittance really, but gold has become scarce in this post-apocalyptic age. The line is full of people waiting to trade earrings, wedding bands, or the occasional tooth for passage.

When I reach the gate, I move through without paying. There is a sudden sound like a train or rocket. I find my way blocked by a sword of flame. The Angels train their eyes on me. As with most Angels, these are clad in traditional white, flowing robes that casually reveal the flesh beneath.

There are things you don't notice about Angels until you see them up close. They have no eyelids or body hair. They lack navels and have no pores. They are immense, titanic, and statuesque. Their swords smell of victory. There is a single, tense moment during which neither of us moves. Then quietly, the second Angel leans down and stares at me. He blows gently to part the hair from my face. His breath smells of lilacs and roses. He studies me carefully. Then, as quietly as he came down, both he and his comrade withdraw, and I pass without further incident.

Beyond the Grigori, I walk into Elysia, the great open plaza where the feet of the Divine Colossus are planted. Looking upward, I can see human construction crews laboring to weld the massive steel framework into place. Below them, Angels plaster the metal skeleton with a skin of molten gold. Nearby, the monolith's head rests with eyes of cold steel and hair of liquid fire, fashioned from the few memories the Angels still have of the image of God. I cannot help but recall the face of the beast Gog-Magog as he rose out of his Middle Eastern desert prison. In the face of God I see the Beast's reflected back, or is it the other way around? The eyes are the same, and the mouth. Yes, all God's creations share His eyes and mouth.

I remember when Metatron, the Voice of God, decreed, perhaps in desperation, the construction of the golden idol. He spoke in a strange, human voice that was full of confusion, "The Fallen are defeated. We are victorious. Yet what price our triumph? The Celestial City lies in ruin. Millions of the Sons of Adam have been slain, millions more escorted beyond the infinite. The Three Who are One are lost to us. Our envoys have searched Eternity, and their efforts have been fruitless. We are lost, abandoned, forsaken. The Seraphim, the Seven Archangels, have taken consul, conferred, and decided. The Hierarchy must have an apex. The Sons of Adam must have a God."

Behold now! We have a new god for this new age, a figurehead for the Angelic Order, something to believe in. This is why the Angels have need of gold. I leave the plaza, careful not to let the Attendant Angels, the Ishshim, see my tears.

I make my way into the squalor, what some residents call the Hanging Gardens. Here, I trudge through more madness. Like the Penitente, these people seek an end to their suffering. Unlike their more ecclesiastical cohorts, the Hung make no plea to the Father. Instead, quietly, calmly, even politely, they commit suicide. Over and over again they die. In the beginning, poisons were popular and it took some time for the supply of toxic substances to become exhausted. Stockpiles of ammunition were quickly depleted, as well. Stabbing has never been popular. Jumping was once a preferred method, but those who are prone to its use often find themselves unable to muster the physical coordination to try it a second or third time. Drowning simply does not work. As a result, hanging has become popular. Thus were created the Hanging Gardens.

The gardens are quite lovely, even in winter. It has become tradition for the Hung to dress in their finest wardrobe and outfit themselves with the brightest, most outlandish neckwear they can find. Some take the time to color coordinate their ensembles to ensure that the fine details of color in their faces and oxygen-starved skin are highlighted. The streetlights and telephone poles of this part of the city are wrapped with the twisting, swinging bodies like so many holiday decorations. Thankfully, the Cherubs have made a sport of cutting down the older of the Hung on a regular basis. They come by in small gangs, flashing switchblades back and forth, hungry for a bit of sadistic fun. Watching one of the Hung gasp for breath and change colors seems to always be good for a few laughs.

I pass a street vendor hawking wares for this obscene neighborhood. His voice is a singsong of hopelessness, "Ropes, thin ropes, fat ropes, white ropes, black ropes, fine ropes." He stops me. "A rope for you, friend?" I have no need of ropes and I tell him so. "No harm in asking, friend, now is there? No harm at all. Besides, I knew from the start you weren't no regular Hung. You ain't got no scars around your neck. No, you ain't here for no ordinary rope. No, sir, you are not. I can tell. I use to be somebody, you know. I used to be a psychiatrist. I know what people are thinking. I know what people need. I know when they are looking for something special."

"I suppose then you have something special? Something I need?" I respond, doing my best to hide the sarcasm in my voice.

"Indeed I do, sir, indeed I do!" He reminds me of a fisherman who has just hooked a big one. "I have a poison guaranteed to kill. Guaranteed, I tell you. These three guys out in the Valley, they took it nine days ago. They ain't moved since. They dead. They are gonna stay dead, too. I swear. They are dead forever. You could be too. For a price."

I drag my eyes up and down his thin frame. "Will you take these in trade?" I offer him six juicy apples.

His eyes grow wide in greed and he snatches the fruit from my hand. "Done!" And the apples are gone. He shoves a greasy, glass vial into my hand and moves off without saying a word. After ten yards, his pace picks up, and he breaks into a run before I have a chance to look at the jar. The contents are blue and viscous. The liquid clings to the sides like oil or grease. Even without taking off the lid I can smell the stuff, laundry detergent, or some similar cleanser. Nothing more. No miracle poison; laundry detergent. I throw the vial into a sewer and move on.

My course takes me past the city library, or what is left of it. The windows and doors are all gone, shattered and broken; their frames are stained with soot and ash. Through gaping, toothless mouth-like doors, I see derelicts shuffling through the stacks carrying torches to guide the way. There are other fires burning as well, larger fires with smoke that smells of old paper, ink, and leather. The librarians are burning the books. Not all at once mind you, just those that have been deemed useless. Philosophy went first I suppose, followed by science and perhaps government. They must be at least up to history by now, or perhaps economics. I mount the steps and leave apples as a dark gift to these traitors to reason.

By noon I reach the Celestial Administration Complex, a vast city of surreal architecture in what was once Anaheim. The happiest place on Earth is now a shining fortress of refuge for the Angels who now dwell among the mundane. Divine fire adorns the artificial mountains and luminous clouds float through the streets. Dog-faced angels that reek of sweat and blood guard the gates. Few humans are allowed inside. Again, I pass without incident. Metatron is waiting for me.

Angels do not pace. When they become impatient an odd reflex places them in a fugue state from which they cannot estimate the passage of time. Metatron awakens from this state when I enter the room.

His voice is oddly human. "This is your fault. You knew this would happen. We should kill you for this. We should cast you screaming into the pit. We will have vengeance."

I stare at the displaced Angel, the former Voice of God. My gaze is cold, dark, and direct. "You will do nothing," I tell him. "Your time is over. The chorus of God has been chosen, and your voice was found too discordant to belong. The age of God and His rule are over. It is my time. There shall be a new age and a new God. I assure you it will not be the sad monolith of gold you are so fervent in constructing."

Metatron's face betrays his fall into humanity as it reflects the all too mortal emotion of bewilderment. I feel sorry for him. I feel sorry for all of them. The Angels, so nearly divine but still imperfect. Part of the plan, but not privy or aware of its details, goals, and consequences. I part my hair to reveal my Mark, the Mark of God.

"I am Cain, Son of Adam, Son of God. My parents tasted the fruits of the Tree of Knowledge. In doing so, God planted His seeds, tended His orchard, and harvested the best of fruits. Yet, as with all harvests, there is still fruit left on the tree. Most of the fruit is overripe, bruised, or diseased. With these meager remains the pickers may do what they want. Most will eventually fall and rot away, returning to the base from which they came. Some of the remains, however, are simply not ripe, not yet ready to harvest. Given time, some will yield the sweetest fruit of all."

I pull the last apple from my pocket. "This is the fruit of the second tree, the Tree of Ignorance. From its seeds a new Eden shall grow. As with the original tree, man will be offered these fruits. These are not the fruits of knowledge or immortality. Rather, they are the fruits of ignorance and oblivion. Man must return to his origins. He must be without sin and without mind, as the beasts in the field. This is my mission, cursed to me by the Lord from the beginning. I will lead man from the light and into the darkness."

I watch as realization, then rapture overcomes Metatron. With this new dawning, his need fulfilled, Metatron slowly dissolves away into the ether of creation. All around the world, faithful Angels dissolve into nothingness. In the midst of it all he speaks; Metatron actually speaks, "The Prophecy is fulfilled. The Alpha and the Omega. In the End . . ." and he is gone.

And then there is a second voice; a voice for the world, and it speaks to the world, "In the Beginning . . ."

"There was darkness," I respond. I close my eyes and wait for the world to begin again.

— THE STUMP AND THE SPIRE —
by Joseph Lallo

If you want to get to the root of something,
you're going to have to dig.

I T IS A USEFUL BIT of wisdom in any walk of life. Time has a way of covering things up, after all. To get to the essential truth of a thing, the place where it all started, you will have to brush away the layers left behind by the passing years. The words may mean different things to different people, but the wisdom behind them remains. When a healer says you must dig to the root, for instance, he means you must find the cause of an ailment. When a diplomat says you must dig to the root, she means you must learn why a war began. The words could mean a dozen different things; it only depends on who is doing the speaking, and who is doing the listening.

On this day it was William who was doing the listening. He was a young boy of ten who had grown up working the land with his parents and his sister. The one doing the speaking was William's father, and he was not a diplomat or a healer. He was a farmer, and when a farmer says you must dig to the root, he is holding a shovel and pointing to a tree stump. Farmers don't have time for metaphors.

"Father, I can't dig out a whole tree by myself," William objected.

"I did it when I was your age. It just takes time," his father said, handing the boy the shovel and tousling his hair. "It will do you good to get some proper work done, and this stump is long overdue to come out."

William looked to the stump again. It was an ancient gray thing, the remains of an oak that had been dead the day they found it. The tree had been on the land since long before they had taken it over the previous season, and it was at the center of a patch of barren and lifeless field. It had been simple enough to cut down the trunk, and after a bit of sawing and chopping it provided some much needed firewood. As for the stump, they had been in too much of a hurry to take care of it thus far. The growing season was short, and the planting season shorter. During those months, their time was better spent elsewhere. Now the harvest was over, and the air was already taking on the harder nip of the long winter ahead. There was no better time to dig out the stump and see what could be done to nurse the soil back to health. It wasn't a terribly large job, all things considered. The stump was only half as tall as the boy and perhaps equally wide. The tangle of roots beneath it was daunting though, particularly considering how deep it likely ran.

"But it'll take me forever!"

"Just do as much as you can do today, then come back tomorrow. It'll be done before you know it," William's father assured him with a firm slap on the back. "And do your best while the weather is still warm, because once the ground starts to freeze it'll be that much harder."

"But—"

"*William,*" he said, his voice stern and his gaze hard. "Remember what happens to little boys who disobey their parents. A dragoyle will come along and eat your toes in your sleep."

"Yes, Father." William had been hearing stories about dragoyles for as long as he could remember. They were supposed to be evil creatures left behind by the D'Karon, dark wizards from long ago who had come from another world and nearly conquered this one. Dragoyles were said to be vicious monsters, and the D'Karon were the blackest of evils, but mostly they seemed to exist specifically to frighten little boys into doing what they were told. William had stopped believing in them years ago, but he knew that once his father started talking about them, the next words would be punishment.

"So what are you going to do?"

"I'll dig up the stump, Father."

"That's my boy," he said.

William sighed and put the shovel to work, hacking at the first of what would be many, many roots. The boy wasn't shaping up to have what one might call a farmer's physique. He was short for his age, and he'd never lost his baby fat, despite plenty of hard work on the land. His temperament left something to be desired as well. Whereas his father could think of no finer way to spend the day than getting his hands dirty tilling the soil, William had other interests. The boy would much prefer to while away the hours sketching shapes on the ground, daydreaming, and asking questions his parents wouldn't have known how to answer even if they'd had the time and inclination to do so. It was a source of great concern for William's father that the boy didn't show much interest in the family work, but he was a simple man and confident that a few more summers with spade in hand would make the boy see the light. After all, it had worked for Layla, William's sister.

Layla was four years older than William and taller by a head and shoulders. Though she still gave her parents plenty to worry about, she was at least happy enough working on the farm. She tended to the animals and was never shy to take up a rake or a hoe if an extra set of hands were needed. It had left her with a fit build and boundless energy, which was something of a mixed blessing. Though her parents were grateful for her help and enthusiasm on the fields, they would have preferred a bit less energy afterward. She already had a habit of getting into trouble when the day's work was through, and it would only get worse as her thoughts began to drift toward more amorous pursuits.

As the sun was hitting its highest point, Layla paid her brother a visit. She was wearing her dirt-encrusted work clothes, and in her hand was a familiar cloth sack.

"Lunchtime, Willy!" she chirped.

The boy looked wearily at his sister as she offered him a smile and set the sack down beside the stump.

"So Dad finally decided to have you dig something up," she said, untying the corners of the sack to flatten it into a tablecloth of sorts. Inside was a pile of golden-brown pockets of baked dough and a leather water flask.

"Yeah. All by myself," he replied. He wiped his hands on his pants and eagerly tried to stuff an entire dough pocket into his mouth. They were a treat his mother had concocted when she grew tired of her family attempting to eat their midday meal while in the fields. After most of her bowls were lost or broken, she started baking meat, gravy, and vegetables into a pocket of dough so that they could eat with their hands.

"He does that. Remember when he made *me* dig up all of those bushes when *I* was ten? It is like a test. Do it right and you're a grownup."

"It's hard, it's no fun, and I'm only doing it because I have to," he said through a mouthful of meat and dough. "What's that supposed to teach me about being a grownup?"

Layla smirked. "That about covers it I think." She slapped him on the back. "You always were the fast learner."

"Does that mean I can stop?"

"Nope. Being a grownup is for good." She grabbed a pocket of her own. "Besides, what *else* are you going to do?"

"I don't know. Anything. Think about stuff. Let my mind wander."

"You know what Dad says about that sort of thing." She adopted a gruff voice and an educational tone. "Things that wander tend to get lost."

"Don't you ever wonder about things?"

"Like what?"

"Well…like why do they call this place Oddspire Fields?"

"That's easy. Because of the spire," she said, pointing.

Just beyond the fence at the edge of their land, about a dozen yards away from the stump, was a spire. It was ancient and worn by the elements, but one could still see the intricate designs that had been carved into its surface. It was about twice as tall as Layla and jutted out of the ground at an odd angle. "It's a spire, it's in the fields, and that's odd. Oddspire Fields."

"But how did it get there? The closest place with spires like that is New Kenvard, and that's miles away."

Layla treated the question with her usual level of diligence. She gave it half a thought, then shrugged and took a guess. "I suppose people liked it better that way. Anyway, eat up. Plenty more digging before this thing is out."

William nodded. The two finished their meal and each went back to work. For a while he continued to think about the spire. New Kenvard was a long way away. If someone had really taken the spire from one of the roofs of the old buildings and installed it here, he couldn't imagine why, and they'd done a poor job of it besides. It was standing at an odd angle and didn't have so much as a path leading to it. When he was done turning that mystery over in his head, he started to wonder why no one else had been curious enough to find out the answer. It seemed like no one really cared how things were, or about the mysteries of the world. Not anymore, anyway. Now they just cared about their own little corner of the world and how to get by. As the day rolled on, his thoughts were eventually reduced to variations of "This tree sure has a lot of roots," and "I wonder how much more I'll have to dig."

The last answer, he learned several days later, was *plenty*. The tree may have been dead, but in its day it must have been mighty, because the roots seemed to go on forever. William hacked through the ones he could, but the main taproot was as thick as his arm and as tough as nails. Day after day he dug deeper, trying to find a point where the root was thin enough to chop through. In the evening of the seventh day, when the hole beside the stump was now well over his head, his shovel struck something strange nestled among the roots.

It wasn't a stone or a particularly stubborn root. He'd struck enough of *them* to be a veritable expert. Leaning his shovel against the wall of the pit he'd dug, he got down on his knees and clawed at the object with his hands. It was extremely entangled, whatever it was, but the roots around it were thinner and more brittle than he'd encountered thus far. With a bit more digging, he managed to unearth what turned out to be a small metal box. It was only about two square-feet around and a few inches thick, but it was unlike anything he'd seen before. Rather than being rusted beyond recognition, the box was barely corroded. It was a dark gray color, and when he hauled it out into the fading sun he could just make out some thin engravings forming a complex pattern. One side had a delicate hinge, and the other had two latches. From the looks of it the roots had managed to work their way inside, snapping one of the latches and providing a glimpse within. He twisted and turned the box in the dim light, trying to catch a peek of what it held, but before he could see anything useful, he heard his mother's voice calling him home for dinner. He tucked the box under his arm and climbed out of the hole, scurrying toward the house.

Their home was a simple one, consisting mostly of one large room. The fireplace, which currently had a heavy iron pot hanging in it, filling the home with the smell of boiling cabbage, nested along the wall opposite the entrance. The room had a table and a few chairs, and the family used it for almost everything but sleeping. For that, there was a pair of bedrooms, one for the children and one for the parents. Outside the house, the family was lucky enough to have its own well and a barn a bit further away.

William ran to their barn to stow the shovel. With the tool in its place, he made ready to bring the box to his father, but something stopped him.

Like most people these days, William's father had little use for a mystery. He tended to dismiss things he didn't understand as unnecessary distractions from planting or harvesting. If William showed this box to his father, he would simply tell William to throw it away, or perhaps take it so that he could see about selling it at the market. Granted, William reasoned that selling the box *was* probably the best idea…but not before he'd had a chance to take a closer look. He lowered it carefully to the ground beneath the feed trough, brushed some hay over it, and hurried to the house. He tried to take a seat as his mother dished out the cabbage soup she'd prepared.

"Uh-uh-uh. You know better than that. You're filthy. I don't want you eating with a filthy face and filthy hands. The bucket's by the door like it always is," she scolded.

William grumbled and pushed open the door. A heavy wooden pail filled with clean water from the well hung on a hook outside. He splashed enough on his hands and face to get rid of the bulk of the accumulated soil from the day's digging, then hurried back. When he shut the door behind him, his father and sister were taking their seats. His mother put a hearty bowl before each member of the family before she sat as well. William hungrily dug into it. A full day of shoveling was enough to make any meal a banquet.

"There, you see. A good appetite is a sign you've been putting in a good day's work. You've made a lot of progress, William, I'm proud of you. Another few days and we'll be able to hitch the oxen to that stump and pull it out."

William simply nodded and industriously went to work emptying his bowl, as though doing so quickly enough would win him a prize. When the meal was through, he made a show of stretching and yawning.

"I'm really tired, Father," he said. "I'm going to go to bed early, all right?"

"Of course," his father replied. "Get a good night's sleep. Maybe if you get an early start on it tomorrow, you can have the job done by nightfall." He watched with a smile as his son carried his bowl to the washbasin, then gathered his nightclothes and went to his room. "You see, Clara? I knew giving him an important job would turn him around," he said proudly.

"He just needed some time, Tom," said William's mother. "And you just needed to have faith in him."

"Isn't it good to see your brother finally showing some interest in the land, sweetie?" he asked Layla.

The girl pursed her lips and looked to the bedroom door. "He's interested all right," she remarked with a raised eyebrow. "Dad, I'm a little tired too. I think I'll turn in."

"Good night, then. Maybe if the two of you are up early enough and finish your work, we can take a trip to New Kenvard."

"Sounds great, Dad," Layla said, standing up to kiss him on the forehead. "Good night."

He watched as she got herself ready and slipped into the bedroom as well, then smiled to his wife. "We're raising a great couple of farmers, Clara."

"I've always thought so, dear," she said.

William struggled to stay awake in his darkened bedroom. He hadn't been lying when he said he was tired. A week of digging from sunrise to sunset would be enough to make anyone exhausted and sore, but he forced himself to stay awake until heard his parents retire for the night. Once their door was shut, he crawled out of bed as quietly as possible and eased open the shutters to his window. They swung open with the whisper of a scrape. He held his breath and looked toward his sister. In the light of the moon, he saw her still motionless in bed. He released a sigh of relief, then pulled himself to the sill and promptly tumbled to the ground.

He sat up and shook his head, then winced and waited for his parents to swing their window open and order him back to his room, or his sister to poke her head out and demand to know what he was up to. A few moments passed with nothing, but he should have expected as much. They all worked as hard as he did. It would take more than a ten-year-old plopping down on the grass to wake them. He brushed himself off and ran barefoot to the barn. For many people, the air would have been a bit too brisk to be running around in one's pajamas, but Oddspire Fields was a part of the northern kingdoms. Locals like him tended not to bother with a coat until it was below freezing.

William grunted against the barn door and tugged it open. The unmistakable fragrance of large animals wafted out from inside, but there was little moonlight and few windows, so the interior of the barn was pitch black.

"Darn," he muttered. "I should have brought a—"

"Looking for this?"

The voice came out of nowhere, startling William. His panicked brain told him to run, but without selecting a useful destination first, he only made it three steps before colliding with the barn door and falling to the ground. Dazed, he blinked until the smirking face of his sister came into view. She was holding an unlit lantern in one hand and had the other outstretched to help him to his feet.

"You know, for such a bright kid, you're lousy at running away from home," Layla said, pulling him up.

"I wasn't running away from home," he defended, brushing himself off.

"Then what are you doing out here?" She set the lantern down and sparked it to flame.

"Nothing!"

"Just felt like visiting the cows? Come on, Willy. What've you got?"

He crossed his arms and huffed. "Fine, I'll show you. But you can't tell Mother and Father until *I* say, since I found it."

"That depends on if it's juicy enough to be worth getting me out of bed," she said, ruffling his hair.

The pair slipped into the barn. William's father was primarily a farmer, but to work the land properly he kept a pair of oxen for plowing and hauling. The family also had a horse and cart for taking the harvest to the market and the family to town when the need arose. Add to that their two cows, the coop of chickens beside the barn, and a few sheep they'd picked up the previous season and Layla had her hands full keeping the animals fed and healthy. She raised the lantern.

"Easy everyone. We're just visiting," she cooed to the livestock when their arrival caused the inevitable stir. The animals had all gathered themselves at the far side of the barn for some reason, and her words did little to calm them. "Never seen them do that before," she mused. "I wonder what's gotten into them."

"Over here," William said, digging into the hay beneath the trough. "Bring the light. And close the door."

Layla pushed the door shut and crouched down beside her brother as he revealed the treasure he'd unearthed earlier that day. Somehow it looked even more mysterious in the light of the lantern. The flickering flame caused shadows to dance across the designs on the surface, deepening the appearance of the etched lines. Twisting the box made shimmers run along the shapes and sigils, almost seeming to make them pulse with light.

"Ooo," Layla remarked. "*That's* a fancy box. Where'd you find it?"

"It was buried under that tree! What do you think is inside?"

She shrugged. "Well it's half-open, so probably dirt and bugs now."

"Well yeah, but what *else*? I'm going to try to get it the rest of the way open." He took two of the trowels from their place on the barn wall and wedged them inside the opening the roots had made. He eagerly tugged and twisted them.

"Look at *you* getting so excited. How come I never see you get so giddy on the farm?"

"Because nothing *interesting* ever happens on the farm," he grunted, fighting with the remarkably sturdy little box. "When was the last time anything on the farm was half as amazing as—" He gave one more yank. "—this!"

The box popped open and both siblings leaned close, excited to see their discovery. As expected, a fair amount of soil had found its way inside, along with some withered and blackened bits of root, some dead beetles, and some shriveled worms. He brushed them away with a grimace until he'd cleared off a bundle of grimy fabric. The cloth was strange. It was finely woven, so much so that it was almost as smooth as silk. The surface glittered slightly in the light, even through the layer of dirt. The bundle was almost the same shape as the box, a rough rectangle with an irregular bulge, and there was a black ribbon securing it shut. He tugged at the ends like a child opening a long-awaited present and unwrapped the cloth. Layla's eyes widened with anticipation…then her shoulders sagged when she saw the contents.

"Congratulations, Willy. You found a book and a stick," she said flatly.

He didn't reply. Unlike her, the sight of the book didn't wipe away his enthusiasm; it set it aflame. He picked up the tome, a thin volume with a strange purple-black leather cover and bound with sinewy twine.

"It's a book, Layla. A book! I've never seen one this close before."

"Well sure, Willy, but what good is it going to do us? I can't read and neither can you. I don't even think Mom and Dad can. The stick is kind of pretty though."

She reached down and picked it up, turning it in the light of the lantern. It was some sort of silvery wood, as thick as her finger and perhaps a foot long. Like the box, it was covered with fine engravings, but these were far more intricate. It tapered slightly from one end to the other and was perfectly straight. Both ends were rounded.

"I know I can't read, but with a book, maybe I could learn," he said. He flipped through the pages. They were covered with shapes far more complex and varied than he'd ever seen written anywhere else…not that he'd seen very much writing.

"Dad will teach you everything you want to know about running a farm. What do you need to learn to read for?"

"To learn everything *else*," he said. "Hold the lantern closer."

Layla looked to the dwindling flame.

"I guess it was low on oil. Come on. Maybe the moon will be enough."

He gathered the book and hid the cloth and the box while she snuffed out the lantern flame. The moon was low on the horizon. To get the best light, they made their way to the far side of the barn. While William pored hungrily over the pages, Layla continued to inspect the carved wood.

"How do you figure they got the carvings so fine?" she asked. "They're so intricate, I can't even make out the smallest ones."

"I don't know. Mom said they make fine jewelry in South Crescent. Maybe that's where it's from."

"That's silly. Why would someone come all the way from across the sea with a carved stick, then bury it in a field?"

"I thought you said *I* was the one who asked too many questions."

She shrugged. "It isn't the first time I've picked up a bad habit. Oh, darn it!"

"What is it?"

"There's a mole. Get out of here, you little pest," she said, waggling the stick angrily. "If you ruin even one stalk of wheat I'll—"

There was a sharp crackle and a brilliant flash of violet light. William looked up from the book in time to see a glimmering bolt of black and purple lance through the air and strike the ground, narrowly missing the scurrying mole, and blackening the earth where it had been.

Layla stood perfectly still, eyes as wide as saucers. The artifact was still in her hand, held in precisely the same position. After a few stunned seconds she held it out at arm's length, then dropped it to the ground.

"What did you do?" William yelped.

"I don't know! I thought about how I wanted to get rid of the little monster and then, zap!"

The siblings looked at the stick. Its tip still glowed faintly, and the engravings had an undeniable shimmer to them now.

"It's a...it's a magic wand. Willy, *you found a magic wand*!"

For a moment they both kept a cautious distance. Then at the same instant, they dove for it.

"Give it to me! *I* found it! You already had a turn!" William whined.

"Oh no, Willy," she said, planting a hand on his forehead to hold him at bay. "You picked the book, you stick with the book." She snagged the wand. "Go get our boots. We'll go out in the field. I want to see what sort of tricks this thing can do."

After a clumsy fumble through the darkened house that made it clear his parents were harder to disturb than he'd ever imagined, William returned, and they went on their way toward the stump. Layla reasoned that since William was already digging there, anything that needed covering up could get a few scoops of loose soil over it, and no one would be the wiser. Considering how little interest she seemed to have in learning, Layla could be fiendishly clever when it came to getting away with things. As they walked, though, William became increasingly uneasy.

"I don't know, Layla," he said, face uneasy. "The more I think about it, the more I feel like this is a bad idea."

"That's why thinking is bad sometimes, Willy. Dad says if you want to start doing something, the best way to start doing it is to start doing it."

William considered the words for a moment. "Sometimes Father's sayings don't make much sense."

"Makes plenty of sense to me. Just play with your book."

"The moon's behind clouds now. I can't even see it."

"Hmm. Well, let's try this."

She raised the wand and swirled it in the air. A thin streamer of blue-white light began to trail behind it. A few more twirls conjured a sort of wreath of light, more than enough to illuminate the page.

"Wow. How did you *do* that?"

"I just thought about doing it and it happened."

"I wonder if that means I can do the same thing with this."

He looked at the book's unfamiliar symbols and imagined being able to read them. At first nothing happened. Then he felt something in his mind start to stir. First one at a time, then in whole lines, the shapes on the page changed. They didn't look any different, but now a sequence of squiggles and runes seemed to have meaning. Each represented a word or a thought.

"It's working. It's working! This says 'The Ways and Workings of the First Wave Casting Wand.'"

"And you said *Dad's* sayings don't make sense," Layla said. She collected a few medium-sized stones and set them on top of the stump. "I'll bet you I can hit these from over by the fence."

For a few minutes, Layla took crackling potshots at the stones while William flipped through the pages of the book, ravenously consuming the contents of each one.

"This thing is hard to aim," she remarked as a third blast in a row went lancing into sky. She squinted and lined the wand up carefully, then gave it a flick. A bolt of energy struck one of the stones, shattering it. "Ha! Those moles had better watch out now! Did you find anything good in there?"

"I think this book is written to tell you all of the things the wand can do." He glanced behind him. The spot along the fence that Layla had chosen to stand for target practice was a stone's throw away from the region's namesake spire. He eyed it in its place on the other side of the fence, then turned to her. "Let me try it for a second."

"In a bit. I'm just getting the hang of it."

"Come on, I'll give it right back."

Reluctantly, Layla handed him the wand. He steadied the book in one hand and held the wand in the other. After a few moments of looking at the page he closed his eyes, then opened them again and waved the wand at the spire. There was no immediate effect.

"What was supposed to happen?"

"It says I should be able to 'reveal all that needs to be known' about the spire."

"Leave it to you to pick something *boring*. Give me the wand back, I—"

The air around them shuddered, then the world seemed to vanish into darkness. In front of them, where the spire had been, there was only a long and irregular stone. Along the surface, the stone began to spark and flash, falling away in tiny chips. The chips fell faster and faster, eventually revealing the rough shape of the spire. As it became more detailed and refined, the world around it began to fade back into place, but it wasn't the farm. It was a city, ancient and primitive. The chips falling away to give the spire ever-greater detail were now falling under the expert bite of an artisan's chisel. The artist moved so swiftly that he was little more than a shimmering blur. Above them the sun streaked from day to night and back again with such velocity that there seemed to be perpetual twilight. In no time the spire stood in all of its freshly crafted glory. Next the whole world around them began to shift and slide, whisking by while the spire remained stationary. It was as though its position and angle were locked in place with respect to its observers. The work of art was slung with ropes, heaved onto a boat, then dangled from scaffolds and affixed atop a castle. For a few glorious moments William and Layla were drifting in the sky beside a magnificent tower while below them a city began to assemble itself. It should have been terrifying to be hanging in the air high over the ground, but the awe of the sight washed the fear away.

"What is this place?" Layla asked breathlessly.

"It looks like New Kenvard...only different. I think...I think it might be *old* Kenvard."

The flickering of day/night slowed until the scene was moving slowly enough for them to make out individual people going about their lives. In the distance, beyond the walls, a force of red-clad soldiers gathered. Arrows were launched, fires were started, and then the soldiers broke through the walls, washing over the city like a tide. When the soldiers receded, the city was in ruins. Without so much as a moment's pause in respect for the fallen, the day/night returned to its blinding speed. Though they passed in seconds, what must have been years of time rolled by with few changes to the scene below. New buildings appeared, and a steady stream of soldiers flowed from them, but little else seemed to occur. Then the sun slowed once more, and in the distance a form in the sky revealed itself, a dragon with a woman on its back. It whisked through the city and darted into the doors at the base of the tower beneath them. A heartbeat later the dragon erupted from within, now with a strange looking creature as its second passenger. Next a blinding flash of blue light blotted out the landscape for an instant. The world twirled around them, and finally the spire came to rest in its current location. The scene flickered with day and night for a few moments more. A tree sprouted, grew, withered, and died. The farmhouse and the fence appeared. Finally the sun set one final time and the ghostly images of William and Layla themselves appeared, played with the wand, then stepped into their present positions.

A full minute passed before either of the children could coax their minds into producing words. Layla was the first to speak, her eyes fixed in wonder upon the wand.

"What else does the book say this can do...?"

The hours of the night seemed to sweep by as swiftly as they had in the visions the spell had shown them. One by one they worked their way through the pages of the book, testing spells that seemed interesting. Knowing what the shapes on the page meant, it turned out, wasn't quite enough. Many of the spells contained words of which they had no clue of the meaning, or sequences of words they knew, but which didn't make sense when put together. After a few spells, Layla began to understand that the wand wasn't simply doing whatever she wanted it to do. It could do a variety of things and was selecting the one closest to what she had in mind. Some of the more abstract spells took a few tries to cast, but before long they had nearly reached the last page.

"Try this one. It says it will 'produce from raw material a temporary, simplified, dragon-type puppet under the caster's permanent control,' whatever that means," William said.

"A puppet? Why would there be a spell for making a puppet?" she wondered.

"Maybe the wand was supposed to be used for entertainment. That's what *we're* using it for."

She shrugged and tried to conjure to mind a reasonable approximation of a "dragon-type puppet," then flicked the wand. The bolt of magic sparkled toward the mound of earth William had created through days of digging. They waited a few seconds, but nothing seemed to happen.

"That one was another fizzle. What's left?" she asked.

"Just one more," he said. "It just says, 'The most important of spells. The beginning, the entrance, the keyhole. A door large enough for four.' What could that be?"

"Only one way to find out."

"Are you sure we should? The sun's almost up. We've been doing this all night."

"As long as we've already lost a whole night's sleep, we might as well finish things," she said.

Layla pictured a keyhole in her mind, then waved the wand vaguely toward the stump. A slow wave of black wafted along in the path behind the wand's motion. The wispy darkness drifted like a ribbon of gossamer caught in the wind, then began to coil in on itself above the stump. The wand shook lightly, then tugged itself from Layla's fingers, floating forward until it hung in the air just below the coil of black. A filament of brilliant blue light burst from the tip, feeding the coil and causing it to tighten and swirl.

"Oh. This might be a good one," Layla said, crossing her arms and waiting for the spell to run its course.

For a time the coil merely swirled with steadily increasing speed.

"I wonder how long it will take," William said.

"Hopefully not too long. I don't want it to still be going when Mom and Dad wake up." At the sound of tumbling soil, she looked at William, then at the mound beside the hole. At first she gasped, but then a smirk came to her face. "Oh, look, the puppet spell did work."

Emerging from the pile of dirt was a creature that at a glance certainly seemed to be "dragon-type." It didn't look *exactly* like a dragon. For one thing, it was tiny, perhaps the size of a cat. For another thing, it looked almost like it had been chiseled from stone. Its long neck and tail had a segmented look to them, and except for the wings, the features were all very rough and crude, formed from a purple-black hide similar to the book's cover. There were no eyes, only sockets that had an ember-orange glow to them. Its mouth was a jagged beak hanging slightly open. After stepping free of the now greatly reduced mound of soil, it stood motionless, staring at them.

"Ugh. It's an ugly little thing," Layla remarked. She furrowed her brow. "Why does it seem familiar?"

She turned to her brother, who was staring with eyes wide with fear.

"What's wrong?"

"It's a dragoyle," he said with a frightened hush.

She looked back at it, then back to her brother. "The monster things? The ones Dad always told scary stories about? Yeah, I suppose it does look a bit like one of them."

"Did you picture one when you cast the spell?"

"Not even close. I pictured a dragon made of wood with strings on it. Why would the wand make a dragoyle?" Her mind churned for a moment, sifting through the stories that the dragoyle brought to mind. Then the answer struck her, and her eyes widened as much as her brother's. "You don't think...what if...what if that is a D'Karon wand? The D'Karon were the wizards who made those things, right? Why would a wand make a dragoyle if it wasn't one of theirs?"

"The D'Karon are wizards who came here from another world... and we just cast a spell that said it was a door..." he said.

She looked back to the wand. It was crackling with energy. "We need to stop the spell!"

Layla rushed toward the wand and tried to reach for it, but a spark of energy leaped out from it and struck her hand, causing her to recoil in pain. William flipped madly through the book.

"It says the only way to stop a spell is to cut off the source of power. We can't just take the wand. We have to break it," he said.

"But I can't even get close!"

The swirl was getting larger now, almost as large as the stump, and there was a foul-smelling wind rushing out of it. Just at the edge of hearing was a mixture of chilling noises, like voices chanting in an unknowable language. Layla panicked, grabbing stones and hurling them at the wand. The fear coursing through her took any precision from her throws, and any stones that came close were zapped away by the wand.

"Go get me more rocks!" she cried out.

William scrambled to obey, spotting a decent one a short distance away, but before he could reach it, the little dragoyle sprang into action, clamping down on the rock with its mouth and dropping it at Layla's feet.

"Why did it do that?" she asked, her mind in no condition for any more puzzles.

"It...it is a puppet. You control it."

"You're right!" She turned to the monster. "Dragoyle, destroy the wand!"

It snapped to the task, bounding toward the wand and shrugging off a blast. It clamped down on the artifact, heaving a breath of blackness while it shook and chomped. There was a hissing whine, almost like the wand was screaming in pain, and finally it fractured in a burst of light and fell to the stump. The instant it broke, the dragoyle fell lifeless, and the swirl began to slow. Layla wiped beading sweat from her forehead.

"Okay, the wand is gone. What happens now?" she asked.

He flipped to the end of the book, and his eyes traced over the page, the words now illuminated by the first rays of the rising sun.

"I can't understand the words anymore," he said.

"I guess that makes sense. All of the spells are going away. Did it just get colder?" she asked, pulling her nightshirt a little tighter.

"Just windier, I think," he said. He looked across the brightening field. The tufts of grass and remaining stalks from the harvest were beginning to bow under the force of the wind, but they weren't moving in the sweeping wave that he was used to. They were bowing in a curve...and all directly toward the shrinking swirl. "Grab onto something! The wind is blowing toward that thing!"

They sprinted toward the fence, but its widely spaced slats were already rattling dangerously in the wind. If the gale grew strong enough, it wouldn't anchor them for very long. Crawling through it and fighting a rush of wind that threatened to drag them backward, they made their way to the spire and wrapped their arms around it. The wind intensified. Soil and earth were spiraling into the black swirl. It sucked up the book, shredding it to pieces as it did, and made short work of the dragoyle's remains as well. The stump was shaking and straining at its weakened roots. Above it, the swirl was barely the size of the fist, but the air rushing into it howled deafeningly.

With a crack like a whip, the stump pulled free, colliding with the ball of darkness and splintering into a galaxy of tiny fragments that disappeared inside. Now the mass of black was the size of a marble. And now it was the size of a pea. Now a pinpoint. The air shook with a resounding roll of thunder and burst of energy as the swirl finally vanished completely, taking the maelstrom with it just as swiftly as it had come.

The children let a few long moments pass before they were willing to release their grip on the spire. When they did, they took some time to observe the scene of chaos revealed by the rising sun. The stump was gone, and a good deal of the earth beneath it had gone with it. A few slats had been ripped from the fence and hurled far into the field. Each of the siblings was plastered with dust and dirt, their hair and eyes wild. Their jangled nerves had not yet permitted anything as complex as speech or rational thought to fall into place by the time they heard their names echoing across the field. They looked toward the farmhouse and saw their father rushing in their direction, still in his nightclothes. Layla and William both hurried to him, hugging him tightly.

"What is going on here? Your mother and I woke to a terrible sound and found your room empty."

"We—" William began.

"We woke up early to...to finish the stump," Layla said. She was always quick with a lie when the situation called for it. When the truth involved dark sorcery and nearly summoning an ancient evil, the situation *certainly* called for a lie.

"You what?" their father asked. He looked around, spotting the scooped out pit of earth and the scraggly remnants of roots sticking out from its edges. "Good heavens. You certainly did a thorough job of it." He looked around. "Where did you put it? And where did you put the soil?"

"A man came by. He had an empty wagon. We convinced him to haul it away," William offered, slowly picking up on his sister's ideas.

"If you were digging, where are the shovels?" their father asked, now legitimately confused.

"We put them away," Layla said.

"Then why are you out here?"

"We were trying to figure out how to fix the fence. It broke when we were loading the soil."

The confused farmer looked around at the shattered and scattered slats. "And the noise? What was that?"

"There was a windstorm. It passed quickly, but it made a mess," Layla said.

He looked into the frazzled and anxious faces of each of his children. Their story didn't make any sense, and he seemed reluctant to believe it, but in the absence of a better explanation it was enough.

"We'll discuss it later. Next time you plan something like this, tell your mother and I so we won't be worried."

"I don't think we'll be doing something like this again, Dad," Layla said.

The trio set off back to the farmhouse. William glanced over his shoulder at the spire.

"Father?" he said.

"Yes, William?"

"Since the stump is gone, can we go to New Kenvard like you said… after a nap."

"Perhaps."

"Do you think anyone there will be able to tell us about the history of the city?"

"I imagine so."

"I'd like to hear about it."

"Yeah," said Layla. "I think I would too."

— AN EQUITY IN DUST —
by R.S. Belcher

DURING THE EARLY HOURS of Shallow the watch discovered the Duke of White Rapture burning on the catwalk, his hot ashes drifting downward to join the skulls and dust.

His murderer leered at me through the crumbling outer walls of the Hive. Bloated and red, it straddled the terminal between dark earth and bruise-blue sky.

Things weren't fixed out here anymore unless decay threatened the Hive's core. It made people uneasy. Most haunted places do. Angry victims of the Bug had died cursing as they beat their bloody fists against the seals, begging to be allowed inside the inner dome.

My magistrates, fifteen strong, were with me. Led by Wren, they fanned out at his silent signal and began to secure the scene of the crime. Wren spoke to the guards who had made the discovery.

Guardsmen also called to the scene stood sullen watch, their radios occasionally crackling with police chatter. They did nothing. They knew better than to interfere in attendant politics.

Knoris' magistrates, attired in the tan and gold of their patron, grudgingly gave ground to my people who, like Wren and myself, bore the Halloween livery of our Duke—haystack yellows, jack-o'-lantern oranges, and fire-ember reds upon night-pure jet.

Galia and Knoris were engaged in hushed conversation, appropriately choreographed, with their backs to my approach. My fellow high attendants grew silent. They turned to greet me hidden behind masks of sheet-white kabuki paint and smiles that held all the sincerity of jackals baring their teeth.

"Ah, there you are Finch," Knoris said. He was tall and wide, once with muscle but now creeping to fat. His head was shaved and he wore his duke's mark across his forehead in black tattoo. "Good Shallow to you. We wondered what was keeping you."

"It would appear an *error* was made in the instructions the watch were given about notifying me first," I said.

"Well you really can't blame the watch," Knoris said, smiling. "For over a century I've been the one they reported to in such distasteful matters. It's only natural they would have some difficulty in adapting to the new arrangement."

"I don't blame the watch. It's easy to understand their forgetfulness," I said. "As I'm sure your attendants have also forgotten that they now no longer bear the magisterial authority to disturb this crime scene."

Knoris darkened beneath his pale paint. I saw the minute constriction of his pupils, watched his body give off twelve of the twenty-seven signs of increased distress we had been trained to notice and conceal in the temple. I felt a mild disgust that he had allowed himself to become so easily read.

As shaven acolytes in the Temple of the Servant, we were always instructed to treat attendants of the Beloved with all of the respect and politeness we would to the Beloved themselves also, but with none of the deference.

"I'm sure that too was merely an omission in orders." I made the slightest bow of my head, then showed my own jackal smile.

"Of course, Finch," Galia said, her voice like oiled leather. "We merely came to provide our patrons with any relevant information they should know about Duke Kolvino's demise."

Her pale hand opened like a bloom to reveal the silver signet ring with a large eye of yellowed ivory. It was Kolvino's.

"Knoris' second found it among the ashes of the Duke's remains," she said.

The anger poured into me but I remained cool stone and inscrutable smoke; no outward sign betrayed my core. I remembered my lessons.

Was it real? Had they planted it and, if so, why? I didn't have time for this nonsense. It was time for quick answers and Knoris had already showed me the easiest way to get them.

"How fortuitous you found it," I said. "But I must inquire why the high attendants of the Duchess of the Iridium Mask and the Duke of Hounds were out in the fringes at such hours? My people tell me you beat the watchmen here."

I let the accusation hang in the air, a crippled thing waiting to be made whole by their reaction. Sadly, Knoris took the bait. He couldn't help himself.

"You go too far, Finch! You dare to include the names of our Patrons in this scandalous affair? Be assured this slight will be redressed!"

"And be sure," I interjected, "your interference in this inquiry, which I must assume was undertaken with your patrons' knowledge, shall be reported to my Duke and will figure prominently in his own report to the Queen's Court."

Knoris was hot under his sizeable collar, but mention of Her Dark Majesty doused his fire quickly. He had raised the stakes by threatening to enter the Beloved into this, I merely upped the ante.

Galia, the smarter of the two, quickly stepped in to try to minimize the damage done.

"Finch, Knoris misspoke himself. No one questions your Duke's authority in this inquiry, or your service in this matter. What say you, we provide you with the signet and any other knowledge our people have gathered and we retire and leave you to your work? It shall be as if we were never here, yes?"

"Of course." I plucked the signet from Galia's palm and showed them my back as I walked away. "Good Shallow."

They retreated from the walkway quickly, with their entourage in tow.

Wren, who had been watching the exchange with some amusement, approached. He signaled the watchmen to step in to finish the search of the walkway and to cover the ashes and blackened skeleton of Duke Kolvino.

"Sir," he asked, "do you believe they had anything to do with this?"

"If they had been involved, they would not have been here when we arrived."

Galia and Knoris' patrons were allies of Kolvino in the High Court and I doubted this was the result a split within their alliance. They were here without their Patrons' knowledge, searching for scraps of information to curry favor. "No, Knoris' reaction proved to my satisfaction that they had no hand in the Duke's demise," I said. "I think they were here to see just how far they could push me."

Wren snorted. "Not very far, it would seem. I have sent for Duke Kolvino's High Attendant, Perin," Wren said as he watched the last of Knoris' agents disappear down the iron stairs.

"Perin? He's Kolvino's consort as well?"

"Yes sir, I believe he is," Wren said as he jotted a note in his small notebook. "They were quite the item some time back, as I recall. Quite the scandal, I hear. Some kind of gift or title the Duke wanted to bestow upon Perin that was forbidden for a high attendant, or some such," he said and waited for me to fill in the remainder of the Court gossip to which he had not been privy.

I smiled at his long, bland face, a face I had come to count on over the last thirty years.

"You should spend less time culling scraps of idle chatter from old ladies in the Basement Quarter. It was not that scandalous a matter. It was rare for one of them to think so highly of one of us to risk royal censure just to bestow a gift on a consort."

"Must have been true love," Wren said flatly.

I shrugged and began the work at hand.

The Hive is home to over three and a half million human beings and a handful of the Beloved. Like the sprawling human cities I remembered from childhood, just before the Bug, the Hive never truly sleeps, is never truly silent. It constantly moves and moans like a fever patient, tangled in damp sheets and mazes made of dream.

I made my way down Aktic Street. It was lit by strings of small electric plastic lanterns hanging between the wood and canvas dwellings, plywood kiosks and nylon dome tents that lined the narrow winding way.

If I had revealed the crest upon my leather tunic under my long coat, people would have given me a wide berth out of fear and respect. I kept it hidden. I did not need fear and respect. I needed to be jostled and shoved. I wanted to smell stale sweat and pungent hash smoke. I craved to hear laughter and shouts of anger, to be a part of the river of humanity all about me.

The endless night under the great dome was filled with the whispers of lovers, the cries of babies and the barking of dogs. Music from battery-powered radios mixed with the babble of a dozen languages.

Faces of all colors and ages drifted past in the shadows of the dwellings. My own face had changed very little since I had began taking the sacrament on my twenty-fifth birthday; the Beloved's grace kept me young, but inside I felt my age.

Kolvino's spire, Pale Gnosis, was a column of shimmering, white marble with a great, ivory-veined staircase spiraling upward from its base. Terraces, large and small, intersected with the winding carved stairs, far above me.

Wren and a small party of my men confronted a group of Kolvino's attendants outside the large glass doors to the spire's lobby. Perin wasn't among them.

"Your master has perished. This dwelling is no longer under the protection of royal rules of domain. I am Prefect of the Queen's Justice Minister. My magistrates and I are investigating the Duke's demise, as required under royal edict, and you will provide us with full access to this building. Now"

The eldest of Kolvino's attendants frowned for a moment then nodded, more to his fellows than to me. "Of course, Prefect," he said.

As we entered the spire, I took the elder aside.

"Where is High Attendant Perin?" I asked him softly.

"He...has been gone since yesterday's deep. I do not know where he is."

"Show me his quarters."

I had sent Wren and the others to examine Kolvino's quarters and the sacrament hall. After all this time there was still only one of the Beloved that I claimed to comprehend at all. I would learn nothing from the god, so I decided to spend my time with the servant; someone with whom I had infinitely more in common.

Perin's apartment was similar to my own at Raven's Spur. I drifted from bedroom to closet to library, but found only shrill order.

An irregularly shaped tablet of ancient clay hung suspended from wires, dividing two rooms. It was covered with wedge-shaped columns of alien symbols. They had been pressed into the moist clay when even the Beloved were still young.

I stepped past it, into Perin's studio.

Decades ago, I had flirted with the arts but found I had neither the ability nor the patience for it, so I dropped the notion of creating beauty and stuck to hunting facts.

Perin had none of my flaws. His work, mostly in oils and charcoal, was subtle and powerful, a soul attempting to understand the infinite, trying to understand *them*.

The only other item of interest was a small number of older paintings, less accomplished, almost juvenile. Their subject was an older woman and two young girls. From the looks of the women they were residents of the Basement Quarter. The paintings held a place of reverence on a low stone table in Perin's bedroom, almost like a shrine. I picked one up, remembered my father, and slipped it into my pocket.

Raven's Spur is an obsidian wing of dark glass and black metal, almost stabbing the dark dome that was the sky of the Hive; an eternal starless night.

As I ascended in the glass elevator towards the aviary, I saw the worn granite column that was the spire of Knoris' Patron, the Duke of Hounds, vaulting upward from his Quarter of the Hive miles away. To my left, far in the distance I could see the massive figure hewn of marble the color of dried blood - the spire of the Duchess of the Red Miracle.

The elevator lurched and stopped. Vast black swarms of birds swirled about the spire in ever-shifting patterns like living Rorschach blots. Even through the heavy glass of the elevator's walls I could hear their shrill cries.

The aviary was cool stone, shadow and babbling water. A rotunda opened to the Hive's skyline through massive windows in the domed ceiling allowed the birds access in and out of the Spire. Statuary and gurgling fountains crouched in dark alcoves all around the room.

At the center of the Aviary was a wide, low dais surrounded by a sparse stand of sycamores and a few marble benches. White light fell down in a ring upon the dais from spotlights mounted in the ceiling.

A statue of shimmering alabaster with bronze wings like an angel's stood upon the platform; all smooth stone and pooled shadow. Birds lighted upon its outstretched arms and shoulders, oblivious to my entry into the hall.

I waited quietly at the dais' edge for over an hour, listening to the night song of the birds echoing. One hour turned into two, then three.

At last, the statue moved, drawing its "wings", a scalloped cloak, about its pale, perfect body. The birds scattered with startled cries of alarm, dark motes flying upward as if carried by their own screams.

The Duke of Dying Leaves turned his eons-old eyes upon me.

"They don't know," The Duke said with all the earnest wonder of a child. "They have no comprehension within their brittle shell of awareness, what they sound like to one outside their simple universe of need. To them it is nothing but a process, like breathing, or eating, no concept of the beauty. How sad and how wonderful,"

I remained silent, letting his vast consciousness envelop my mind. It often reminded me of a dim childhood memory of an ocean wave crashing over me, too big to be jumped. He went on forever in all directions.

"How goes the inquiry into poor Kolvino's demise Finch?"

"Disturbing, my Duke," I said. His physical dimensions seemed to diminish to something my mind could contain as he descended the dais. "The Duke's High Attendant, Perin, is unable to be located at present. I fear that whoever slew the Duke may also have killed Perin."

"You dismiss the notion that Perin may be your criminal and has fled?" The Duke asked as we began to wander the Aviary.

"I...find that highly unlikely, my Duke."

"And why is that?"

"He was Kolvino's consort and more importantly, his High Attendant. We are incapable of such disloyalty."

This answer amused the Duke. He paused and turned his gaze full upon me.

"Because you could not betray me, Perin could not do the same? Oh, Finch, have you learned so little about your kind even after all this time?"

"I do not speak of what human beings are capable of. Perin is an Attendant; we are a breed apart. No Attendant would do that to one of the Beloved. We care for you as you care for our people"

The Duke smiled. It was a thing of dark stains and sharp bone. It rippled through the illusion of his ethereal beauty like a stone breaking the tranquility of a pool.

"You are correct," the Duke said. "In the long history of my kind, a human raised to the position of Attendant has never betrayed our trust. You are of our blood through the sacrament. You share in our power and the promise of eternal life through faithful service, but never before in history have we lived so openly among you as we do now, never in such a confined geography. Familiarity breeds contempt.

"At any rate, the Royal Court demands answers as to what happened. See to it."

The thoughts churning within me were difficult to keep in that small, dark box in my mind, hidden from the Duke. The box was a gift, given unknowingly to me by my father. His memories resided there along with my own secrets.

"As you wish, my Duke. I am meeting with Dr. Bandrel at the scene an hour after shallow. I will report all my findings to you as I have them."

"Very good," the Duke said. He plucked a dark bird from flight and examined its frightened eyes.

"Finch," he whispered to the bird, reading the bright black eyes of his captive. The bird squirmed within its cage of pale, cadaverous, fingers. The Duke released it. It fluttered up beyond the Aviary's ceiling and out into the darkness.

He turned with a flourish of his great scalloped cape that rustled like his namesake. His human guise expanded, and then diffused into the darkness like a drop of ink in water.

The cries that echoed in the great hallway that led back to the lift were a frenzied amalgam of scream and song that traveled with me long after the lift had departed the Aviary.

I regarded the red dawn from the worn steel catwalk where Kolvino had perished.

Turning away from the killer, I looked down at the piles of bones and dust around me. My father's remains rested here with all the other generations drained to satisfy the hunger of Kolvino, my Duke, and the other Beloved of the Hive. Now one of their own joined the ash of mortals, all equal now. As the dawn crept across the carpet of skulls, I wondered what had passed through Kolvino's ancient mind as death had come to him.

Though they had enjoyed briefly death's cold company, the Beloved no more understood death than I did. They were still subject to it. I liked to believe they still knew fear and regret in their final moments, it made them seem more understandable.

Dr. Bandril's labored breath announced his arrival.

Bandril's skin was like yellowed paper. His long tangled hair was the color of fireplace ash. He wore robes of purple and black that announced his station. He had been old when the Bug had nearly destroyed humanity and the Beloved had shown themselves to the survivors. Now, he was the High Attendant of Her Dark Majesty and royal surgeon for the Hive.

Bandril was accompanied by one of his students, a heavy-set man, who helped him up the stairs.

"Couldn't pick my nice, cozy house to meet me in, could you, Prefect Finch?" he said gulping for air. He steadied himself on his young apprentice and then rested against the rail of the catwalk.

"I thought you might wish to view the crime scene yourself, master physician," I said, flicking away my cigarette into the bone yards and bowing in Bandril's direction. "I thought perhaps you might have missed something or had…"

"I miss nothing," Bandril snapped with a hiss and spray of spittle. "My agents are well trained, better than your clumsy magistrates. They provide me every detail, every insight. I have already visited this place many times, High Attendant. Why should I bother to actually come here?"

"Of course, doctor. I mean no disrespect. What news have you?"

The old man reached out a wrinkled claw to his assistant. The apprentice opened a cracked leather medical bag, faded white with wear, and handed Bandril sheets of green and white striped computer paper. The Doctor examined it with rheumy eyes.

"You realize, of course, that when the Beloved are exposed to direct sunlight, it produces a violent and virtually complete exothermic reaction at the cellular level. Almost nothing remains after they have been consumed.

"I was able to acquire a small trace of fatty tissue clinging to the underside of the catwalk you and your men bumbled about on for hours. Not much, really, just a tiny speck of grease. It was sufficient for a chemical examination, however. Would you like to know what I found?" he asked, like a petulant child, teasing.

"Yes," I said, "please."

"A powerful coagulant," Bandril cackled, brandishing the green-and-white computer analysis paper like the royal scepter. "Some type of hematological ester, a manufactured molecule that produces tremendous viscosity in human blood. It would have caused one of the Beloved great pain and terrible difficulty in movement for many hours as it froze the blood within their veins. A most efficient way to render such a powerful being impotent, yes?"

Poison. A dreadful connection snapped close in my mind. I tried to push it into my mental box.

"Then this was definitely introduced into the Duke's body? There is no way this could have been any sort of disease or natural condition?"

Bandril looked at his assistant, for strength, and then sighed.

"I detest repeating myself. I said it was man-made. I have studied our divine benefactors and their anatomy for over two centuries, while you were still a temple boy. The drug was introduced into Kolvino's body, most likely by a gradual process, since such a chemical would require time to build up sufficient dosage to overcome one of the Beloved's preternatural stamina. Yes, yes, many hours of exposure to the chemical would be required."

"What would this chemical do to the blood of a mortal?" I asked already knowing the answer.

Bandril snorted as if the question was not worth the effort. "Why, kill them, obviously. Slowly, painfully, I would hazard; very painfully."

The Temple of the Servant was a wide, squat dome of stone the color of bleached bone encircled by great rings of smooth blue-gray granite stairs. Four massive arches of shimmering obsidian set at equidistant points around the temple lead into the cool, cavernous interior. The Temple was at the very center of the Hive; in truth, it was its heart.

I entered through the eastern arch, along with hundreds of vessels that had come to offer tithe to the Beloved. "Offer" may not have been the correct word; it implied a choice in the process.

Speakers mounted inside the entryway carried a mellow, parental voice repeating instructions and direction in a variety of languages.

"Today you undertake the most awesome responsibility of your existence. Your sacrifice serves the good of all. Through you, the Beloved and all of Humanity remain strong and vital. Please wait patiently for an Attendant to obtain your information."

Two young attendants with radio headsets and tablets screened the vessels as they entered: name, address, and Red Lottery number. It was all encoded on a plastic card worn around the neck. The same card had hung around my father's neck.

Most of the people in line looked more bored than frightened. Several watched the televisions mounted on the wall as the line slowly shuffled forward, or looked at the pictograms in the newspapers. A few of the children rocked nervously back and forth, nervous and excited at this first time of being called.

It had been very different two hundred years ago. The Hive then was little more than a vast, hollow concrete cave with tattered survivors within and the Bug, hungry and hot, without. The Red Lottery was almost always a death sentence in those days, but the odds of staying alive were better with the Beloved than with the Bug.

I had first entered the Hive when I was 10 years old, holding my father's hand through our Biohazard suits. We shuffled in along with thousands of other refugees with no place to go, now that our world had become a graveyard. My father's face seemed indistinct to me now behind the plastic shield of the suit, but his muffled voice had lingered with me over the centuries, like my memories of the sun.

"It will be all right, Aaron. Don't be afraid. We'll take care of each other, son."

"Prefect Finch?"

The voice shook away the vague shadows of my fading memory. It was one of the attendants from the entrance. She was standing beside me.

"Yes, Bora, isn't it?" I said, stuffing my father back in the bolthole in my mind.

"Yes, sir. I understand that your new duties will require more attendants. I would very much like you to consider me for induction into the House of Dying Leaves."

It was a bold move. I would never have had the nerve to do it myself at her stage of initiation.

"You have completed your training here at the temple?"

"Yes, Prefect. I am awaiting selection to a household and I would very much like to be selected by yours. I know two of my fellows were recently inducted for special service."

"You do understand that the House chooses the Attendant, not the other way around?"

This seemed to deflate her somewhat but she hid it well. Very good.

"I apologize for my enthusiasm, High Attendant. I only meant..."

"I understand," I said. "I will review your records and speak with your instructors. If I deem it appropriate, I will discuss the matter with the Duke."

"Thank you, High Attendant," she said, a smile peeking through her discipline and nervousness. I tried to recall what it was like to be that young.

"Where is Attendant Kestrel at this hour?"

"The Hall. She is teaching."

"Why do we serve the Beloved?" Kestrel asked the assembled acolytes, a sea of shaved heads and crimson robes.

Behind her was a sweeping view of the main donation floor. On the floor, attendants went about the business of collecting tithes of blood from hundreds of vessels, strapped to donation tables.

Slender intravenous tubing dangled down from the ceiling, like lazily drifting tentacles from some giant man o' war. A brief whisper of praise for good citizenship in the vessels' ear, a needle slid into a plump blue vein, bee-sting quick. The dark, potent liquor of their hearts crawling upward, through the tubes.

Attendants helped pale, staggering vessels, whose number had come up too often, into the recovery rooms. They would be treated, returned to their homes and their lives, until the next time their number came up in the Red Lottery.

"By our service and loyalty does the covenant that saved the human race remain intact," Kestrel intoned as she paced before the assembled hall of fresh faced acolytes. "But it's much simpler than that, isn't it?"

Her hair was the color of autumn leaves—gold and fire. Her eyes were green spring promise. Her lips were the color of dried blood. She wore the same crest and colors as I.

"Survival," she said. "Boil down all that noble and selfless verbiage and you get simple survival. We serve the Beloved because it is what we must do to survive as a species."

Her eyes locked with mine. She nodded faintly.

"Pretty words from a textbook that mean nothing to you will not gird your heart for the toll centuries of service will inflict. You must cling to what you really know, in your marrow, in your heart. Those things will sustain you.

"Students, I must retire for a moment," she said. "In my absence you are to meditate upon the reasons you desire to serve."

"What do you want, Finch?" she asked in the hall.

"That substance we once discussed, that was never to be used, has been used to murder Kolvino."

"What?" Her surprise seemed genuine but with Kestrel it was always hard for me to be sure. I could never read her, even when we were children.

"Has it begun?"

"And if it had, Finch, whose side would you be on?"

She walked quickly down the hallway, her sandals echoing in the empty hall. We ducked into a small study alcove, off from the main corridor.

"You told me the plan to use the drug had been vetoed, that too many agreed with the warning I gave you."

"A very passionate plea. Pity you didn't have the nerve to give it yourself."

"I am not a party to your little rebellion," I said.

"And yet, you come to me now, alone, not with your hounds. You whisper in alcoves with me, Aaron. Why is that?"

"You know damn well why. Because you and your fools will get us all killed.

"If they even suspected your little network existed, they would kill every Acolyte, every Attendant, in the Hive. They might not stop there. Imagine it, every man, woman and child in the city strapped into those infernal machines day after day, bred and milked like cattle without even the pretense of freedom and humanity to cling to.

"How long do you think it would take, Julia? Without us to keep the rabble in line, keep them from annoying the Beloved with the demands of their existence? With being human?"

I turned away from her. My anger recessed back into the vault of discipline I had allowed it to escape from.

"And my name is no longer Aaron," I said to the wall.

"Aaron...Finch," she said, "Those 'rabble' are your people, enslaved in this tomb. Better to die free than live like this."

Her hand came to rest upon my shoulder and I realized I could no longer remember the last time I had experienced the touch of another human being. I reveled in the simple feeling of connection, of empathy.

I suddenly realized just how seductive Kestrel's rebellion really was. To feel whenever you wanted, however you wanted. To not have to guard your mind and emotions constantly from beings that could read both like examining bacteria under a microscope. To trust in touch and scent and all our old instincts that had lain fallow so long in this, their world.

I brushed the hand away and turned back to face her. She was close to me. I breathed in her life and exhaled it in a sigh of regret.

"You were an infant when you first came here," I began. "I remember you running, laughing, down the halls of this temple when you were three. You don't remember the Bug, the way it killed, what it did to us when everything began to fall apart. We were finished and then they stepped out of the shadows and saved us."

"They saved themselves," she said, stepping back from me. "Like farmers trying to save their crop from blight."

"Yes, and that's why I trust them more than I trust us. Where do you think the Bug came from? Some lab where we were trying to perfect a way to kill as many of our own as efficiently as we could. The Beloved don't scare me; what we can do to each other, that's terrifying.

"We are their food; they need us. It's in their best interest to keep us alive and happy and quiet. They saved us out of enlightened self-interest and they will continue to keep us alive and relatively free as long as we don't make the price of our freedom too high."

Kestrel ran a hand across her face. Her shoulders dropped like someone weary from a long journey.

"You must have heard the same stories I have, she said. "The blood orgies, the indiscriminate killings with no lottery, no warning. A pretty face strikes the fancy of one of them and then that pretty face disappears. The rumors of an arena somewhere where we are slaughtered like animals for their amusement.

"Could anyone live as long as they have and remain sane? Tell me Finch, if even some of the rumors are true, are you so sure they can be trusted? That they deserve your loyalty?"

"Duke Kolvino's demise was not an assassination?" It was time for the masks again.

"Someday, high attendant, you will have to choose a side," she said. "No. We did not sanction Kolvino's murder."

"Do you know Kolvino's high attendant, Perin?"

"Yes," she said. "He recently joined us. I did not recruit him myself. I remember being concerned because his loyalty to Kolvino was said to be as strong as yours is to the Duke of Dying Leaves."

I ignored the barb. "Did he have access to the drug?"

"He could get it from one of our sources," she said. "You suspect him as the killer? Why?"

"If he joined your group, obviously his loyalty was not as steadfast as reported."

Unless...*the faces from the paintings on their small shrine.*

"Are your people hiding him?"

"If we were, I wouldn't tell you." The space between us was back to its proper distance—two nemeses, circling the same singularity of mutually assured destruction.

"No matter. I'll find him," I said.

Wren was leaning against a crumbling concrete wall across the street from the old woman's home. The rain cycle had just begun and my oldest and most-trusted magistrate had the hood on his worn leather coat pulled tight to ward off the cold reclaimed water as it fell from the dome's dark ceiling.

"Anything?" I asked as I approached him from the alleyway.

"I think I'm getting a cold," he sniffled. "Other than that, they are all in there and they had company."

"Oh?"

"Two of them. I made them for attendants, but I didn't recognize either of them. Looked like their hair had just grown back in."

"Young?"

"Even if it weren't raining, they would be wet behind the ears."

"Are they still in there?" I asked, trying to light a damp cigarette.

"No, milord. They left about an hour ago. The old woman definitely looked relieved to see them go."

"I know two of my fellows were recently inducted for special service," Bora had said at the temple.

"Thank you, Wren. Go home."

"All the same to you, sir, I'd just as soon stay for a while."

"No."

"This has gotten political, hasn't it?"

I nodded and gave up on the cigarette, tossing it into the rushing waters of the gutter at out feet.

"I hate political," he said, barely audible over the rain.

"Go home, Wren. I'll be fine."

As I crossed the empty street, I wrapped my coat tighter around my body, hiding my badge of office. I knocked on the battered tin door. The house number was marked in shaky lines of black spray paint.

A slender blade of light appeared as the door was cracked and the face of an elderly woman peered out. Fear glazed her eyes.

"Hello," I said softly. "My name is Aaron; I'm an associate of Perin's. I wonder if I might come in."

The Duke of Dying Leaves allowed me to wait in the cool echoes of the Aviary for over an hour while he sang to his smallest servants.

Then en mass, they ascended in a shrieking whirlwind of sound and motion, circled him for a moment, and then departed through the openings in the dome.

His eyes were dark wells as he regarded me.

"Yes, Finch?" he said.

His voice rumbled in my thoughts. I knew he was even now searching for the reason for my unexpected arrival to the Aviary in the folds of my brain. I retreated to my father's fortress, my box, as I lowered my eyes and addressed him.

"I have found Duke Kolvino's murderer."

"Excellent," he said, with obvious amusement.

"You," I said, managing to raise my eyes to meet his alien gaze. In that instant I knew with every cell in my body that I was about to die.

There had seemed to me to be no intervening travel from where he had been to where he was now. He smelled faintly of the damp earth.

"Pray tell," he said.

"You forced Perin to kill his master, his lover. Kolvino was plotting to win Her Dark Majesty's favor and gain back the position of the Justice Minister for his ally, the Duke of Hounds," I said. "That was why Knoris and Galia were sniffing about. They knew a plot was afoot, they just didn't know the details of it.

"You had no intention of allowing Kolvino to tip the balance back to his side, so you had a few of your newly recruited attendants visit Perin's family in the Basement Quarter weeks ago. They were seen there again last deep.

"I spoke with his sister, now quite old, and his two nieces. They said nothing just as Perin and your attendants instructed them to do. An old woman and two children, all frightened that you will come in the darkness and gobble them up. How does that make you feel, my Lord? Remind you of the good old days?"

"My feelings are irrelevant," he said, oblivious to my tone.

All the anger, all the bewilderment that I had felt countless times for junkies and alleyway murderers who ruined lives without comprehension bubbled up inside me. It was pathetic enough for human beings to do this to each other, but the Beloved...with eons of existence...I buried my rage; it would only serve the Duke in this.

"Your men threatened to kill his family if he did not help you destroy Kolvino and turn over the secret he had learned, the secret that he was going to give Kolvino.

"Yes, Kolvino used him too, I suspect. Turned his love into a tool to gain him some petty upper hand in your political wars. Or maybe, just maybe, he did it all for Kolvino's love, unbidden. A gift to make up for the damage Perin had done to his lover's status. But once he discovered the secret, he knew. He knew that he and Kolvino must both die to protect it.

"He was told that his sister's Red Lottery number would pop up quite a few times if he did not cooperate. At her age, she wouldn't survive that for long."

"As well you know," the Duke whispered, "from...personal experience."

I swallowed hard. My eyes burned. Calm...control.

"Tell me, where is Perin now?" the Duke asked.

"He's dead. I found his body in a sewer pipe not far from where Kolvino was slain. His secret died with him"

"You have surprised me yet again, my friend," he said.

He was close to me. There was a cloying stench of the grave carried with each word, decaying syllables bubbling up from a rotted soul.

"With time you learn to measure a man, Finch, and my measure of you was that you would never be able to go on as such a reliable agent if I confided in you in this skirmish in the game. So I relied on lesser agents that could easily be removed without questions or inconvenience. Regrettable that I could not trust you in this, but it is simply the price I had to pay for all of your other assets. After all, you are only human."

"Yes," I said.

"But that will change." He expected me to fall into step beside him, so I did.

"With Kolvino's domain vacant, One of the high attendants will be given Exalted Communion by Her Dark Majesty and join our ranks. My allies and I will assure it is you, Finch.

"What explanation do you want me to give?" I said, lowering my head to examine the worn stone path, the thick grass.

"Kolvino went too far, in High Sacrament with Perin," the Duke said as if he were staging of a play. "Having slain his beloved consort, wracked with grief, he destroyed himself in the rays of the dawn. Very romantic, don't you think?"

"Yes, touching."

"Is there any evidence to contradict such an account?" he asked as we neared the great doors at the end of the path.

"No," I said honestly, having collected all of Bandril's findings and samples and having disposed of Perin's body myself. I had given his sister coin and told her to lose herself among the masses of the Basement Quarter. Even I had no idea where she and the girls were now.

"Then it would seem that this has all worked out to our satisfaction," the Duke said as we paused at the doors. "You have shown me you are ready to wield real power. You possess the experience, and now I know you possess the discretion as well. You will honor my household as one of the Beloved, Finch."

"No, milord, I will not," I said. "Before coming here to give you my report as your Prefect, I was bound by the duty of that office to notify the Prime Minister of your suspected involvement in the matter of Kolvino's demise,"

I felt the heat draining away from my body, the Duke's form growing larger, broader, and less human before my eyes.

"I have been commanded to appear before Her Dark Majesty and the entire Court to present my findings," I said.

The force of the slap would shatter my skull like cheap pottery. It stopped inches from my face, defying all the laws man understood about velocity and energy, but the Beloved answered to older, darker laws.

"Your findings..." the Duke rasped. He was a gaunt, tattered scarecrow now, all jagged shadows and flashing yellow teeth. Snap, snap.

"I will be required to disclose the admissions you have made during this audience, my Lord." Every human instinct screamed in me to flee. "Unless you command me as your high attendant to remain silent."

"You would stand mute before Her?" the Duke said incredulously. "She, who is mother to us all? She who defied the Goddess and who all Beloved fear as your kind fears us? You would defy her at my command?"

"Yes," I said. "For while the Prefect is required to report the suspicion of any Beloved involvement in a high crime to Her Majesty, there is nothing in the Codex that requires an attendant to betray the confidence of his master to anyone."

"Surely there will be disagreement upon such an argument, if anyone even has the gall to posit it," the Duke said. Ever the consummate politician, he was already turning the jewel of the problem over and over, looking at each facet. He nodded after a moment.

"My faction will have to raise the argument," he said, coming to the conclusion I had hoped he would. "If not, then the Queen will rip the facts of this from you and..." he let his thoughts trail off as the implications settled in.

"And you and your co-conspirators will be joining me on the Rock of Suffering," I said.

"It will not come to that," the Duke said. "Others will not want to give her the authority to question our attendants in such a manner. Everyone has too much to lose.

"This will bring down much disgrace on my house. I will appear to have had Kolvino dispatched in the court of public opinion, even without an ounce of proof and will now look to be covering up the matter. You have cost me, Finch, and you have cost yourself a chance to be free from the shackles of mortality."

"The order, My Lord?"

"I swear this; you will never become one of us, Finch. Never."

The Duke spun, giving me his back as I opened the great doors.

"The order, Lord?" I began to walk through the doors, my back to him as well.

The cold was like that of deep space; his anger was a star of heat in my mind.

"Say nothing," he said.

"As you command, my Duke."

The doors closed upon the aviary. As I walked down the hallway to the lift, the screams of dying birds mingled with the howl of a wind made out of rage.

On the southern stairs of the Temple of the Servant I reclined, looking out over the mountains of concrete and glass lit by a hundred thousand electric fires.

"How did it go?" Kestrel asked as she sat down on the step above me.

"It was a stalemate. The Queen didn't want to pry too deeply into the affairs of the others for fear of unifying them against Her, and no one wanted their dirty secrets getting out to the entire court."

"The entire court," Kestrel said. "What was it like, seeing Her Dark Majesty?"

The images leered at me in my mind. I remembered a room full of hungry, shrill ghosts, cold and crowded. I remembered chanting, a great crystal case, and a hand emerging from within as it slowly opened. The rest of it was denied me by my mind out of mercy.

"I don't remember much of it," I said. "I don't want to go back."

"What happened to Perin?" she asked, changing the subject.

"He was a plant, sent by his lover and master to infiltrate your group," I said.

"I don't believe that," she said defiantly.

"Believe what you want," I continued, "He was torn between his master and lover, his family and the secret of your group.

"Kolvino refused to allow Perin to bring his sister and her family into his household. He was jealous of Perin's last human bond and wanted the old woman to die, so he would be the only thing in Perin's world. That's what Perin's sister said, anyway."

"Perrin understood what would happen if word of the underground got out. He took the way out that destroyed the least lives. He killed Kolvino by taking the drug and then having his lover drink from him. He left him for the sun to do the rest.

"The drug killed him, Kestrel, horribly. He curled up in that sewer pipe and hoped the rats would find him before there was any trace of the drug left. He saved us all, you and your revolution, the rest of the attendants, and his family. Maybe the entire human race, as well."

"He will be remembered as a hero of the revolution," she said."

It took too much effort to laugh. I shook my head and took a drag on my cigarette.

"What will keep the Duke from exacting revenge on you now that he's off the hook?"

"He's far from that. His reputation is very shaky now in the court. I am his saving grace. I was the one he named as Prefect and I've delivered the goods. The whole court knows that now. They may hate me for opening this can of worms but they all know I'm not just his lapdog. Besides, I got the better of him in this. He'll try to beat me, break me, but not kill me. There is no gloating in that."

A group of acolytes, headed for dinner in the grand hall, passed and greeted Kestrel. She nodded to them. We were silent until they had passed.

"Plus he thinks I learned the secret Kolvino learned, and he wants to get it out of me, so he'll keep me close."

"That secret is us," Kestrel said. I nodded.

"Your people had best behave too," I said, smiling over my shoulder.

The darkness above us concealed the true roof of the world, but we both knew it was there. Like some Gnostic model of the universe, a fake sky beneath a false heaven. Beyond it all lay cool night and glittering testimony to long dead stars.

"You'll have to choose a side someday, Aaron," she said as she walked slowly back up the stairs to the temple.

The teeming, breathing chaos of the Hive was below me. My father's kin, my kin, lived in ashes, lived in slavery, but at least they lived. And from ashes, new life could arise, or so the old stories said; freedom as brilliant and burning as the source of all life and light.

"I have," I said, looking across the Hive, basking in the invisible sun.

— CENTURIES OF KINGS —
by Marie Brennan

I HAVE KILLED KINGS, lured emperors to their doom; destroyed courts, brought countries to war; for thousands of years I have brought chaos with me wherever I go, death not enough to stop me, and I regret none of it.

And now the hunters pursue me through the wood.

Tamamo-no-Mae. Pao Sze. Dakki. These are but a few of the names I have answered to in my life. Wife, concubine, whore. I have answered to these as well. Two thousand years is a long time – more than one name can bear.

They blur together in my mind, the kings I have killed. Few last for more than a year, and then I move on. Not all have been kings. But men of power, yes; the poor or unimportant do not interest me. I go from land to land – China, India, Japan – where I am does not matter to me so much as who I find there. Toba is the most recent, but it began with Zhou.

I remember the days in Zhou's court as if they were yesterday, though they lie centuries distant. The court of the last Emperor of the Shang Dynasty, the man said to be more dissolute than any other in China. I could tell such tales of that court – tell of the day he demanded that seventy-two ladies of the highest blood strip to their skin and dance, in public, for his entertainment. When they refused, he had a ditch dug before his palace, and he filled it with snakes and lizards and biting insects; when it was full his guards threw the women into the ditch, and their screams filled the air. And he laughed and asked if I did not find it amusing.

I found my amusement elsewhere. A few words in the right ears, and trouble was seeded; you cannot murder seventy-two ladies of the highest blood and not expect rebellion in response. Zhou expected it, but his arrogance had robbed him of allies. His enemies stormed the palace compound late one night, and he died in his favorite pavilion, perishing amid the flames.

The fire did not begin outside, with the invaders. It began inside, from a tipped lamp.

I died in that fire with him, but by then it did not matter; I was finished with Zhou.

This much I will say for the hunters: they are noble men. Many have chased me in their time, but few have been as distinguished as Miura-no-Suke Yoshiaki and Kazusa-no-Suke Hirotsune. Retired Emperor Toba set them on my heels, and they are determined, more determined than many who have gone before them. This is the third time they have pursued me. The first time, I gave them the slip, and the second, their horses faltered before I did. Again they return, though, and now we flit through the hills and woods of Shimotsuke-no-Kuni, across the Nasu Plain, our feet as swift as leaves driven by the wind.

They may catch me; they may kill me. It does not matter. However many times I die, I will always find my way back.

I returned to China years later, during the dynasty called Zhou. Not the same name, but it echoed nonetheless with memories of snakes and screams. The Emperor then was Yu, twelfth of his line, who cast aside another woman for me. He wanted to make me smile: a harmless enough goal. But flowers and jewels brought no light to my face; the antics of monkeys and dogs were to me as indifferent as the changing of the moon.

Could he have succeeded, had he known how to pursue his goal? Years had passed since my time in Zhou's court, true, but not so many – not nearly so many as have passed now. Perhaps I could have smiled, then, for some cause other than bitterness or vengeful amusement. Perhaps.

But that was centuries ago, and who can say now what might have been?

A court functionary suggested it to him. Yu lit the signal-fires, meant to summon soldiers to him in case of need. The soldiers rushed to the courtyard, all in haste, and when I saw them there…

I laughed.

Yu misunderstood. He heard in that laugh nothing of harm. But I saw the soldiers milling over the paving-stones, and I heard the angry mutters of the lords, and I saw that Yu was a fool, and that his foolishness would bring him down. It was for *that* I laughed.

He saw me laugh, and was pleased; and, as I had known he would, he lit the signal-fires again and again, all for my sake, and every time I laughed louder.

I laughed the loudest of all when the father of the woman Yu had cast aside returned with an army, and he lit the signal fires one final time.

I laughed, not because the soldiers came, but because they did not. And Yu perished alone.

I do not know where the two noble hunters found their horses; these are not the ones they rode before. They pursue me without pausing, thundering across the plain toward the peaks of the Nasu Mountains, and although I am swift, I cannot outrun them.

Fools. This chase is for nothing. Toba will perish. And so may I, it is true; but that will accomplish nothing save to make these noble warriors feel proud. They will congratulate each other, and return home, and be given the feast of heroes – but they cannot stop the cycle, nor turn it back.

They cannot undo the past. No one can.

Zhou set this in motion two thousand years ago. Let them blame *him*, if they will.

Some kings I bring down through war or rebellion; others waste away. So it was with the Retired Emperor Toba. I was a mere servant-girl when he first cast his eye upon me, but such considerations did not stop him; my beauty was unsurpassed, my hair a shining river of blackness, my skin as perfect and pale as the moon, and the scent of my body was never marred by sweat or dirt. In darkness, I glowed with my own light.

That much was obvious to see. The rest, he discovered with time. We listened to music, and I amazed him with my knowledge of it. We viewed the moon, and my poems were gems, more precious than any the others could compose. He questioned me on Buddhist teachings, and found my answers wise beyond even his comprehension.

Two thousand years is a long time. I have learned much, and forgotten nothing.

Toba sickened before long. But someone in his cloistered court had more sense than most; someone dispatched a messenger to summon the great diviner Abe no Yasuchika to the Sendo Palace. Many of that kind are frauds, but Yasuchika had eyes that saw much, and when he turned those eyes upon the emperor's sickness he saw what I had done.

Oh, indeed, he saw much. But not all.

He saw the life draining from the emperor, draining from him to me. He saw my pointed ears, my golden fur, my nine tails. He saw the centuries of slaughter stretching behind me.

But he did not see where it began.

They chased me from the palace with dogs and bows, sent warriors to hunt me down. The word echoed in the halls of the Sendo Palace: kitsune! And I fled, abandoning my human mask, flying over hills in the form of a fox.

Yasuchika never guessed what he failed to see. He never saw the playful young fox spirit that once lived in China, free from care. He looked away too soon, and did not see an emperor take interest in her; nor did he see her fox-father refuse, knowing too well the corruption of humans.

Yasuchika closed his eyes, and did not watch as the great Shang Emperor Zhou, noble and wise, with the mandate of heaven behind him – a foolish, human conceit! – sent his soldiers to take the fox against her will.

That is where it began. But this, Yasuchika did not see. For he believed he had seen enough.

We have reached the base of the mountains, the noble hunters and I. My strength is at its end. Soon they will catch me, and then I will die.

I have died before. I no longer fear it. Toba will die as well, and that is all I ask for now.

Zhou is dead; Yu is dead; Toba will soon join them. The names of those I have brought down form a list whose recital would last hours. I take pride in that list, as I take pride in little else. What is beauty to me, or immortality, or the nine tails I have earned? What are love, joy, peace? These inner things, valued things, were taken from me long ago, and the outward things matter not at all. What matters is that Zhou has paid, and Yu has paid, and Toba will soon pay for *his* own crimes.

Oh, I heard what the ladies-in-waiting said, whispering in the corridors of the Sendo Palace as Toba weakened and moaned. He is a good man, they said. A wise ruler, guiding the country from behind the throne, retiring out of the light of court so he may concentrate on more important things.

Perhaps it is so. But his crimes would have come soon enough. They always do.

I learned that lesson from Zhou, centuries ago. Humans are of two kinds: mindless cattle, and the iron-fisted tyrants who herd and devour them. Those without power, and those who abuse the power they have.

Toba had power, and in time he would have used it for evil. For that, I have delivered justice. It is what I do.

The arrows thud into the dirt around me. I dart and leap, changing direction, but as I slip between the trees, I see something flash by.

A slip of paper, tied to the branch of a tree.

I realize at last that this chase has been different. My hunters have been herdsmen, leading me to this trap. Enchantment forms a net around me, and behind it I feel the hand of Yasuchika. He will bring his holiness to bear against me, Buddhist prayers, Shinto charms, and perhaps this is how I will die.

Holy men have killed me before.

The hunters pull their horses up short, shouting words I cannot hear. The chanting of Yasuchika fills my ears, and now, too late, too late, I feel what he is doing.

He will not kill me. He will do worse.

My hind paws drag in the dirt, cease to move. I cannot lift them. I rear up and am frozen thus, held by the trap I entered so carelessly. I curse this blind monk, who does not see that what I do is right and good, that it is *necessary*. He calls me an oni, a demon, and now he will bind me to this spot. My body grows heavy and stiff. I cannot move. He has caught me well, stealing my freedom, my ability to transform, leaving me on the edge of the Nasu Plain as nothing more than a twisted stone.

He won that day, and he lost.

The diviner put an end to my centuries of kings. He trapped me in this body of stone.

But my spirit survives.

Now my victims must come to me, and I care no more for justice. They call me the Death Stone, the Murderer Stone, an object filled with malice and hate. Those who understand avoid me, but there are always the strangers, the travelers, the ignorant.

The fools.

The enchantment that put me here will not last forever. Someday it will wane, and I will break free once more. There will be no mercy for the humans then. I will kill them as I find them, draining out their life, and no monk babbling prayers will trap me, ever again.

For I have learned the lesson of Zhou, the lesson of Yasuchika. Power is what matters, not the use to which it is put. I was a fool to think otherwise. I am a demon indeed, and will bring hell to them on earth.

ABOUT THE AUTHORS

Tad Williams has held more jobs than any sane person should admit to—singing in a band, selling shoes, managing a financial institution, throwing newspapers, and designing military manuals, to name just a few. He also hosted a syndicated radio show for ten years, worked in theater and television production, taught both grade-school and college classes, and worked in multimedia for a major computer firm. He is co-founder of an interactive television company, and is currently writing comic books and film and television scripts as well as novels.

Tad and his wife, Deborah Beale, live in the San Francisco Bay Area with their children and far more cats, dogs, turtles, pet ants and banana slugs than they can count.

Marsheila (Marcy) Rockwell was born an indeterminate number of years ago in America's Last, Best Place. A descendant of kings, pilgrims, Ojibwe hunters and possibly a witch or two, she spent the first few years of her life frolicking gleefully in a large backyard that is now part of one of the nation's largest Superfund sites. Perhaps that explains her early penchant for fantasy and horror--the first book she ever read (at the tender age of three) was L. Frank Baum's *Ozma of Oz*.

Fast forward two decades. Marcy graduated from Last, Best Place State University with a degree, not in Creative Writing, as may have been expected, but in Civil Engineering—because even then, she knew writing alone would never pay the bills (her mistake, of course, was in thinking that engineering *would*). But while she worked as a registered Professional Engineer for several years, she never forgot her true passion, sparked by that early love of books, and in 2005, after more than ten years of writing and submitting short stories and poems, she finally landed her first book contract.

Marcy now lives in the desert in the shadow of an improbably green mountain with her Naval officer husband, their three sons, the requisite Black Lab, and far too many books. In odd moments stolen from her family and her writing, she can be found browsing eBay for unusual Wonder Woman figures or Seabees sweetheart jewelry from WWII.

Jeff Mariotte was born in Park Forest, Illinois. He moved away from there at the age of six, when his father, a civilian working for the Department of Defense, was transferred to Paris, France. Since then he's lived in Arlington and Reston, Virginia, Worms and Schriesheim, Germany, San Jose, San Diego, and Arizona.

He graduated from San Jose State University with a degree in Radio/TV/Film. He has worked delivering the Washington Post, in a comic book store, fast food, selling encyclopedias door-to-door, and as maintenance supervisor for a large regional shopping center. He was the manager of Hunter's Books, La Jolla when his first fiction was published. He has been VP of Marketing and Senior Editor for comic book publisher WildStorm Productions, Editor-in-Chief for IDW Publishing, and a freelance writer. He and his wife Maryelizabeth Hart and partner Terry Gilman are the owners of Mysterious Galaxy, an independent bookstore specializing in mystery, science fiction, fantasy, and horror.

He currently lives on the Flying M Ranch in Arizona with his wife and two dogs, in a house filled with books and comics and toys and music and laughter.

He is passionate about—among other things—reading, the deserts and mountains and forests of the American West, modern and historical politics, photography, independent bookstores, and whatever else strikes his fancy at any given moment.

Kenny Soward grew up in Crescent Park, Kentucky, a small suburb just south of Cincinnati, Ohio, listening to hard rock and playing outdoors. In those quiet '70s streets, he jumped bikes, played Nerf football, and acquired many a childhood scar.

Kenny's love for books flourished early, a habit passed down to him by his uncles. He burned through his grade school library, and in high school spent many days in detention for reading fantasy fiction during class. In those days, his sixth grade teacher encouraged him to start a journal, so he began jotting down pieces of stories, mostly the outcomes of Dungeons & Dragons gaming sessions. At the University of Kentucky, Kenny took creative writing classes under Gurny Norman, former Kentucky Poet Laureate and author of *Divine Rights Trip* (1971).

By day, Kenny works as a Unix professional, and at night he writes and sips bourbon. His latest releases are *Rough Magick* (GnomeSaga #1) and the "Dead West" series, which he co-writes with Tim

Marquitz and J.M. Martin. He now lives in Independence, Kentucky, with three cats and a gal who thinks she's a cat. His website is www. kennysoward.com.

Betsy Dornbusch writes urban and epic fantasy, science fiction, and dabbles in thrillers and erotica. Her short fiction has appeared in print and online venues such as *Sinister Tales, Big Pulp, Story Portal,* and *Spine tingler,* and her work is in the anthologies *Tasty Little Tales and Deadly by the Dozen.*

Betsy's been an editor with the ezine *Electric Spec for six years and regularly speaks at fan conventions and writers' conferences. Her first full length novel, Archive of Fire* came out in 2012 to great reviews and the first of her epic fantasy series, *Exile,* came out in February, 2013. She's the sole proprietor of Sex Scenes at Starbucks (http://betsydornbusch. com), where you can believe most of what she writes. In her free time, she snowboards, air jams at punk rock concerts, and just started following Rockies baseball, of all things.

Keith Gouveia lives in Florida with his wife, Lisa. He is a mechanical engineer by trade and writes fiction in his spare time. Among his works, he recommends *Death Puppet: Revolt of the Dead* and *The Screaming Field: A Novel of Scarecrow Terror,* both from Coscom Entertainment, as well as his fantasy novel, *The Goblin Princess,* published by Lachesis Publishing and the well received *Animal Behavior and Other Tales of Lycanthropy*—check it out, if you dare.

Kevin has also edited the anthology, *Bits of the Dead,* published by Coscom Entertainment, and released his self-published title, *Behind The Stained Glass,* called by Charles Gramlich "a world worthy of Oz and Wonderland with a touch of Dante's 'Hell' thrown in."

Jeff Salyards grew up in a small town north of Chicago. While it wasn't Mayberry, with all the doors unlocked and everyone offering each other slices of pie and quaint homilies, it was pretty quiet and sleepy, so I got started early imagining my way into all kinds of other worlds and universes that were loud, chaotic, and full of irrepressible characters and heaps of danger. Massive explosions. Tentacled aliens. Men with sharp swords and thousand-yard stares and secrets they would die to protect. Clearly, I was a full-bore dork.

Royal Crown bag full of multi-sided dice? Check. Blood-red hooded cloak? Check. Annual pilgrimages to Renaissance Faires? Check. Whacking other (curiously athletic and gifted) dorks with rattan swords in the SCA? Check. Yes, I earned my badges, thank you very much.

My whole life, I've been fascinated by the fantastic, and of course this extended to speculative fiction of all kinds. Countless prepubescent evenings found me reading a worn, dog-eared copy of *Thuvia, Maid of Mars* (it sounded so much dirtier than it was!) or *The Frost Giant's Daughter* (high hopes for that one too!) well past lights-out, flashlight in hand, ignoring the repeated calls to turn in. That's as quiet and harmless a rebellion as you can have, and my parents mostly sighed and left me to it.

So, no one has ever been surprised to hear that I was working on (or at least talking about working on) some sci-fi or fantasy story or other. But it took years of flirting with various projects, flitting from one to the next without the hint of complete commitment, before I finally mastered myself enough to finish a novel. And longer still before I finished another one that was worthy of being published.

But wonders never cease. And here we are.

My debut novel, *Scourge of the Betrayer,* is a hard-boiled fantasy published by Night Shade Books in May, 2012, and will be followed by *Veil of the Deserters* in May, 2014. I'm so excited I'm beginning to annoy myself. I am represented by Michael Harriot at Folio Literary Management, and couldn't be happier. His savvy, smart advice has been invaluable on this journey. I suspect he has a secret stash of 20-siders somewhere in his desk.

I live with my lovely wife, Kris, and three daughters in a suburb west of Chicago. I am indebted to Kris in countless ways for her steadfast encouragement, support, and thick skin in dealing with a prickly, moody writer. I don't always like living with me, but she has a choice and stays anyway.

And before you are tempted to mention it, I am fully aware that siring three daughters is certainly karmic retribution, particularly when they all transform into teenagers. I cling to the hope of discovering at least one of them reading covertly in the middle of the night. That kind of transgression I can handle.

William Meikle is a Scottish genre writer now living in Newfoundland. He has 20 novels and several hundred short stories in genre presses, anthologies and magazines. His current bestseller is the sci-fi novel *The Invasion* with 20,000 copies sold and counting. When he's not writing Willie drinks beer, plays guitar, and dreams of fortune and glory.

Ian Creasey was born in 1969 and lives in Yorkshire, England. He began writing when rock and roll stardom failed to return his calls. His first story was published in 1999, and since then he has appeared regularly in magazines such as *Asimov's Science Fiction*.

His story "Erosion" featured on the 2009 Locus Recommended Reading List, and was reprinted in three Year's Best anthologies. "Erosion" is the lead story in his collection *Maps of the Edge*, alongside sixteen other SF tales.

Ian's spare time interests include hiking, gardening, and environmental conservation work... anything to get him outdoors and away from the computer screen.

Hi. I'm **Mercedes M. Yardley**. I have two broken laptops, three kids, a husband, and no time to write, although I try my very best. I like to write stories. I like to write poems. I like to write essays and sometimes they're funny, sometimes they aren't.

I'm the author of *Beautiful Sorrows, Apocalyptic Montessa and Nuclear Lulu: A Tale of Atomic Love,* and *Nameless: The Darkness Comes, which is the first book of The Bone Angel Trilogy.* I specialize in the dark and beautiful. I blog at abrokenlaptop.com.

Pete Rawlik's first professional sale was "On the Far Side of the Apocalypse" to the legendary magazine *Talebones* in 1997. Since then his work has appeared in *Crypt of Cthulhu, Morpheus Tales, the Lovecraft Ezine, Innsmouth,* and the anthologies *Dead But Dreaming 2, Horror for the Holidays, Urban Cthulhu,* and *Worlds of Cthulhu.* He is a regular contributor to the *New York Review of Science Fiction* and *Tales of the Shadowmen,* an annual anthology series focusing on heroes from French literature, comics and film. His first novel, *Reanimators,* came out in 2013 from Night Shade Books.

Joseph Lallo, though having written several novels, is slow to consider himself an author. Educated at NJIT, where he earned a Master's Degree in Computer Engineering, the world of Information Technology is where most of his bills are paid. When not crunching numbers, he owns and operates BrainLazy.com along with two friends. There he posts random rants and editorials regarding the world of humor, entertainment, and technology. He made his home in Bayonne, NJ, where he had lived all of his life until the success of his books allowed him to buy a home in Colonia, NJ. His novels and short stories are available via Smashwords.com.

R.S. Belcher won the grand prize in the Strange New Worlds SF-writing contest. He runs Cosmic Castle, a comic book shop in Roanoke, Virginia.

Marie Brennan is the pseudonym of Bryn Neuenschwander, an American fantasy author. Her works include the Doppelganger duology (*Doppelganger* and its sequel *Warrior and Witch*, respectively retitled "Warrior and Witch" on later printings); the Onyx Court series; and numerous short stories. The first of the Onyx Court novels, *Midnight Never Come*, published in May, 2008, in the UK, and in June, 2008, in the USA; it received a four star-review from *SFX Magazine*.

As an undergraduate at Harvard University, Bryn served as co-chair of the Harvard-Radcliffe Science Fiction Association. After graduating from Harvard, she pursued graduate studies at Indiana University, studying folklore and anthropology; in 2008 she left graduate school without completing her PhD in order to pursue writing full-time.